"What are y[ou doing?" she
asked as she [...]

"Just walking a la[dy...]

"I am home. This [...]

"You never know [what might] come out in the dark." He covered the distance to the back porch, opened the door to the house and ushered her in.

"Thanks for letting me watch the foal be born tonight," he said.

She turned to face him again. "You're welcome. At least you weren't totally useless. You made the phone calls, and you brought my coat."

Jud laughed. "So happy to be of service, Ms Mayor. Aren't you glad you changed your mind and let me stay in the foreman's cabin here?"

"I guess so. But keep out of my way," she said, retreating to the shadows within, "unless you want me to change it back again." The thud of the house door punctuated her order.

"Not a chance," Jud said softly, walking across the open ground towards the foreman's cabin. "I'm not leaving until my business here in Homestead is done."

He glanced over his shoulder just as a light upstairs winked out. "And that business, Miranda Wright, definitely includes you."

Available in May 2007 from Mills & Boon Superromance

The Prodigal Texan
by Lynnette Kent
(Home To Stay)

Unexpected Complication
by Amy Knupp
(9 Months Later)

The Girl Who Came Back
by Barbara McMahon
(The House on Poppin Hill)

A Man She Can Trust
by Roxanne Rustand
(Blackberry Hill Memorial)

The Prodigal Texan
LYNNETTE KENT

DID YOU PURCHASE THIS BOOK WITHOUT A COVER?
If you did, you should be aware it is **stolen property** as it was reported *unsold and destroyed* by a retailer. Neither the author nor the publisher has received any payment for this book.

All the characters in this book have no existence outside the imagination of the author, and have no relation whatsoever to anyone bearing the same name or names. They are not even distantly inspired by any individual known or unknown to the author, and all the incidents are pure invention.

All Rights Reserved including the right of reproduction in whole or in part in any form. This edition is published by arrangement with Harlequin Enterprises II B.V./S.à.r.l. The text of this publication or any part thereof may not be reproduced or transmitted in any form or by any means, electronic or mechanical, including photocopying, recording, storage in an information retrieval system, or otherwise, without the written permission of the publisher.

This book is sold subject to the condition that it shall not, by way of trade or otherwise, be lent, resold, hired out or otherwise circulated without the prior consent of the publisher in any form of binding or cover other than that in which it is published and without a similar condition including this condition being imposed on the subsequent purchaser.

MILLS & BOON and MILLS & BOON with the Rose Device are registered trademarks of the publisher.

First published in Great Britain 2007
Harlequin Mills & Boon Limited,
Eton House, 18-24 Paradise Road, Richmond, Surrey TW9 1SR

© Cheryl B. Bacon 2006

ISBN: 978 0 263 85781 8

38-0507

Printed and bound in Spain
by Litografia Rosés S.A., Barcelona

Dear Reader,

My first job out of university involved physiology laboratory research, which was every bit as dull as it sounds. To perk up the day, we listened to the radio while we worked; since this was Nashville, Tennessee, the station of choice often played country music. One day a colleague of mine – obviously not a fan – complained that "every country music song talks about Tennessee or Texas!"

And why not? Texas, especially, has earned a pre-eminent place in the American legend, with the Alamo and the Rio Grande, with ranchers, Rangers and rustlers, with cattle drives and, yes, country-and-western music. I've enjoyed writing a story set against this unique and romantic background, particularly in a series with four equally unique and romantic Superromance authors.

As *The Prodigal Texan*, Jud Ritter returns to Homestead, Texas, only to discover how much about his home town remains the same. Most people – including his own brother – still believe the lies that circulated about him all those years ago. If Jud is to redeem his reputation, he'll have to prove to the people of Homestead just how much he has changed.

Mayor Miranda Wright has worked long and hard to transform her beloved town for the better. Now she must count on Jud Ritter to save Homestead from oblivion. Can she trust this one-time bad boy with the town's safety? Should she trust him with her heart?

I hope you have a good time with Miranda and Jud and the people in Homestead, Texas. Please feel free to write to me at PMB 304, Westwood Shopping Centre, Fayetteville, NC 28314, USA or visit my website at www.lynnette-kent.com.

Happy reading!

Lynnette Kent

To Kathleen. An editor in a million.
With many thanks.

I'm grateful, as well, for the chance to work with Roxanne Rustand, KN Casper, Linda Warren and Roz Denny Fox in developing the HOME TO STAY series. From brainstorming to nailing down the smallest details, you folks were creative, co-operative and downright fun!

CHAPTER ONE

May

THE DAY STARTED WITH A FUNERAL.

By five o'clock, Miranda Wright had endured as much neighborly nosiness, listened to as many insinuations and waded through all the close-minded arguments she could stomach. With a slam of the door and a twist of the key, she abandoned her Wright for Mayor campaign office, skipped town without speaking to a single prospective voter and took the long way home. With luck, a breezy ride through the wide-open Texas countryside would restore her peace of mind.

Since the meandering back road she traveled led pretty much nowhere except to her farm, she was surprised to come over a rise and find a black truck parked on the shoulder at the bottom of the slope. Engine trouble, maybe. And no cell phone would work in the deep trough between the two hills.

Despite her mood, Miranda did the neighborly thing and stopped a few yards behind the tailgate of the black Ford 250. No flat tires evident, no smoking engine. Just the driver, sitting motionless at the wheel. Sick? Disabled? Dangerous?

Wishing she could replace her navy funeral suit and high-heeled shoes with jeans, boots and a rifle, she stepped up to the driver's window. "Everything okay?"

Then she saw who she was dealing with.

"If it isn't Ms. Mayor-to-be," Jud Ritter said, giving her his one-sided smile. "How's it going?" He took a swig from a half-empty whiskey bottle. An identical bottle lay on the passenger seat. Empty.

"Hey, Jud." The man had attended his mother's funeral this morning. He had a right to drown his sorrows, but not behind the wheel. "What are you doing out here in the wilderness? You should be at home with your dad and Ethan."

He barked a laugh. "Not likely, Ms. Mayor-to-be. 'Don't bother coming back,' was the phrase, as I remember it. 'You don't belong here.'" He helped himself to another drink, then held out the bottle. "Want some?"

"Sure." Miranda took it, stepped back and poured out a golden stream of whiskey. The sharp tang of liquor rose from the pavement. As she handed him the empty bottle, Jud stared at her, eyes narrowed, lips pressed into a straight line.

Finally, he shrugged. "That'll teach me to be polite." Groaning, he stretched an arm down into the foot well on the passenger side. "Good thing I know my limits." He sat up again with a third bottle in his hand and proceeded to break the seal.

That was so like him—Homestead's most infam-ous bad boy, a law unto himself, always finding a new way to flout the rules and make somebody mad. The citizens had heaved a collective sigh of relief when he'd left town after high school.

Miranda opened the truck door. "Come on, Jud. Get out. You can't drive under the influence of two quarts of whiskey."

"I know that," he said, stepping down to the road. He staggered a little, then caught his balance. "I'm an officer of the Austin police department. I wouldn't drive drunk, even in this redneck refuge."

She gritted her teeth against the insult. "You can't just park here until you're sober, either. Who knows what could happen?" Why she even cared was a question Miranda couldn't answer. She and Jud had squabbled and snapped and sniped at each other the entire twelve years they'd been in school together. The most humiliating moments of her adolescence had Jud Ritter's name attached.

"Nothing's gonna happen." He looked at her, his brown gaze as guileless as a little boy's. "I'm not bothering anybody as long as I'm parked on public property. I'll spend the night under the stars, like a good cowboy should. Come morning, I'll take my hangover and head back to Austin."

Leaving the driver's door open, he sauntered to the back of his truck, let down the tailgate and hitched himself up to sit on the edge. Miranda reached into the cab and took the keys out of the ignition, guaranteeing he wouldn't be going any-where till she decided he could. She'd give them back in the morning when he'd be suffering, but sober.

"Have a seat," Jud said. "It'll be a nice sunset in just a little while."

Maybe if she humored him, he'd agree to let her drive him to Homestead's only motel to sleep off the booze. Or she could take him home, dump him on the bed in the guest room. Her mom wouldn't mind—she'd always had a soft spot in her heart for handsome, arrogant, uncontrollable Jud Ritter.

Still regretting the absence of comfortable clothes, Miranda shrugged out of her suit jacket and stowed it—along with Jud's keys—in her truck.

"Aw, don't go away," Jud called. "We could have our own class reunion."

"We didn't graduate together," she said, walking toward him. "I got held back twice, remember?"

"Oh, yeah. Well, we're both graduates." He toasted her with the bottle. "To dear old Homestead High." Another swig. "So I hear you're going to save the town single-handed. Like the Lone Ranger."

She hitched herself onto the tailgate beside him, then took a second to pull her skirt down as far as it would go. "Not single-handed, but I've got a plan that could bring people and opportunities back to Homestead."

"Some kind of land swap?" He was drinking steadily, and she almost wished she could join him, relax a little. Jud had always made her nervous. He'd been everything she wasn't—handsome as sin, with the physical grace of an athlete and the charisma of a politician. An encounter with Jud in the school hallway had usually left her feeling as stupid and confused as most people thought she was.

She took a deep breath. "A giveaway, actually. People must agree to build on the property, or renovate an existing building, live there for a year, and then they can sell it or continue in residence as the owner."

"Where do you get the giveaway land?"

That was the touchy part. Miranda swallowed hard. "When the K Bar C Ranch went bust, the county seized the property for back taxes."

Jud chuckled. "So that's why my dad is so pissed about you running for mayor. He merged his ranch into that K Bar C investment deal. Now he's lost the family plot, so to speak."

"I know."

"Considering the Ritters have held that land for over a hundred years…" He shook his head. "I think that's one vote you won't be getting."

"You don't mind?"

"Nah. I gave up any right to the Ritter legacy when I left home. They're right—I don't belong here. Thank God."

He didn't say anything else for quite a while. The sun dropped behind the hills around them, bringing a quick, cool twilight. Stars popped out one by one, white sparks in a purple Texas sky.

"See, I told you it would be a nice night." Jud chugged from his whiskey bottle, then let himself fall back in the truck bed. "Great for stargazing. You ever go stargazing, Ms. Mayor?"

"I live on a ranch," she said without thinking. "I see the stars all the time."

"No, I mean real *stargazing*." His grin was white in the near darkness. "With a guy."

She felt her cheeks flush with heat. "Not recently."

"Ever?"

"None of your business." She scooted forward on the tailgate. "I'm going home."

Strong fingers closed around her wrist. "Aw, come on." He pulled backward, but she resisted. "I'm not talking about anything besides watching the sky."

"I'll bet you say that to all the girls."

"Most of 'em," he said, and took another swig.

But never to *her*. Miranda figured she was the only female in Homestead anywhere near his age that Jud Ritter hadn't gone out with. He'd asked once, or so she'd thought at the time. What a travesty that had turned out to be.

"Relax," Jud said, his voice now definitely slurred. "Lie back and look at the sky." He tugged on her wrist again.

Miranda flattened out on the truck bed, feeling every ridge in the liner on her back. "This isn't a very comfortable place to watch the sky."

"You get used to it. Sure you don't want a drink?"

"I have to drive home."

Jud shrugged. "Up to you." He took a noisy gulp of whiskey, then handed the half-empty bottle to her. "Do whatever you want to with that. I'm done."

She held the bottle for a while, fighting the urge to take just one swig. Her experience with liquor consisted of eggnog punch at Christmas and champagne for New Year's Eve. Plus the occasional long neck beer at a party. But she caught the rich oak aroma from Jud's breath on the air, and her mouth watered for a taste. Just one.

Finally, though, she put the bottle at her side.

"Not tempting enough?" Jud rolled to face her, elbow bent and head propped on his hand. Full darkness had fallen, but they were close enough that she could see all the details of his face—the straight slant of his nose and the angle of his cheekbones, the shape of his mouth, the spark of laughter in his eyes. "What does tempt you, Ms. Mayor?"

"Pecan pie. Fast food cheeseburgers."

"Guess you don't get too much fast food out here in the sticks."

"Just Bertha's kolaches."

"She's still cooking?"

"Breakfast every day but Sunday."

"Nothing ever changes." After a silence, he said, "Do you have weaknesses for something besides food?"

She was beginning to feel drunk herself, listening to his voice, whiskey warm. "Horses. Never met one I didn't love."

He rubbed his knuckles up and down her lower arm. "Men, Miranda. Don't you have a weakness concerning men?"

"Nary a one," she lied, as goose bumps broke out all over her body. "Haven't found a man yet I couldn't live without."

His fingers touched her cheek. "You just haven't met the right guy."

"I've met all the men I'm likely to here in Homestead."

She should sit up, get down, go home. Jud Ritter was bad news, as at least one girl in Homestead had learned the hard way. He was drunk enough to seduce Miranda, for lack of anyone better, but she wasn't drunk enough to succumb. She didn't think she could get that drunk without passing out first.

Then he kissed her.

She gasped, tasting the liquor on his breath. And there was more…the firmness of his lips moving gently and deliberately over hers, the faint lime scent of his aftershave. She put up a hand—to stop him?—which came to rest on his shoulder, square and solid under his shirt. Without thought, she lifted her other hand to his hair, running her fingers through the short, sleek strands, pausing to cup the nape of his neck, the curve of his head.

And now they were both involved in the kiss, as he coaxed her response with patience and persistence and—dammit—expertise. She wouldn't have him thinking she was a total novice, though that might not be far from the truth. By the time she was finished with him, he'd know he'd been kissed....

Somewhere along the way, though, her intentions grew wispy, then evaporated altogether. Mouths fusing, releasing, the clash of teeth. Hands exploring with long, savoring strokes or desperate clutches at sweat-slicked skin. Night air cool on heated bodies pressed ruthlessly together. Tension building, desire pounding in her veins. This, *this* was the reason she'd waited. *He* was the reason....

"Jud." She whispered his name, and he stopped his exquisite torture of her breasts to look into her face. She saw his eyes focus.

In the next instant, he took his hands off her body and jerked away. Choking, growling like a rabid wolf, he partly fell, partly jumped out of the truck bed, hit the ground on his hands and knees and stayed there, swearing.

Miranda lay on her back where he'd left her, staring up at cold stars in a black sky, her mind an absolute blank.

"What the hell are you doing?" Jud dragged himself to his feet using the edge of the tailgate. "You let just any sonofabitch maul you?"

He grabbed her hands and drew her to sit up, like a rag doll who'd lost half her stuffing. "Any woman with half a brain would know better."

She put a hand to her head, where her brain used to be. "I didn't—" Past and present swirled together...she might have been sixteen again, standing at the door to the high school gym where she was supposed to meet Jud for the homecoming dance. He'd *said* to wait for him there, in the note she'd found in her locker.

"Are you crazy?" he'd demanded, when she stepped out to claim him. She showed him the note, and he laughed. The crowd of kids watching them laughed, too.

"If you had half a brain," he'd said, "you'd know better." Then, with his arm around his date, he'd walked past Miranda into the dance.

"Pull yourself together," he ordered, with a wave at her wrecked blouse and wrinkled skirt. "Go home, before you get tarred with the same brush they used on me. That'd ruin your election chances, for sure."

When he reached for the whiskey, Miranda focused enough to grab it. "No. I'm not leaving you a single, solitary drop." Scrambling on her knees to the other side of the truck, she launched the bottle into the darkness beyond her vehicle. The satisfying crash of glass shattering on asphalt announced her success.

Jud swore again, even more fluently.

Still kneeling, Miranda fixed her bra and drew the edges of her blouse together. One of the buttons had popped—or been torn off. She'd have to wear her jacket into the house and hope her mother didn't notice.

When she scooted to the end of the tailgate, Jud held out a hand. Miranda told him what he could do with his hands, his truck, and the rest of his life before she hopped down without help.

He grabbed her shoulder and pulled her around to face him. "Look, I—"

As she pivoted, Miranda slapped him with the full force of her turn. "Don't talk to me. I don't care what you think. I was stupid—gee, that's a surprise. But I'll get over it, all the easier if I never see your face again."

She'd reached for the door handle of her truck before she remembered that she had his keys. "I'll send the sheriff out in the morning," she yelled. "He'll have your keys."

"Hey," Jud shouted, and started running. "You can't—"

But Miranda was behind the wheel with the motor roaring before he'd covered half the distance. She backed into a plume of dust, skidded onto the pavement and gave Jud a wave as she passed him, already doing forty-five.

She didn't slow down until she reached the driveway at the farm. And only then did she acknowledge the tears running down her cheeks and dripping off her chin.

CHAPTER TWO

December
Four years later

TRADITION IN HOMESTEAD, Texas, demanded that every bridal couple drive away from the ceremony in a suitably decorated vehicle. Noah and Greer Kelley would be no exception. While their reception—a hoedown and barbecue—continued in the town park, friends of the happy couple went to work on Project Newlywed. The groom had parked his truck in plain sight as a decoy while trying to hide his bride's red Blazer, a futile effort that gave the decorating committee the opportunity to embellish two vehicles, instead of one.

"I brought tin cans," Miranda told the crew surrounding Greer's car. "Plus string and crepe paper."

"We'd better hurry and get this done, then." Wade Montgomery, the sheriff of Loveless County, surveyed the Blazer. He held a can of shaving cream in one hand and a white shoe polish applicator in the other. "I can't imagine Noah's going to wait much longer to have Greer to himself. I remember thinking I'd never get Callie away from our wedding reception."

Kristin Gallagher wrapped a ribbon around the antenna and tied a bow at the top. "I imagine Greer has some ideas of her own," she said, with a glance at her husband, Ryan, who was assisting Wade with the shoe polish.

Miranda caught the sexy grin Ryan sent his wife in return and felt her cheeks heat up. There had been a rash of weddings in Homestead recently—all her friends seemed to be pairing off, leaving her the odd woman out. An old maid was what she was, an old maid who still lived with her mother.

But this old maid was the town *mayor*. Miranda couldn't help being proud of what she'd accomplished, for herself and for the hometown she loved.

"What can I do?" Ethan Ritter took the

bag of tin cans Miranda still held and set it on the ground. "Kayla's going to come looking for me any min-ute." Ethan was another recently married citizen, a man who, more than most, deserved some lucky breaks in his life. And his wife, Kayla, definitely counted as good luck.

Once the group had done its best—or worst, depending on how you looked at it—the participants stood back for a moment to admire their handiwork. Miranda happened to be facing the Loveless County courthouse, so she was the first to notice a man approaching from the far side of the square. A long, lean drink of water he was, wearing boots and jeans and a chambray shirt under a leather jacket, but no hat on his head, cowboy or otherwise. The sun sat low in the sky behind him, leaving his face in shadow. He walked with a distinctive limp and she knew of no one in town who'd been injured lately. Obviously he wasn't a local.

"Who's that?" she asked, of no one in particular.

"I don't know," Ryan said, squinting into the sun.

When she glanced at Ethan, she found his

eyes hard, his mouth set in a straight line. "That's my brother Jud."

Miranda put a hand over her belly button, just at the spot where her stomach had suddenly shrunk into a tight, throbbing ball. Four years felt like no more than four hours, as humiliation flooded through her. How could she face Jud Ritter again in the light of day? In front of her friends? And his brother, for heaven's sake! Could she retreat to the reception in the park before Jud arrived?

Other questions occurred to her as she watched him limp toward them. Why the hell had he come back? What right did he have to spoil an otherwise terrific afternoon? Did he seriously think anyone wanted him here?

His brother evidently didn't. As Jud drew close, Ethan stepped out in front of the group, a barrier nearly as effective as a stone wall. He didn't say a word in welcome, or even acknowledgment.

The move forced Jud to stop some distance up the sidewalk. "Hey, Ethan. How are you?"

Ethan hesitated before accepting the handshake his brother offered. "We're fine."

When Ethan didn't say anything else, Jud

looked past his shoulder to the party in the park. "That's some shindig going on. What's the occasion?"

"A wedding. You probably don't remember Noah Kelley, and his wife, Greer Bell."

"I do remember Noah, in fact. And Greer." He turned to Wade. "Hey, Sheriff. I thought you were in charge of preventing vandalism."

"I've learned when to turn a blind eye," Wade said as they shook hands. "Some of us read the Austin newspaper, you know. We heard about your little 'accident,' even way out here. A citation for going above and beyond the call of duty, wasn't it?"

"I was just doing my job." An unspoken message passed between the two men, before they turned in different directions.

Jud nodded to Ryan, standing just behind Miranda. "Hey, Gallagher. How's it going?"

"Great." Ryan stepped forward to shake Jud's hand. "Let me introduce you to my wife, Kristin." He put an arm around the petite blonde and drew her forward. "Kristin, Jud and I used to run wild together, back in high school."

Jud held her hand a moment. "I always

knew Ryan would choose a beautiful wife. I'm glad to meet you."

Kristin looked him over with an appraising eye. "I also manage the health clinic here in Homestead. If you need some help while you're here, please come by."

"I'm okay," Jud said with a shrug. "Just an accident at work."

His wary gaze traveled to Miranda's face. "I understand you won your election and rescued the town from disaster. Very impressive." His flat tone drained the compliment of any meaning. He didn't offer a handshake.

She dropped her own half-raised hand to her side. "I—"

"Ethan!" Kayla Ritter stood on the edge of the party nearest the street. "Ethan, they're getting ready to cut the cake. Are you finished?"

"You bet." Ethan started toward the park without so much as a nod to his brother, followed by Wade and the Gallaghers. Miranda lingered to gather the remnants of Project Newlywed. When she straightened up, she found Jud had collected a couple of shoe polish bottles and a length of ribbon.

"These were in the street." He eased the

trash into the bag she held in her arms, which brought his hands close to her chest. "What's the fine for littering?"

"Life behind bars with no possibility of parole," she said without thinking, desperate to put some distance between them.

Jud snorted. "I believe that. This always was a straitlaced town."

Was he talking about *her?* "Having standards doesn't make us straitlaced." With her heart pounding, Miranda turned on her heel and headed toward the park and the wedding party. After all, *he* was the one who'd stopped, that night. She would have let him go all the way….

To her dismay, Jud fell in beside her. "There's a fine line between having standards and being narrow-minded."

She stopped in her tracks to confront him. "Only to someone who's determined to defy good sense and decency."

He stared down at her, his dark eyes narrowed under lowered brows. "I wondered how long I'd be here before somebody threw my past in my face."

"Did you think I—we'd all forgotten?"

"I guess I hoped that just maybe, after

fifteen years, people could let go of the past." Shaking his head, he gave a weary sigh. "Dumb, Ritter, real dumb."

When he didn't say anything else, Miranda turned toward the party again. After only a few steps, though, she realized Jud wasn't coming along. Despite herself, she glanced over her shoulder to see if he'd gone back the way he came.

Instead, he was staring up at the oversized statue of Hilde Schnorrberger guarding the entrance to Homestead Town Park. Hilde had followed her land-hungry husband to Texas, but when she reached the bank of Pecan Creek, she'd tied her bonnet to a tree and refused to take another step.

"Things have come full circle, haven't they?" Jud looked from Hilde's face to Miranda's and back again. "A woman founded the town and now a woman's running it."

Miranda set her jaw. "You object to the idea of a woman in authority?"

"Not at all." He gave her a wink and a half smile. "I'm fine with having a woman on top."

Heat flared over her throat and across her face, but Miranda refused to be baited.

"Then you'll feel right at home in Homestead, won't you?"

"That," Jud said quietly as she walked away, "is what I'm here to find out."

NAN WRIGHT stationed herself at one end of the long table borrowed from the Methodist church to hold the potluck dishes folks had brought to Greer's wedding reception. Her other option for passing the time was to go sit with the older ladies—mothers and grandmothers—as they gossiped about the latest love affairs, the newest pregnancies, the possible divorces. Nan kept telling herself she would never get that old.

Just as she wedged a spoon into the creamy goodness of macaroni and cheese, a jolt in the food line brought someone new to her end of the table.

"Delicious," Cruz Martinez said. When she looked into his face, he winked at her. "The food, too."

He reached for the spoon she'd just added to the dish and Nan watched in fascination as his fingers closed on the metal handle, still warm from her touch.

Cruz grinned as he moved to the next dish,

green bean casserole. "Are you having fun over here?"

She glanced around to be sure nobody was listening. "Not exactly."

"Me, neither." He spooned a helping of creamed corn onto his plate. "Why don't you come out from behind there and dance with me?"

"I—"

"Pardon me." Clarice Enfield reached across the table to serve herself a helping of scalloped tomatoes. "What are you doing standing in line over here, Cruz? You should be out on the dance floor with one of these cute young girls. Nan, where's Miranda? She'd be perfect for Cruz, don't you think?" She elbowed him in the side. "You two lovebirds could live in the cabin and Nan could live in the farmhouse like she does now. How perfect would that be?"

Once Clarice had moved on to the salads, Cruz leaned over the table. "How about you and me in the cabin and Miranda in the farmhouse?" he murmured.

Nan couldn't help smiling. "Hush! Next thing I know, all these motormouths will be talking about me. Go sit down and eat."

"Dance, later?"

"Shoo," she said, without committing herself.

As she looked along the length of the table, she caught Rae Jean Barker's eye. Rae Jean operated the beauty shop in downtown Homestead and considered herself the source for local news. As Nan watched, she turned and whispered something to Millicent Niebauer, who had stepped up to take her turn in the food line. Millie ran the local newspaper, the *Homestead Herald,* with her husband Hiram.

"I do like that young man you have working for you," Millie commented as she moved in front of Nan. "He's trustworthy and competent. And so attractive." She sighed. "I bet girls all over the county are dreaming about him."

"I expect so," Nan said warily.

"I imagine he'll set his sights on one of them soon, decide it's time for him to get married, have some kids, find his own land to manage."

"No doubt."

"And all those females who thought he was so handsome will be left sad and lonely. Maybe feeling a little foolish, even."

Nan met Millie's gaze. "Maybe."

The reporter shrugged. "That's the way life works." She moved on, no doubt fully aware of the knife she'd stuck between her victim's ribs.

When Cruz came back, Nan was prepared. "No, I can't dance."

"Why not?"

"I've got to get the table cleaned up."

"Later?"

"I don't think so. Why don't you dance with…" She saw the warning flares in his eyes. "Why don't you go talk to Wade? Callie's busy, and he's all by himself."

Cruz started to say something, then shut his mouth, turned on his heel and walked away.

Nan spent the rest of the reception hanging around the mothers and grandmothers. Maybe, without realizing it, she'd already gotten that old.

SINCE HE HADN'T BEEN invited to the reception, Jud decided to keep a low profile. He headed for the traditional party post for unattached males—the precinct around the keg.

With a tall plastic cup full of ice-cold beer in his hand, he leaned back against a tree, grateful for the chance to ease his barely healed leg and get his bearings before he actually tried to mingle.

Closest to him were the young studs, as he was sure they thought of themselves—he certainly had at nineteen and twenty. Like many of their kind, they spent the evening chugging their beer and making lewd comments about the girls preening for them on the other side of the dance floor. Jud didn't know most of the boys' names, but two of them he could identify by the fact that they were identical twins. Allen and Abel Enfield had the misfortune to take after their mother, with her frizzy red hair, freckled complexion and tendency to put on weight. The boys were big, beefy, and more than a little drunk.

"Mary Louise sure looks hot today." Jud wasn't sure which twin made the comment. "I bet I could get her to give me some, if I got her away from this stupid party."

The other boys greeted the suggestion with hoots and laughter. "Yeah, right," his brother said. "Just like last weekend. You were talking so big. And what'd you walk away with—a kiss on the cheek?"

That question started a scuffle, and Jud

thought he was going to be called upon to prevent bloodshed. But when a silver-haired man with a drooping mustache and wire-rimmed glasses approached the keg, the knot of grappling boys instantly fell apart.

"This," he said in an old-fashioned drawl, "is a wedding reception, not a tavern. If y'all can't behave, leave immediately and I'll deal with your bad manners myself later." He stared down the Enfield boys, then looked around at their cohorts. Something about the way he held his silver-topped cane constituted a threat. "Any part of that order y'all don't understand?"

A chorus of shamefaced "No, sirs" answered him.

The gentleman smiled. "Good. Now go ask those nice young ladies to dance. And keep your hands where everybody can see them."

The motley crew dispersed, and the man turned to Jud. "Boys will be boys, as I'm sure you remember. How are you, Jud? Good to see you back home."

"Thanks, Mr. Enfield." He disengaged as quickly as possible from the former mayor's handshake. "Looks like Homestead is getting to be a pretty lively place."

"Yes." Enfield's smile held no warmth. "Yes, Mayor Miranda's grand plan has certainly stirred things up, as I expect you'll find out. Are you staying in town very long? You and Ethan must have a lot of catching up to do. Last time you were home was your daddy's funeral…no, that's not right, is it? You didn't get here for that one. Your mother's funeral, must've been. Quite a while ago."

"Yes, sir." Jud deliberately relaxed his hands. He couldn't punch out a guest at a wedding reception, no matter how much he deserved it. "I was in the hospital when my dad…died."

"Suicide is always such a tragic business." Arlen clicked his tongue. "But I know you don't want to talk of this right now. Give my best to your brother—I'm sure I'll be seeing y'all around. That's the thing about small towns, isn't it? Everybody always knows what everybody else is doing."

He turned to watch the crowd for a minute and Jud stood still, wishing the man would go away.

"I remember a time," Enfield said with a

sigh, "when farm laborers knew their place and stayed there."

Jud followed his line of sight and saw the bride and groom laughing with a man who displayed his Hispanic heritage in his tanned skin and sleek black hair.

"Ah, well." He turned back to Jud. "Enjoy the party." When Enfield gripped his shoulder, Jud fought a strong urge to grab hold of the man's wrist and twist. Hard. The former mayor's sly digs had been one of the most unbearable aspects of living in Homestead. Something else that hadn't changed.

Enfield ambled away. With his teeth still gritted, Jud freshened his beer and went back to surveying the crowd. His attention lighted immediately on Miranda Wright, maybe because she was taller than the rest of the women, maybe because he hadn't expected her to look so beautiful.

That had been the problem four years ago, too. In the middle of his mother's funeral, he'd looked up to see Miranda straight across from him…warm, lovely, concerned.

He'd remembered a scrawny girl, all arms and legs, with tightly braided pigtails, an overbite and a learning disability that caused the teachers to keep her back in several grades. *Miserable Miranda* had been her nickname, often called out in a singsong voice. As Jud recalled, the moniker fit more often than not. He recalled, too, how she challenged the boys to races, to arm wrestling, to any kind of physical contest that she thought she could win. More often than not, she was right.

Somewhere, sometime, the pigtails had given way to a thick chestnut mane flowing around her shoulders. The dentist who'd corrected that overbite should get a medal, because now what a man noticed about Miranda's mouth was those full, kissable lips. Scrawny no longer applied, either—she had a figure perfectly proportioned for her height, with generous curves and long, shapely legs.

Jud had retained enough good sense to avoid her at the service, and afterward at his dad's house. But when she'd shown up just outside his truck window while he tried to drown himself in whiskey, he'd lost the last of his pickled brains.

He didn't recall every detail of their encounter, but he remembered enough. And so did Miranda—the fact that she still held it against him had been obvious in her face a few minutes ago.

So he would put her on his list of apologies to be made, along with most of Homestead's population. Not in front of friends, though, and especially not in front of Brother Ethan, the man with a permanent stick up his butt.

Looking over the crowd, Jud found his brother slow-dancing with a cute redhead who must be his new wife, judging by the lack of space between their bodies. Good ol' Ethan would never seduce a woman and then drop her like a hot brick. Faithful, loyal, honest…if Homestead had ever sponsored a scout troop, little Ethan would have been the poster boy.

Jud visualized a poster of himself with a big red *X* across the picture and the message Warning! Headed Straight for Hell! Do Not Follow! The glances he was getting from the guests at the party, the whispers he could see winnowing through the crowd, assured him his reputation remained intact.

On the dance floor, couples broke apart and then rejoined as the band commenced a two-step. Jud straightened up away from the tree as he saw Wade Montgomery coming toward him, accompanied by the man who didn't "know his place," according to Arlen Enfield.

"Join me," he told the sheriff, holding up his beer. "I don't like drinking alone." Usually.

"Don't mind if I do." Wade drew a cup for himself and one for the other guy. "Jud Ritter, this is Cruz Martinez, the foreman on Nan Wright's farm. Cruz, Jud is Ethan's brother."

Martinez offered a firm handshake. "Pleasure to meet you."

"Same here."

"I knew you'd need a place to stay," Wade said, "and I didn't think you'd…uh…want to crowd in at Ethan's house, with the kids and all."

Nice guy, Wade, and tactful. Jud had never known him to be anything but loyal and honorable in the twenty-five years they'd been friends.

"Cruz lives in a cabin out on Nan's ranch," Wade continued, "and he's got plenty of room. He says he'll be glad for some company."

Jud recognized a bad idea when he heard one. "I thought I'd…uh…stay at the Rise and Shine, out on the highway. I don't want to put anybody out, especially the bride and groom on their wedding night."

"You don't want to stay at the Rise and Shine," the sheriff assured him. "The cockroaches rearrange the furniture every night when the lights go out."

"Yeah, but—"

"Everybody in town will know your comings and goings if you stay at the motel. Tripp Dooley still owns the place and he still goes through the guests' luggage while they're out of the room. I've never caught him stealing, but not for lack of trying. Chances are good he'd compromise your investigation, especially if any of the locals are involved." He blew out a deep, frustrated breath. "And they practically have to be."

Jud held up a hand. "Okay, I give in." He'd just avoid Mayor Wright on her own land as much as possible, and wrap up his business—personal and professional—fast. "Thanks," he told his host.

"No problem." Martinez shrugged. "Wade

says you're looking into some of the trouble we've been dealing with around here."

"Anything I can do."

"We had a break just this week," Wade said. "The kid who played some tricks on Greer Bell's guest ranch—"

"That's Greer Kelley, now," Martinez put in.

"Right. The Sunrise Guest Ranch. This kid's kinda slow, and when a stranger offered him cash to play a couple of 'harmless' pranks, he agreed. He's been too scared to identify who paid him until this week."

"You picked up the guy?"

Wade nodded. "Yesterday. He's sitting in my jail, not saying much of anything. I figured you could use your big-city interrogation techniques to make him talk. Or we could try straight torture. My dad has this bullwhip at his house…"

"You're a violent SOB, Montgomery. I always knew that."

The three of them laughed together, then Wade went off to find his wife. Martinez was giving Jud directions to the foreman's house on Hayseed Farm when shouts broke out from the crowd.

"There they go!" The westward flow of bodies indicated that Noah and Greer were escaping toward the park entrance.

Bringing up the rear of the procession, Jud arrived on the street in time to see the bride double over with laughter at the appearance of her car. Amidst a deluge of tiny purple flowers, Noah Kelley ushered his wife into the vehicle, stared at his shaving-cream-coated hand for a disgusted moment, then ran to the driver's side. Cheers, whistles and rattling tin cans followed the couple out of town as the Blazer disappeared into the sunset.

Once the bride and groom had left, their guests didn't linger. Soon the park was empty except for the cleanup crew composed of the couple's friends, including Cruz Martinez. Jud didn't want to show up at his host's house before the man got there himself, so he decided he would help out where he could. Thanks to a couple of bullet holes in his torso and one in his thigh, his shoulder and leg still weren't up to heavy lifting. But he thought he could manage some of the lighter chores.

His brother and Ryan Gallagher were folding up chairs and tables.

"Looks like there are plenty of these to go around," Jud said, closing the seat of one chair. "Mind if I help?"

"Have at it," Ryan said.

"Don't put yourself out," Ethan said at exactly the same time.

Ryan shifted his gaze from Ethan to Jud and back again. "Uh…Kristin needs me for something," he mumbled, and was gone in the next second.

"Real finesse," Jud told his brother. "Could you have been ruder?"

Ethan didn't glance in his direction. "If I set my mind to it, I probably could. You don't have the least responsibility for clearing up after this party. Why bother?"

"My mother taught me to be polite."

"I'd say you missed a few lessons. Like 'honor your father…'" Ethan shook his head. "No. I'm not going to do this. You're so hot to fold chairs, be my guest." He let the chair he was holding fall to the ground and walked away to help his wife dismantle the food tables.

At the very thought of food, Jud's stomach rumbled—he hadn't eaten since leaving Austin at noon.

"I guess you didn't get anything to eat."

Miranda picked up the chair Ethan had dropped, folded it and set it neatly in the rack.

"No big deal. I'll get something later."

"On your drive back to Austin." She nodded, as if he'd told her his plans.

He took some satisfaction in correcting that obviously comforting assumption. "I'm staying in town for a few days."

"What?" From her horrified stare, he might as well have announced his plans to commit serial murder. "Why?"

"Because I want to."

"But...where will you stay? I mean, Ethan—"

"Wouldn't have me within ten feet of his fence line," he finished for her. "Right. That's okay. Somebody else offered me a room, and I accepted."

Turning to take down a table, she shrugged a careless shoulder. "Who would that be?"

"Cruz Martinez said I could bunk in with him."

"What?" Her screech drew the attention of people all over the park. She let the table fall and planted her hands on her curvy hips. "Cruz Martinez invited you to stay in his house?"

"And I'm grateful. I wasn't looking forward to staying at the Rise and Shine. Especially since Tripp Dooley still runs the place."

Her glare could have burned through steel. "Well, it's just too bad for you that you're going to be staying there after all."

Jud gave her an innocent look. "I don't understand."

"You understand perfectly, Jud Ritter. My mother and I own the Hayseed Farm." She marched up to him and stuck a finger in his chest. "And I'm telling you right now that there's no way I'm having you staying anywhere on my property. Got that? No way in hell!"

CHAPTER THREE

MIRANDA KNEW Jud had deliberately driven her to lose her temper, just the way he'd done when they were in school. She couldn't count the hours she'd spent in detention because of his teasing.

At least Homestead's mayor would not have to suffer detention for fighting. On the other hand, yelling at Jud didn't do much for her image as a mature, competent official.

She stepped back. "I really don't think you'd be happy staying at our place," she said more calmly. "Wade and Callie have lots of room, or there's Greer's guest ranch…."

"I'd rather not horn in on the newlyweds, if it's all the same to you."

"Well, there's—"

"Look, I'll stay out of your way," he said. "You don't have to fear for your virtue or your livestock. I just need a place to crash."

Miranda couldn't let it alone. "You haven't been home for more than a night in fifteen years. Why the urge to stay on now?"

Jud opened his mouth, and she thought she might get an answer. But then Wade stepped up beside them.

"I'm responsible for that, Ms. Mayor. Let's meet in your office Monday morning about ten and I'll explain what's going on." Wade drew Jud away to meet his wife, and Miranda had to be satisfied with what little she knew.

Twilight came early in December, and they finished cleaning up the park in near darkness. Finally, Miranda climbed into her truck and let her head fall back against the seat. "I'm exhausted. Baling a field of hay is an easier day's work than throwing a party."

In the passenger seat, her mom chuckled. "That's why we're farmers, not event planners, or whatever they're called."

"Now that's a horrid thought—a continual round of parties to plan, set up and take down." Miranda shuddered. "Just kill me."

As they drove out of town, they passed Cruz's bright blue truck still parked on the curb, with Jud standing at the driver's open door.

"Was that Jud Ritter?" Nan turned her head to stare out the rear window.

"Didn't you see him at the party? He showed up while we were decorating Greer's Blazer."

"No, I didn't." Her mother dropped back into her seat. "I guess I wasn't paying attention. Did he come back for the wedding?"

"He didn't even come back for his own brother's ceremony. He wouldn't say exactly why he's here, but Wade has something to do with it. We're going to meet Monday so he can explain."

"I'm surprised he was talking to Cruz, though. I don't think Jud's been home since Cruz came to town."

"Wade very kindly arranged for Jud to stay at Cruz's place while he's here."

"What?" The sharpness of the word was completely unlike her mother's usual drawl.

"I don't like the idea, either. I mean, Cruz leases the house, but you still own it, and I'm not sure where he gets off having somebody else stay there."

"Oh...well, of course, Cruz is free to have friends stay with him." Nan raked her fingers through her cap of sleek silver hair.

"We didn't object when his brother came up from Mexico."

"Yes, but—" What did she mean to say? "Jud just plain makes me uncomfortable."

"I know. I remember the tears he cost you all those years ago. But you've both grown up. I doubt you'll even notice he's in town."

Miranda glanced into the rearview mirror and saw two sets of headlights following her as she turned off the highway into their private drive.

"I'll notice," she growled. "Jud will make sure of that."

JUD SLOWED DOWN as he approached the entrance to Hayseed Farm, allowing the two trucks in front of him to get well ahead. Thanks to his childhood feud with Miranda, he'd never set foot on Hayseed Farm during his years in Homestead. This was his first—and maybe his only—chance to satisfy his curiosity.

On both sides of the narrow gravel lane, winter hay had sprouted, narrow green shoots standing ankle high in row after row, acre upon acre. Miranda's mother had managed the farm since her husband died, when

Miranda was only three. For thirty years, Nan Wright had single-handedly planted, harvested and baled hay for local livestock farmers. Like any farm kid, Miranda probably helped out as soon as she was able.

Zeb Ritter had sure as hell put his sons to work in the fields and the barn, practically as soon as they could walk. Jud had hated every minute of every chore. He still remembered the burn of resentment in his belly, the desperate desire to get away.

The hay ended at a line of pine trees bordering the yard around the house—a white, two-story farmhouse, nearly a century old by the looks of it, with wide porches on all sides and a red tin roof shaded by pecan trees and live oaks. A branch of the driveway led directly to the house, where Miranda's blue truck was parked, but Jud followed the curve around the tree line and headed toward the back of the farm.

Behind the house stood a good-sized barn, painted red to match the tin roof, with brown-fenced paddocks and pastures stretching into the distance. He vaguely remembered Miranda doing some barrel racing in the junior rodeos. Jud had hit the pro circuit as soon as they'd let him have his card, so he didn't remember whether she'd actually won or not. His own winning streak had burned out so quickly, the memory was just a blur.

Beyond the pastures sat a log cabin with a stand of pines behind and a field in front planted with hundreds of silver-leafed shrubs. Cruz Martinez's truck sat close to the side of the house. This must be the place.

Jud pulled in beside the Z71 and cut his engine. The country night surrounded him—a quiet, wintry darkness, unbroken by streetlights or the growl of machines, textured by the rustle of pine needles and grass blades as the wind passed by. He hadn't experienced this kind of silence in…how many years?

His heart thudded against his ribs as he recognized the answer. Four. Most of four years had passed since he'd lain in the back of his truck looking up at the stars, listening to the spring sounds of frogs and crickets and whip-poor-wills.

Four years since he'd nearly ravished Miranda Wright in the back of that truck. The memory gripped him like a bad hangover, complete with regret for ever taking that first drink and, even worse, that first kiss. He usually played with women who knew the score, a category which definitely excluded Mayor Miranda.

But at least he'd stopped in time. She might have had her feelings hurt, but he hadn't done anything unforgivable. He'd just been a stupid jerk.

"Damn." Shaking his head, Jud got out of the truck and pulled his duffel from behind his seat.

As he reached the porch steps, Cruz Martinez opened the front door of the cabin. "Come in, make yourself at home." He led the way into warmth and light and a room neater than any bachelor pad Jud had ever seen.

"Take the room at the end of the hall," Martinez said, pointing down a dark passage. "There's a bathroom right next door. More important—" he grinned as he heard Jud's stomach rumble "—the kitchen is at the back of the house and there's plenty of stuff for sandwiches in the fridge."

"Sounds great."

Grabbing a jacket, Martinez went back to the front door. "I'm going to check on the barn. Walk over after you eat and I'll give you a tour. Or hit the sack, if you want. Just treat the place like your own."

"Thanks. Hey," Jud said. "What's planted in the field out front? All those silver bushes?"

His host grinned. "That's Miranda's pet project. She's been nursing those lavender plants for a couple of years now."

"Lavender? For perfume?"

"She's got all sorts of plans for marketing. I don't understand most of them." He winked at Jud. "I think it's a female thing."

"In other words, clear as mud."

"Exactly."

Left alone in the cabin, Jud set his bag down in the assigned bedroom, noting with approval the king-size bed. His four extra inches over six feet didn't fit well in small spaces. He used the bathroom, washed his hands, then flipped back the shower curtain, wondering if he'd be taking showers on his knees.

What caught his eye, though, was a scrap of lavender lace draped over the towel bar at the opposite end of the tub from the water faucet. Jud reached out and caught the fabric between two fingers, pulling it off the bar. A bra, he realized, lace cups and satin straps with a small bow in the center.

"Well, well," he said, his jaw tight. "No wonder Ms. Mayor was so upset to hear I was staying with Cruz Martinez."

Resisting the urge to break something—Miranda Wright's neck, for a start—Jud carefully put the garment back where he'd found it, flipped off the light and went to make himself something to eat.

AFTER AN AFTERNOON spent in skirts and dress shoes, the Wright women changed clothes as soon as they got home. Wearing jeans and a sweater, Nan came downstairs a few minutes later to find her daughter snuggled into the sofa in the living room, TV remote control in hand.

Miranda looked her over. "You're planning to go out? Something wrong?" She wore her favorite sleepwear—a faded, stretched-out, long-sleeved T-shirt over flannel pajama pants decorated with penguins on skis. She'd scrunched her hair into a ponytail. Dusty, the golden Labrador retriever, lay in a contented butterscotch curl across Miranda's feet.

Nan shook her head. "Nope. I thought I'd go and check on the horses, is all, look in on the moms-to-be."

"I'll come with you." To Dusty's distress, Mi-randa shifted her feet to the floor and started to get up.

"Don't bother." Nan pushed her back onto the couch. "I'll just walk through. Be back in a few minutes." She held her breath, expecting an argument.

For once, her daughter didn't insist. "Call if you need me," she said, burrowing back between dog and blanket.

"I will." In case she changed her mind, Nan went straight through the kitchen to the mudroom, where she slipped on barn shoes and her favorite jacket. Outside, the night felt a lot colder than it had earlier, and she buttoned the jacket as she hurried to the barn. When she saw the doors had been rolled back, she slowed to an easy walk, so she wouldn't be breathless when she arrived.

With her first step into the barn, Bailey, her buck-skin stallion, turned in his stall to greet her.

"Hey, big man." She slid open the top half of his door so she could rub his face and neck. "I came to see your new baby. He's gonna be a big guy, just like you." Bailey rubbed his muzzle over her hair. "Uh-huh. I love you, too." She kissed his cheek before closing the door.

Starlet's stall was across the aisle. Nan approached and looked through the grate. "Everything okay?"

As she'd expected, Cruz knelt in the straw, running his hands over the soft dun coat of the sleepy foal they'd named Cappucino. "Sure. I woke him up a little, but he's being a good boy." Nearby, Starlet, a sweet little bay mare, chewed a mouthful of alfalfa hay and kept close watch on the human touching her baby. "What are you doing out here?"

"Just checking." She swallowed hard. "I hear you have a houseguest."

Cruz stretched to his feet with an easy grace. He still wore the white shirt, new jeans and fancy ostrich-skin boots he'd looked so good in at the party, and he looked even better without so many people around.

"That's right. Jud Ritter is doing some work for Wade, and I said it would be okay if he stayed with me."

Beside Cruz, Cappucino folded his legs in

awk-ward angles, trying to stand. Starlet nosed her baby to his feet and he immediately began nuzzling the mare's side, looking for his next meal.

Nan backed away as Cruz left the stall. "So, I guess we won't...I won't be seeing much of you for a while." Her clumsy choice of words only struck her after she said them. How often had she told him she loved just looking at him?

He leaned his shoulders back against the stall door and crossed his arms over his chest. "I guess not."

She didn't hear regret in his voice, and she couldn't read his face in the shadows of the barn. "Did you do this on purpose?"

"You mean, did I plan it? How could I? I never met Jud Ritter until this afternoon at the party."

"But..."

Cruz nodded. "But I was willing to accept Wade's suggestion that he stay with me."

"Why?"

"I think you and I need some space."

The width of the aisle between them was too much space, as far as Nan was concerned. "For what?"

"To choose our priorities. To look ahead and figure out where we go from here."

She'd sensed some unsettledness in him lately, but this seemed to come out of an empty sky. "Why do we have to go anywhere? What's wrong with where we are?"

He stared at her for a long minute. "You enjoy hiding behind the widows and old ladies at parties, like you did this afternoon? You don't want to dance with me, have some fun?"

As Nan struggled to frame an answer, he continued. "You think I want to spend my time leaning against the wall, watching everybody else have a good time?"

"Cruz—"

"When I'm with you, what we have together is enough." His broad shoulders lifted on a deep breath. "But I'm tired of living two lives. Having Jud around will keep me thinking straight, maybe long enough to work this out."

Her heart cramped. "I don't mean to force you into living two lives."

"But if you're not comfortable with people knowing about us, I'm not going to broadcast the news. And that requires me to be one person with you and someone different with everybody else in town. I can't even be honest with Miranda—and she's one of my best friends."

"Yes, and you're closer to her in age than to me." Nan bit her lip as soon as she said the words. She hated sounding like a bitter old woman, jealous of her daughter. But if the shoe fit…

In two strides, Cruz crossed the aisle to close his hands over her shoulders. "Which doesn't make a damn bit of difference to the way I feel about either of you."

They were the same height, and now she could see the anger, the pain blazing in his dark brown eyes. What kind of love was hers, that hurt him this much?

"You're right," she said. "I'm not being fair—"

"Fair, hell." His arms came around her, hard. "I'm selfish enough to want to show you off, that's all."

He claimed her mouth with the directness that was so much a part of his nature, and her body ignited for him in an instant, as it had from the very first. She'd been married for five years, yet had not known passion could take her this way. When she lay alone in her bed now, she ached for Cruz beside her. When they were together, like this, she couldn't get enough of him. There were hay bales in the stall behind them. Her knees weakened and she pulled him closer....

Down the aisle, Bailey whickered as he always did when someone approached the barn.

"Miranda," Nan whispered, and turned her face away, pressing her forehead against Cruz's shoul-der. "I should go back to the house. I told her I wouldn't be long."

Smiling slightly, Cruz loosened his hold and stepped back. "See what I mean? I lose my head completely when I'm around you."

"I'll take that as a compliment," Nan said, trying for lightness. She turned to walk farther into the barn, checking on the mares who had yet to drop their foals. Regaining control. "Flora was pacing this morning before we went to the wedding—I'm thinking tonight might be her—"

"There you are!"

Nan whipped her head around to see her daugh-ter silhouetted at the barn door, wearing her barn coat and shoes and her pajamas. Dusty trotted down the aisle.

"I was beginning to wonder if you'd forgotten the way to the barn and wandered out into the night," she teased. "Or been eaten by wild animals." Head tilted, she looked at Cruz, then at Nan again.

"So what's going on?"

Miranda didn't really expect her mother or Cruz to answer the question. Any intelligent observer would understand what was going on—especially after two or three occasions like this one. She just couldn't resist ribbing them a little about their "secret."

"We got to talking about the mares and foals," Cruz said, his voice deeper and a little huskier than usual. "And the party, of course."

"I thought Greer and Noah looked so happy together." After giving Dusty a head rub, Nan came slowly toward the front of the barn. Cruz backed out of her way, keeping the width of the aisle between them. "And we all had a great time."

"Of course," Miranda agreed. "Even Jud Ritter." She looked at Cruz. "Where is your houseguest?"

"I gave him free run of the fridge and left him to it. He didn't reach the food tables at the reception."

"How long is he planning to stay?"

"Couldn't say."

"Wade said he'd invited Jud here to do some work. Do you know anything about that?"

Footsteps sounded on the floor behind her. "Not much more than you do," Jud said. "And he doesn't ask nearly as many questions."

Miranda stood for a moment with her eyes shut tight, thinking about her messy ponytail and lack of makeup, the fact that she wasn't wearing a bra under the old T-shirt and the way the seat of the baggy, *penguin* pajama pants hung down below her butt. Then she opened her eyes and turned around to face him like the adult she was supposed to be.

"Cruz says you finally got something to eat."

"He keeps a well-stocked refrigerator. Not like mine—I don't know if I've ever used more than one shelf at a time."

"Cruz is a good cook," Nan said from the doorway. "Get him to make you his chicken molé sometime. Delicious." She looked at a point somewhere between Miranda and Cruz. "I'm going to take a nap, then come out about ten to keep an eye on Flora during the night. Call me if something happens before then."

As soon as Nan left the barn, Cruz stirred. "I didn't have much to eat this afternoon, myself. Think I'll go get a bite, then come back to the delivery deck. Is that okay with you, Miranda?"

"That's—" Cruz was gone before she could finish her answer. Disconcerted, she glanced toward Jud, standing his ground at the front of the barn.

"Sorry to intrude," he said. "Cruz offered a tour if I walked over. I didn't know you'd be here."

Miranda backed toward Flora's stall. "No, it's okay. I think I can tolerate five minutes in your company. I'll handle the tour…if you're still interested."

Jud hesitated, then nodded. "Sure." He pursued her down the aisle. "How long has Martinez worked here?"

"A little over two years, since Joe Haynes died."

"I remember old Joe. I got the rough side of his tongue more times than I could count."

"He was a good man. And a good foreman for Hayseed Farm, since before I was born. Nan wouldn't have survived those first years after my dad died without Joe."

"Martinez measures up to the job?"

"He's conscientious and works hard. What he doesn't know, he learns fast."

"He keeps pretty much to himself?"

She frowned at the question. "We're friends, the three of us. We usually eat dinner together, catch up on the day. Why all the questions?"

"Nosy, I guess." He looked down as Dusty sniffed at his boots, then pursued a thorough investigation up both pants legs. When she reached his knees, he held out his hand and let her sniff his palm. "Nice dog."

Miranda nodded. "The best. She goes everywhere I do."

"Except weddings?"

She turned away from him to avoid returning his smile. "Weddings and funerals." And wasn't that a stupid thing to say? "Sorry. I didn't mean—"

He shook his head. "No problem."

Embarrassed yet again, she peered through the grate in Flora's stall door. "How ya' doin', mama? That baby comin' tonight?"

Jud stepped up beside her, his presence like a wall of high-wattage lightbulbs on her right side. Her face heated up and her breath got short, but she was damned if she'd creep away from him just for a little oxygen.

"Cute mare," he said quietly, propping his shoulder against the wall. "Is there a reason to be worried? As I recall, most horses drop their foals without help or complications."

"She's eighteen, which is old to be having babies. We lost her foal last time, and almost lost Flora. We don't want that to happen again." In the stall, the mare flattened her ears, shook her head violently and kicked a hind leg toward her swollen belly.

"So why'd you breed her?"

Worry had already shortened Miranda's temper. "So much for letting go of the past. You still think I'm dumb as dirt, don't you?"

He straightened up from the wall. "What the—"

Miranda jerked her attention back to the horse. She caught her breath as Flora dropped to her knees, then rolled to lie on her side. After a motionless minute, the mare struggled to her feet and started pacing again.

"Another process horses seem to handle without help is mating." Miranda didn't bother to look at Jud as she spoke. "We came home one afternoon last winter to find Bailey, our stallion, in the same field with Flora. Somebody had left a gate open, then Bailey tore down a couple of fences…and here we are."

She turned away and reached for the stall door latch, but in the next instant Jud gripped her shoulder with a strong hand and pulled her back around. Standing at her side, Dusty growled low in her throat.

Jud ignored the dog. "Let's get this out of the way right now. If I ever said you were dumb—and I might well have because I was full of myself back then—you have my sincere apology."

He watched as surprise dawned on Miranda's face. She gazed up at him, and he wondered if she was trying to read his mind. In the years since high school, he'd forgotten how intense she could be. But how could he have forgotten those mysterious topaz eyes?

Or had he just never noticed?

Inside the stall beside them, Flora gave a moaning neigh, lay down in the straw again and groaned.

He loosened his hands and Miranda turned to face the stall. "You can do it, mama. Just relax." She wrapped her fingers in the grate, clinging with a force that turned her skin white. "Push, mama. Push!"

Jud had never been good at waiting. "I should go…."

She spared him a second of thought. "Before you do, find the phone in the feed room across the aisle, right by the door. Punch two for Mom, three for Cruz. Get them down here."

In less than five minutes, Nan Wright came running, and Martinez showed up within ten. By then, Jud would have fought anyone who tried to kick him out. The four of them stood in silence outside the stall, watching the mare labor. Miranda's dog paced in the barn aisle behind them.

Finally, the bluish white amniotic sac appeared beneath Flora's tail. Martinez swore. "That's a rear hoof. The foal's coming out backward."

"We have to turn the baby. Get Doc Shaw on his cell phone." Miranda dropped her jacket where she stood and opened the stall door. First, she knelt at Flora's head, stroking the heavy forelock back from the mare's eyes, smoothing her hands over the sweat-lathered neck and murmuring encouragement.

Then, carefully, she moved to the horse's rear end. Cruz went for the phone.

Nan stood in the open doorway. "Miranda was there when Flora was born," she said when Jud looked at her. "The mare trusts her more than anyone else."

Carrying the phone, Martinez came to stand beside Jud. "I've got Doc Shaw," he said. "He's on his way."

"What do I do?" Miranda looked up, and her gaze caught Jud's for a second before shifting to Cruz. "He has to coach me." Face sheened with sweat, eyes wide, she looked desperate. Terrified.

Flora strained, then relaxed. Miranda took hold of the hooves just visible through the amnion and pushed them back into the mare. "It's tight," she said through gritted teeth. "Mom…"

Nan knelt beside her and the two of them worked through the next contraction. Then again, and again. Martinez conveyed instructions from the veterinarian in a low, tense tone. Despite the December chill outside, the humid air in the barn made breathing a chore.

Jud watched for what seemed like eternity as Nan and Miranda pressed and pushed against the mare's belly, trying to manipulate the body within. Though he'd grown up with horses, spent years riding rodeo broncs, he'd never witnessed a breech birth, never seen anyone turn a baby in the womb. He had no idea whether to expect success—or tragedy.

Headlights flashed in the darkness outside the front of the barn. A car door slammed and then an older man with a surprisingly full head of dark brown hair came striding down the barn aisle. "How's it going?"

Martinez said, "Not good," just as Flora groaned with palpable force. Nan and Miranda shouted at the same time. When Jud looked into the stall, he saw the two women flattened against the wall...and two horses where before there'd only been one.

"Looks like I'm too late," the vet said, grinning. "Miranda does seem to make things happen fast, don't she?" He shot Jud a sideways glance as he brushed by. "Jud Ritter. Never thought I'd see you in this town again. Can't find anywhere else to cause trouble? Now what's going on with this baby?"

Miranda was gently rubbing the dark bay foal with towels provided by Martinez. "He's sluggish," she said, frowning. "You better come in, Doc."

The vet moved into the stall as Nan stepped out, rubbing her face with a towel. "Damn, I don't know why I go through this torture every year."

"Because you love watching them grow," Mar-tinez said with a smile. "What would spring be like without a couple of weanlings driving us all crazy?"

"Peaceful? Worry-free? Profitable, without all the medicines to pay for?" She gave a tired grin.

A gasp from Miranda drew Jud back to the stall. Flora was on her feet again, nuzzling the foal as it clumsily, precariously levered itself to stand. With a few nudges from its mom and a guiding hand from Miranda, the baby latched on to a teat and began to suck.

Jud squeezed his eyes shut to clear his suddenly blurred vision.

Once the vet had checked over the colt, Miranda and Dr. Shaw came out of the stall. Miranda turned to slide the door shut and Nan stepped up and put her arms around her daughter's waist from behind. "Isn't he beautiful?"

"Bailey makes great babies. What are we going to name him?"

Nan glanced at Martinez again. "Espresso?"

He tilted his head. "Cocoa?"

Miranda looked at Jud. "Bailey is Baileys Irish Cream."

"Ah. How about Kahlúa?"

They all looked at the dark brown foal, and back at Jud. "Perfect," Nan said. "I love it. Don't you, Miranda?"

Miranda had buried her face in a towel. She mumbled words that might have been anything and continued to hide behind the red terry cloth.

The veterinarian left with promises to return in the morning to check up on Kahlúa, and Martinez walked him to his truck before heading back to his place. After a short argument, Miranda agreed to let her mother take the first watch on the new arrival, with Dusty for company.

"I'll be out at three," she promised, walking toward the barn door, rubbing a hand over the nape of her neck. Jud studied the sway of her hips, the cling of her thin, damp T-shirt to the smooth curves of her back, and felt a hollow develop under his ribs. This reaction to Miranda Wright was something else he hadn't remembered. Wasn't prepared for.

He took a step forward, only to trip over her jacket, still lying on the floor. With his next stride he grabbed the coat and kept walking until he caught up with Miranda outside.

"You forgot this."

She looked dazed as he handed over the garment. "Oh. Thanks. It's cold out here."

A full moon poured light over the winter grass, the white clapboard house and Miranda herself. As she shrugged into the jacket, Jud could see just how chilled she'd been in the pucker of her nipples against the inadequate T-shirt.

That hollow inside threatened to swallow

him. He drove his fists deep into the pockets of his jeans.

When he continued to walk beside her toward the house, Miranda stopped and faced him. "What are you doing?"

"Just escorting the lady home."

"I am home. This whole spread is my home."

"You never know what might come out of the dark."

She walked on. "So I've learned," she said in a dry voice.

He deserved the comment, so he didn't say anything. At the back porch, he opened the door to the house and ushered her in. "Thanks for letting me watch tonight."

She climbed the steps, then faced him from just inside the threshold. "At least you weren't totally useless. You made the phone calls, and you brought me my coat."

Jud gave a short laugh. "So happy to be of service. You might yet be glad you changed your mind and let me stay." The question remained as to whether he would come out of the experience intact. He doubted it.

"I doubt it," she echoed, retreating into the kitchen shadows. "Just keep out of my way, unless you want me to change it back." The thud of the house door punctuated her order.

"Good idea." Jud walked across the open ground toward the foreman's cabin, about a quarter mile down the gravel drive. "The last thing I need in my life is an argumentative, bossy, overbearing…"

He glanced over his shoulder just as a light in the corner upstairs room of the farmhouse winked out. He thought about that lavender lace bra.

"…warmhearted, sexy and absolutely untouchable woman."

CHAPTER FOUR

JUD SLEPT LATE the next morning and had to break the speed limit driving into town in order to reach the church steps as the steeple bell rang the beginning of the Sunday service. Once inside, he leaned back against the door for a moment, allowing his eyes to adjust to the dimness of dark wood and stained glass. He felt too dressed up when he saw the open-collared shirts and slacks worn by most of the men—an interesting change from the days when every little boy put a noose around his neck for church on Sunday.

His suit and tie were not, he was quite sure, the reason several people gawked at him over their shoulders, then leaned toward their neighbors to pass the news. Before the whispering could drown out the music of the organ, he planted himself in the first empty seat he saw, as near to the back of the church as possible.

When he looked to his right, he found Miss Frances Haase, the town librarian, on the other end of the pew, staring down her nose at him as if he were a fifth grader who'd forgotten to return his library book. Jud sent her a smile and got a sniff and a frown for his effort. Facing forward again, he immediately recognized the slope of the shoulders, the set of the ears and the wave in the hair of the man in front of him. Ethan and his family were sitting in the very next row.

Jud didn't doubt Ethan knew he was there. The tension across the two feet between them felt like an electric field, sure to scorch skin if he tried to reach through. Ethan's wife, Kayla, glanced over her shoulder several times, once with an almost-smile. Three kids on her other side stole peeks at him throughout the service. The one little girl looked enough like Kayla to be her daughter, but Ethan hadn't been married even a year, so Jud didn't know where the other girl and the boy had sprung from. He wasn't sure he'd ever get a chance to ask Ethan about them…or anything else.

Yet here he sat—on a hard wooden pew that provoked his leg and chest to throb in protest—betting his brother wouldn't blow him off with the congregation watching.

The service did bring back memories from childhood—those endless hours spent squirming between his mom's disappointed frown and the vise of his dad's grip on his shoulder. Holden Kelley, Noah's dad, had led the church back then, preaching hellfire and brimstone sermons which had fallen on hard ground as far as Jud was concerned. But then, Father Kelley had always predicted a bad end for that oldest Ritter boy.

Noah, on the other hand, delivered an accessible, generous message on forgiveness and old-fashioned charity. Though surprised to see the groom in the pulpit on the morning after his wedding, Jud found himself chuckling at the young minister's words.

Ethan sat stiff as a board through the entire message.

Standing for the final hymn, Jud knew he would get only seconds, at most, to connect with Ethan. What could he say that might compel his brother to listen?

Noah pronounced the final grace in everyday language, and the organ came to life. Jud reached out to tap Ethan's shoulder, but a crisp voice from his right deflected his attention.

"Well, Jud Ritter, I heard you'd returned."

He stifled a groan and turned to meet his fate. "Yes, ma'am. How are you, Miss Haase?"

"As well as could be expected. What have you been up to all this time?"

"I'm with the police department. Down in Austin."

Lips pursed together, she nodded. "Yes, I'd heard you crossed over to the side of the angels. I clipped the article about your citation a few months ago. You appear to be good at your job."

"I do my best." He gave his most charming smile, aware that Ethan and his family had slipped out of their pew and were headed toward the chapel doors.

Miss Haase proved immune to his charm. "Nowadays, perhaps. But for twenty years, I've been expecting you to return the copy of *Lady Chatterley's Lover* you borrowed in the seventh grade."

Jud swallowed hard. "I—"

"If you don't know where it is, I want a new copy on my desk by the end of the week. Now, excuse me."

He stumbled out of the pew, but Miss Haase still stepped on his toes on her way out. Turning toward the back of the church, Jud saw that Ethan had reached the doorway where Noah and Greer stood to greet their flock. A double line of parishioners stood between Jud and his brother. By the time he got to the door, Ethan would be on his way home.

Fortunately, Jud had spent enough time playing hide-and-seek in the church hallways when he was supposed to be in Sunday school that he knew exactly the locations of the exits near the front of the building.

He rounded the outside corner of the church in time to see Ethan shaking hands with Noah at the door. Kayla gave Greer a hug, and kissed Noah on the cheek. Then, finally, they made their way down the steps to the sidewalk.

Jud came at them from the opposite direction. Unlike yesterday, Ethan didn't see him in time to keep him at a distance.

"Good morning," Jud said, with a smile at Kayla and the kids. "Amazing weather for December, isn't it? I'm Jud—Ethan's big brother."

Kayla glanced at her husband's stony expression. "More like May than December," she agreed. "Um...I'm Kayla. This is Megan, my daughter." She eased the little girl forward. "And Brad and Heather. Ethan and I..." She looked at her husband. "Ethan and I are adopting them."

"I'm glad to meet you." Jud nodded at the children. He was determined to keep his temper, but he could feel his face heating up as Ethan continued to stand there without saying a word. "I'm gonna guess y'all share Ethan's love of horses."

"I do," Megan piped up. "I ride Birdsong all the time."

A huge pit opened up in Jud's belly. He looked at Ethan and found that his brother's expression had changed from indifference to outright defiance.

Jud cleared his throat. "That's...nice." Inside him, the voice in the pit screamed, "You can't have Angela's horse!" But he didn't let the noise escape. "Birdsong has always been a terrific pony."

"We canter and trot over crossbars and everything."

In the next instant, Brad and Heather

chimed in to tell him about their horses. Jud tried to look interested, while Kayla wore a nervous frown and Ethan resumed the stone-faced stare.

"Let's get into the truck," Kayla said finally, putting her hands on the backs of the two girls. "Ethan will be along in just a minute. Good to meet you, Jud." She nodded, cast a final glance at her husband and scurried off with the children.

Ethan watched them until they reached the vehicle, then turned back to Jud. "Okay, you engineered this encounter. Say what you came to say and then go back where you belong."

"What I have to say will take a long time. I thought we could get together—"

"No. We don't have anything to talk about that can't be settled in a sentence or two." Ethan turned away and took a step in the direction of his truck.

Jud clamped a hand on his brother's shoulder and pulled him back around. "You're wrong. We've got years of talking to do. Not just the last four, but a decade before that. Why don't—"

"Why don't you get the message?" Ethan

raised his fist and knocked Jud's arm away. "You walked out on this family, and couldn't be bothered to come back when things went bad. You weren't here to help us get back on our feet after the land deal failed. You weren't here to watch Angela die. You weren't the one who walked in to discover that Dad had blown his brains out. You couldn't even be bothered to come to my wedding."

He set his hands on his hips. "You've made it pretty damn clear that you want no part of us or this town."

"I'm trying to tell you—"

"Don't bother. I'm not listening."

Ethan spun on his heel and stalked off toward his truck.

Only when he swerved to avoid a woman in his path did Jud realize they'd drawn a ring of spectators to their argument. Some faces he recognized, some he didn't, but all of them wore an expression of unabashed curiosity that assured him everyone in town would know about the Ritter brothers' confrontation before nightfall.

"Showdown at the Homestead town square," he muttered, heading for his own vehicle. Thank God, they hadn't actually been armed.

Because at this point, he wouldn't put it past Brother Ethan to shoot him down in cold blood.

AS SOON AS ETHAN STOPPED the truck and turned off the engine, Megan, Brad and Heather tumbled out of the backseat and raced for the house, desperate to change clothes and get back to play. Ethan, however, gripped the steering wheel tightly and stared straight ahead. His head still pounded with the fury that had overtaken him at church, and his stomach churned.

"Ethan?" Kayla put a soft hand on his arm. "Are you okay?"

He dragged in a deep breath. "Not really. What right does he have to accost me like that? He doesn't make a phone call in ten years, and all at once we have to *talk?*" A bitter laugh escaped him. "Jud always did have an ego, I'll say that for him."

The house door slammed. Heather and Megan ran down the steps and across the lawn to the rope swings Ethan had hung in a couple of ancient pecan trees. Brad came out a minute later, leaving the door wide-open, and headed for the tree house Ethan had built on the opposite side of the house from the swings.

"He could have had a change of heart," Kayla suggested. "It's been known to happen."

"Too little, too late." Ethan dropped his hands to his thighs and let his head fall back against the headrest. "I don't see how anything useful can come of rehashing the past."

"What do you think he wants?"

"To say he's sorry?" He shook his head. "No. Jud wouldn't feel responsible for anything that's happened. He wasn't here, he can't be blamed—even though everything fell apart almost the minute he disappeared."

"Why did he leave?"

"Because he finally went too far. He got a girl pregnant and then refused to marry her."

"Somebody in town?"

"Della Bowie. She's not here anymore. Once Jud left, Della and her family moved away. Nobody's heard a word from or about them since." Looking back, Ethan pulled in a deep breath. "Mom and Dad were completely torn up over the whole thing—they felt they'd lost a grandchild. Then Angela and I started getting sick, and everything went to hell." He pounded a fist on the steering wheel. "Nothing I did made a difference. I tried—"

Kayla closed her fingers gently over his, stopping the motion. "You know you're not to blame for what happened. Not for Angela's illness, or your parents' despair. We've worked on this, Ethan. You were only fourteen—you did the best you possibly could."

"Right. My dad was losing his shirt over a ranch deal, Angela and I were getting lead poisoning from Mexican candy, and meanwhile Brother Jud's out conquering the rodeo circuit. How's that for fair?"

Kayla tightened her grip on his fist.

They sat in silence for a couple of minutes until Ethan could finally let go of the anger. For the time being, anyway.

He lifted his hand to press a kiss on his wife's knuckles. "I should've warned you about the emotional minefield you were walking into when you said you'd marry me. Second thoughts?"

"Nary a one." She gave him her sweet smile.

"I know a good thing when I see it. You're stuck, Ethan Ritter. For better or worse."

"Thank God," he said, taking the kiss she offered, and a couple more, besides.

But he couldn't help thinking, as he and Kayla walked arm in arm toward the house that, with Jud in town, worse might be a lot closer than they realized.

MIRANDA AND NAN SPENT most of Sunday in the barn, watching Flora and Kahlúa bond. Cruz walked over for a while when the vet came back to examine the foal, but Miranda deliberately avoided so much as a mention of Jud Ritter's name. She'd be even happier to avoid thinking about him altogether. If wishes were horses...

Monday morning, she pulled her truck into the parking space marked Mayor of Homestead, Texas at 9:00 a.m., and climbed the courthouse steps with her usual enthusiasm. Dusty followed right on her heels.

"'Morning, Mayor." Reba Howell, the town secretary and assistant to the mayor, set down her coffee mug as Miranda stepped into the Homestead Town Office. "I hear y'all have a new arrival at your place."

"Yeah, we do." Miranda grinned as she took the morning's mail out of her box. "Kahlúa is just the most perfect little colt I've seen. I could hardly tear myself away from the barn to come to work."

Reba followed her into the mayor's private office. "Oh, you mean you have a new baby horse? That's right, I noticed you and your mama weren't in church yesterday."

Miranda looked up from the mail. "What arrival are you talking about?"

"Jud Ritter, of course. I heard he's staying out at your place. Too bad you missed it—he and Ethan got into a fight, right there on the church lawn after the service."

With great effort, Miranda kept her tone casual. "A fistfight?"

"Well, no. But they were yelling at each other, and at one point it looked like Ethan shoved Jud, or vice versa—it was hard to tell."

"Jud always was something of a troublemaker." An understatement if she'd ever made one.

"I don't know…I thought Ethan was the one who started the argument this time. I suppose he bears a grudge for Jud being gone all these years." Reba sighed and shook her head. "But I tell you, I've never seen a handsomer pair of men. They looked real good, facing each other down outside the church yesterday morning."

"And you'll get to see at least one of them again today. Wade and Jud are supposed to show up at ten o'clock for a meeting." Miranda sat down at her desk, pulled a folder full of papers out of the file stand in front of her and opened it. "Until then, I'll be going over these Home Free applications."

"Right." Reba hesitated in the doorway. "Can you catch the phone for a couple of minutes? I need to...freshen up." At one hundred pounds even and five feet two inches tall, with natural blond hair and a peaches-and-cream complexion, Reba spent a lot of her workday "freshening up."

"Sure," Miranda said, without looking. She pretended to focus until she heard the outer office door close. Then she put her elbows on the desk and pressed the heels of her hands into her eyes. In the corner, Dusty circled three times and then collapsed into her dog bed with a contented sigh.

Miranda was a long way from content. In the space of thirty-six hours, Jud Ritter had somehow managed to monopolize her life. He'd barged in on her friends' wedding reception and weaseled his way onto her property—well, her family's property, anyway. He'd even become an important part of Kahlúa's birth, which would link them forever in her thoughts.

As if she hadn't spent the last four years trying to *forget* the man. She might have gotten over the seduction scene—he'd been so drunk that night, he probably would have kissed any old stray dog that jumped up in the truck bed with him.

But he'd made her feel dirty for surrendering. "I am not making the same mistake twice," he'd said, comparing her to Della Bowie, the girl unofficially voted "Most Likely To" at Homestead High. Everybody knew Della was the easiest girl at school, and she'd reaped the rewards of her behavior—she'd left town pregnant, in disgrace. And though Della never said, everybody knew the father of her child was Jud Ritter. They'd dated all that spring, before graduation. Then Jud had gone....

"I'm back," Reba called from the outer office. Just a minute later, she said, "Hey,

Wade. How are you this morning? And who's this with you? Jud Ritter, it's about time you came back. We all wondered where you got to."

"Good to see you, too." His rich voice held a smile. "Looks like you landed yourself the most important job in town."

Did he have a smooth answer for everything?

Reba gave a trill of laughter. "I do keep things under control around here. Miranda's got so much going on, I'm surprised she knows where her head is, most days. You know she's always been kinda disorganized."

Thanks so much, Miranda muttered to herself. She stood up and walked to the door. "Hey, Wade, Jud. Get yourself some coffee and come on in."

"Take a seat," she told them as they came through the door, then resumed her own chair. "Now, what's this all about?"

Just as Wade sat forward and opened his mouth, a knock sounded on the door frame.

"Cookies," Reba said brightly, bringing in a plate piled high. "I usually make cookies for Mondays, to get the week started off right. These are chocolate chip pecan. Thought y'all might enjoy a snack while you talk. Mayor Miranda loves cookies, though most of us girls do have to watch our figures, don't we?" She smiled at the men, set the plate down on the corner of the desk within their reach, smiled at Jud *again* and finally left the room.

"Eat up," Miranda said, silently vowing not to take one for herself. "And tell me what's going on."

Wade set his mug on the floor and picked up a stack of folders he'd carried in with him. "When you talked to me last month about the possibility of bringing in somebody from outside Homestead to investigate these incidents of vandalism, I decided Jud might be the answer. We've kept in touch, off and on, over the years. He knows the town and many of the folks, he's in law enforcement, and he's objective. So I asked him if he could spend a few days at home to help us get this straightened out."

Miranda stared at Wade for a moment, wondering why men were so incredibly dense. Then she looked at Jud. "And you just dropped everything, including your job, to rush over here?"

Jud leaned forward and braced his elbows

on his knees, holding the coffee cup with both hands. "I'm on medical leave, as a matter of fact. Nothing better to do."

"How kind of you."

He raised his eyebrows in question. "I thought the trip would give me an excuse to reconnect with Ethan, if you want the whole truth. Is that better?"

"Marginally." She looked at the sheriff again.

Wade cleared his throat. "I brought you both copies of all the case reports." He put his stack of folders on the desk. "We've had everything from poisoned vineyards to barn fires, vandalism to malicious pranks."

Jud flipped through the top report. "But you haven't managed to track down the vandals themselves?"

"Like I told you, I picked up the guy who's been paying local kids to cause mischief. But he's just the middleman—this isn't going to stop until we find the source of the money."

"Why would anybody be paying for trouble in Homestead?"

When you used to make it for free? Miranda bit her tongue on the thought. "All the people who've been hit are owners of Home Free land parcels."

Jud's gaze swung to her face. "Somebody wants to sabotage your land giveaway?"

She shrugged. "I guess that's what you're here to answer."

"What happens if you don't find anyone to blame? Aren't some of these incidents just nuisances? In the city, we wouldn't have time to deal with—" he flipped through a different file "—a ruined fence."

Miranda gripped her hands together on top of the desk. "Many of the stunts haven't been so harmless. Kayla Ritter's first grapevine planting was completely destroyed with poison, and her daughter nearly died from an asthma attack caused by cat fur planted in her school desk."

Jud narrowed his eyes.

She nodded. "That's right. Cat fur deliberately planted to make an allergic child sick."

Wade held up his hand to interrupt. "I think the same guy paid Tolly Craddock, the school maintenance man, for that stunt. Tolly's in the jail again, too, but he won't talk."

"Callie Montgomery's house was vandalized by a couple of kids who wouldn't say who paid them. Greer Kelley's overnight guests got lost on a trail ride," Miranda continued, "thanks to trail signs which had been switched. Though it sounds like a practical joke, those women—tenderfoots, all of them—might have spent the entire night out in the open, compromising their safety and Greer's new business. I'm assuming I don't have to explain the threat of a barn fire to you."

He tightened his jaw. "No."

"And every time there's an incident, I get one or more letters from people withdrawing their application for Home Free land. People don't want to move to a town where their animals, their children or their property are at risk. We've made a good start at getting Homestead back on its feet. But there's still a long way to go before we have enough kids to support the schools, enough citizens to keep the shops and businesses open. We need a population increase and a solid tax base, or the whole county will be carrion for any buzzard that flies over."

And she'd have failed, just as the folks she grew up with—including Jud Ritter—always said she would. She'd offered them a plan to rescue the town, and they'd made her mayor on the strength of it. But if the land program didn't survive, Home Free would be just another of Miranda Wright's dumb ideas. Miserable Miranda, Jud had nicknamed her, back in the fifth grade. The name had stuck until she'd left for college.

With a deep breath, she reined in her temper. "All of us have a stake in figuring out who's behind these incidents and putting a stop to them. If you can do that," she said, trying for lightness, "I'll give you the key to the city."

Jud stared at her for a moment, his face unreadable. "That's a beginning," he said, finally. "I'll let you know what else you owe me when I get the job done."

JUD FOLLOWED Wade through the halls of the courthouse, appreciating—probably for the first time in his life—the beautiful nineteenth-century woodwork and floors.

"This place is in good shape," he said. "I never realized how well the town maintained it."

"The brick exterior is a real bonus. They

put in air-conditioning back in the seventies to preserve the interior," Wade explained as they started down the stairs, "and did some plaster repair work. But until Miranda came into office, the place only got cleaned up about once a year. She's made a point of having volunteers come in every month to sweep, dust and keep the windows shining."

Miranda, again. "Sounds like she's been a good mayor."

"This town wouldn't have stayed alive without her." Wade unlocked the dead bolt on a solid door and waved him through. "Back door to the sheriff's office. Make yourself at home."

Jud grinned. "No, thanks."

The Loveless County jail had been paneled with the same stained oak as the rest of the building, but the small windows were high and barred. Four cells, two on each side, faced each other across the wide aisle leading straight to another door locked with a dead bolt.

One cell of each pair held a prisoner. On the right, a man about Jud's age lay on the cot, his booted feet on the sheet and his arm hiding his face.

"This is Hank Darrow," Wade said. "The report on his prints came in this morning, and he's got an interesting history, to say the least. I've been tempted to break out the thumbscrews for help in persuading him to talk, but I thought I'd wait for you."

He gestured at the man in the cell opposite. "Tolly Craddock was the maintenance worker at the elementary school. He's been out on bail, but I picked him up last week for loitering and nonsupport. He won't say why, or who paid him to harm that little girl. But he has a real fancy lawyer. Who's due here—" Wade looked at his watch "—any minute."

With the words, the door on the opposite wall opened and a thousand-dollar suit walked in. Jud had seen the type often enough, defending drug dealers and crooked politicians in Austin courtrooms, which explained his instant shudder of distaste.

"You ganging up on my client, Sheriff?" The lawyer stepped between Jud and Tolly Craddock's cell. "I know law enforcement types when I see them. I'm Raoul Dermody." He held out a hand to Jud. "And you would be?"

Jud ignored the gesture. "Jud Ritter. Austin police."

Dermody looked at Wade. "Couldn't figure out how to railroad my client by yourself?"

Wade opened the cell door without comment, then locked the lawyer inside. "Call when you're ready to leave. I'll think about letting you out."

Once in his private office, Wade dropped into his desk chair. "That man gets my goat."

Jud sat in the chair opposite. "He's the worst of a bad lot. Who's paying him?"

"No clue."

"I'll put that on my To Do list. He didn't seem to see your second prisoner."

"I noticed."

"Did you ever consider listening at the door?"

"No, but those windows are right at ground level."

Jud got to his feet. "Well, then, I guess I'll do my part to keep Homestead clean—starting with the courthouse lawn."

Before ten minutes had passed, Jud had confirmed that Dermody, Craddock and Darrow all knew each other. The three were deep in conversation.

So who was paying the lawyer to protect these guys? And why did someone want to sabotage the Home Free program?

More important, how far would that someone go to stop Miranda Wright?

CHAPTER FIVE

AS SOON AS THE SHERIFF and his prize investigator left, Miranda shut the inner office door and dropped heavily into her chair. With luck, she'd have a couple of minutes of privacy in which to fall apart.

Or maybe not. The outer door opened with a squeak. "Hello? Anybody home?"

"In here, Millie." Miranda stifled her groan and straightened her back. With her unerring instinct for news, the reporter was no doubt here to ask questions Miranda didn't want to answer.

"I was beginning to think everybody had run off, leaving the town with no one at the rudder." Millie shut the door behind her, then perched on the edge of the chair Jud had occupied.

Miranda succumbed to the temptation of a chocolate chip cookie. "The rudder goes anywhere I do," she said, after a soothing bite. "What can I help you with?"

Millie flipped open a spiral-bound notepad. "Well, I noticed Wade Montgomery and Jud Ritter leaving here just a few minutes ago and thought that was an interesting development. I'm sure the readers—and voters—would like to know what kind of official business our prodigal son is doing with the mayor and the sheriff."

"Our prodigal son?" Miranda choked on a laugh. "Are we supposed to be killing the fatted calf for Jud Ritter?" A childhood spent in Sunday school had left her familiar with the Bible story of a young man who wasted his inheritance and returned home penniless, only to have his father celebrate his homecoming with a huge party. "He doesn't impress me as the repentant type."

"I've always thought that boy was driven out of town, even though the official version was that he chose to go." Millie cocked her head like the perky sparrow she resembled. "Between the rumors about Della Bowie's baby being his—which might have been true or not, since the girl was, shall we say, quite free with her favors—and his dad expecting

Jud to do the work of three ranch hands plus keep his grades decent for college, not to mention a streak of wildness that was Jud's alone…well, I just wasn't surprised when he took off on the rodeo circuit practically the day after graduation."

"The whole town thought Jud had fathered Della's baby. Even his mom and dad."

"People see what they want to see."

Miranda propped her chin on her free hand. "Now, Millie, why would Jud's family want to believe something like that about him?"

"If they thought that was the only way to keep him home…" She shook her head. "I'm talking through my hat, as usual. And you're hoping I'll forget why I came over here to begin with. Why did you have a meeting with the sheriff and Jud Ritter?"

The delay had at least given Miranda a chance to collect her thoughts. "It's no secret we've had a few suspicious incidents in Homestead lately—in some cases we've caught the culprits, in some we haven't. Wade asked Jud to keep an eye out while he's here, report anything that might help us put a stop to these disruptions. Homestead is a good town, a safe place to bring up families, and we want everybody to be convinced of that fact."

"Did Jud come specifically to investigate, or is he here for another reason?"

She straightened her back. "I'm not privy to Jud's plans or intentions."

"Well, for goodness sake, you don't have to bite my head off about it." Millie flipped her book closed and snapped to her feet.

"I didn't—"

"You never were an easy girl, Miranda Wright. And you're still hard to get along with. If you're not careful," she said, with a glance over her shoulder as she opened the door, "you're going to be a bitter old maid." The glass in the door window rattled with the force of Millie's slam.

Miranda slumped over until she rested her chin on her hands, lying flat on the desk. Eyes closed, she considered the reporter's prediction.

Had it already happened? Was she a bitter old maid at thirty-three? The single men in Homestead were either young bucks like Arlen Enfield's boys, elderly widowers and hermits, or else dead like old Clyde Braxton, who'd owned the land now making up a good portion of the Home Free Land Giveaway. Most of the guys she'd gone to school with were happily married, like Noah and Ethan and Wade.

Then there was Jud.

She shivered and shied away from the thought. If she wanted a man, it was beginning to look as though she'd have to find one somewhere other than Homestead. But she didn't want to go somewhere else. She was the mayor, and she was doing good things in this place. Or she would be, once the vandalism stopped.

And for that, she evidently had to depend on Jud Ritter—the man who'd run out on his pregnant girlfriend, who'd left his family in dire straits to pursue his own reckless ambitions.

Not exactly a sure bet.

Leaving Reba to her dreams of romance, Miranda, with Dusty at her heels, escaped the artificial air of the town office for the overcast sky of a winter morning. She stood at the top of the steps for a few seconds, taking deep draws of the chilly air and damp breeze. The pecan trees edging the courthouse square had lost their leaves, and she had a clear view of downtown—the businesses, churches and other buildings surrounding the square. Over at the general store, Ed Tanner was stringing Christmas lights around the big front window. Behind the windows, his wife was setting up the annual snowman display, though Miranda couldn't remember a December in her lifetime that had actually produced snow in Homestead. Tradition was tradition, however, and she doubted the Tanners would ever give up that snowman as long as they owned the store.

"We're gonna have to get the town decorations out," Miranda commented to Dusty. "Wade and I can get them up in an afternoon. With your help, of course." She grinned and Dusty wagged her tail. They understood each other perfectly.

Directly across the street, the door to the clinic opened as Miranda started down the courthouse steps. Greer Kelley and her daughter stepped out onto the sidewalk, followed by Kristin Gallagher. Miranda waved and skipped down the last couple of steps, then jogged across the street.

"Hey," she said as she and Dusty came to

a stop. "How's everybody this morning?" Miranda looked at Greer's daughter, Shelby, leaning against her mother's side. "I heard you're not feeling too great. Sore throat?"

Eyes heavy, cheeks pale, Shelby nodded. Greer pulled the girl a little closer and brushed the red hair off her forehead. "Kristin says the strep test is negative, so that's good news."

"There's a virus going around," Kristin said. "I've seen fifteen people with the same sore throat in the last couple of weeks, two-thirds of them kids." She shook her head. "I'm waiting for Cody to bring the germ home from school."

Dusty moved over to nose at Shelby's knees. The girl crouched and put her arms around the Lab's thick, furry neck.

Greer grinned and then looked at Miranda. "Not too sick to cuddle a dog. I think I'd better back out on lunch today, though. Shelby needs to get home to bed."

Shelby jumped to her feet. "Mom! You promised I could have ice cream!"

"But—" Greer looked at Kristin. "What do you think? I don't want to make everybody sick."

Kristin gave her a calm, sweet smile. "I think we'll be okay, as long as we make Shelby eat all of her ice cream by herself. No sharing." They turned as a group toward the corner where the ground floor of the big Victorian house had been converted to Callie's Café.

"Is Kayla coming?" Miranda asked. She hadn't had a chance to talk to Ethan's wife since the wedding last weekend—in other words, since Jud's arrival.

"As far as I know," Kristin said. "One of those sick kids I saw last week was Megan— we were worried that she'd have extra trouble, with the asthma and all. But at the wedding Saturday, she looked just fine."

They climbed the broad steps to the porch. "Stay," Miranda told Dusty, who promptly curled up next to the rail, thumping the wood plank floor with her tail.

"That dog is amazing," Greer said as Miranda held the door for them all to go in. "Does she ever disobey?"

"Hasn't yet." Miranda followed the group in. "I worry sometimes that she's too compliant, but when she gets out on open ground, she's as energetic and joyful as you could ask for. Speaking of joy...and energy," she said, with a wink, "how's married life?"

Greer winked back. "What's a word for better than fantastic?"

Across the dining room, Kayla Ritter waved at them from a big round table. "I was beginning to wonder if I'd be eating alone," she said as they reached her. "How is everybody?"

"I'm sick," Shelby announced, sitting down beside Kayla. "So you can't have any of my ice cream."

Kayla laughed but Greer protested. "Shelby! You move over and let me sit next to Kayla. Then we'll put an empty chair on your other side and everyone else can sit down as far from you as possible."

Miranda sat down beside the empty chair, just as Callie Montgomery appeared. "Hi, Ms. Mayor." She put a hand on Miranda's shoulder. "I'm glad to see everybody. Kayla was getting pretty lonely over here. What can I get you all to drink?"

"Can you sit with us and have some lunch?" Miranda asked. "It's hard to talk to you when you're working."

Callie shook her head. "I'd love to. But Ethel and Wanda both called in sick today so

I'm shorthanded. I'll stop and visit when I can."

They ordered their drinks, then their food and finally settled down to chat. "How's the lavender coming?" Greer asked Miranda. "Do you expect a full crop this year?"

"I do, unless we get drowned by winter rain. My field has good drainage, though, so we'd have to have a real deluge to ruin the plants."

"I found a recipe for lavender lemonade," Callie said, setting out glasses of iced tea and soda, and a ginger ale for Shelby. "Come summer, I'll put a note on the menu that the lavender comes from Hayseed Farm."

"I've been collecting vases for my guest cabins," Greer added. "Really nice shapes in hand-thrown pottery. I thought I'd put sheaves of lavender in them to pick up the blues and purples in the glazes."

Miranda grinned. "We'll make Homestead the lavender capital of Texas before we're through."

"And wine, don't forget." Kayla had moved to Homestead to start a vineyard on the land she'd received through the Home Free program.

"That's right. You can open your winery for tours and tastings—"

"Which I'll cater," Callie said, setting salads in front of Greer and Kristin.

"We'll sell wine and lavender products in a rustic little shop—" Miranda continued.

"And the visitors will all come back to my place for a trail ride and cookout," Greer concluded, "followed by a peaceful night at the Sunrise Guest Retreat!"

Kristin laughed and applauded. "Sounds wonderful. Be sure to send all those tourists downtown before they leave so the rest of Homestead can benefit, too."

"Definitely." Miranda stared with pleasure at the cheeseburger platter Callie had left in front of her. "We've got a couple of land applications from folks who want to start up retail businesses in town. We'll get those empty storefronts filled soon enough."

She cut the huge sandwich on her plate in half, then picked up one side and prepared to take a bite. Her teeth closed on the chewy, slightly drippy concoction just as a hand gripped the back of the empty chair next to her.

"Excuse me for interrupting, but I wanted to extend my best wishes to the bride."

She didn't have to look up. She couldn't possibly mistake Jud Ritter's voice for anyone else's.

"I'm having ice cream," Shelby announced before anyone else spoke. "And I don't have to share it with anybody because I'm sick. Nobody's supposed to sit next to me, either."

"That's okay. I never get sick," Jud told her. Miranda chewed furiously, trying to get her mouth empty so she could shoo him away.

"Then you should sit down," Greer said, beating her to it. "I saw you Saturday at the wedding, but didn't have a chance to say hello. This is my daughter, Shelby."

As Jud took his seat, Miranda tightened her hold on the burger. Ketchup, mustard and a tomato slice squirted out, over her fingers and onto her plate.

Jud glanced in her direction. "Looks like the food here is terrific. Hey, Miranda." He smiled, but there was a challenge in his dark eyes.

Wiping condiments off her hands, she choked out, "Hi."

Greer came to the rescue. "Jud, let me introduce you to some friends you may not know. This is Kristin Gallagher, Ryan's wife."

They both nodded and Kristin said, "We

met Saturday while we were…um…decorating your car."

"You could have stopped them?" Greer demanded of Jud, pretending to be outraged.

He held up his hands in a gesture of surrender. "Since the sheriff was involved, I figured I'd let well enough alone."

Callie stopped at his shoulder. "The sheriff did what?"

"This is Callie Montgomery," Greer said, "the sheriff's wife. Callie, Jud Ritter. Evidently Wade had a lot to do with the shaving cream I washed off my Blazer yesterday. *And* off Noah's truck."

"I know nothing," Callie declared. "What would you like to drink, Jud?"

"Soda, thanks. And I'll have a platter just like Miranda's."

"Coming right up."

"And across the table from you is…" Greer slowed to a stop, suddenly realizing the awkwardness of what she was about to say. "Kayla. Um…Ethan's wife."

"We met yesterday," Jud said quietly.

"Yes," Kayla said.

"I hear you've made Ethan very happy," Jud added. "I'm glad to know that."

Her eyes widened. "Thanks. Welcome ho... back."

Jud nodded and glanced around the table, where eating had pretty much been suspended. "Don't let me interfere with your lunch—I just wanted to say hello."

"You aren't," Kristin assured him. "But we would love to know what's brought you to Homestead, Jud. Everybody I've seen in town this morning is asking that same question."

He took a sip from his cola. "Wade asked me to come, give him a little backup."

"But Wade has a deputy already." Kayla hadn't picked up her fork since Jud sat down. "Virgil Dunn."

"I'm not a deputy. More of an investigator, I guess."

"Investigating what?" Shelby said, too loudly.

Miranda straightened in her seat. He was making a mess of this. "Jud's looking into the vandalism we've had around here recently." She kept her voice low. "Wade and I want to be sure we don't have any more problems. That's all."

"So *you* asked Jud back, too," Kayla said.

"No," Miranda heard herself say, too loudly. "Wade didn't tell me who he'd asked. Just that he knew someone who could help us out."

"That's right, you're a policeman down in Austin, aren't you?" Greer nodded. "You're taking your vacation to help us out? That's awfully nice of you."

"I'm on medical leave, in fact, and figured I might as well spend it here."

"Medical leave?" Kristin asked. "Are you okay?"

"Sure." He shrugged, obviously unwilling to talk about it. Cassie arrived with his plate and Jud gave a big sigh. "Looks great. And I'm starved." He picked up the entire burger and took a big bite, then gave a groan of satisfaction as he chewed. "Oh, yeah."

Her friends around the table grinned and went back to their own food, but Miranda had lost her appetite. She couldn't possibly sit there and de-molish the big burger as Jud was proceeding to do. Echoes of the lunchroom teasing she'd taken as a kid—when she was growing like a weed—bounced around her brain. She should have ordered a salad.

Of course, a salad wouldn't get her through the afternoon she had ahead of her—

training horses, cleaning stalls and loading hay bales. She wasn't a featherweight, but she used up all the food she ate. Dang it, protein was good for building muscle!

That didn't explain the fries, though. Or the apple pie and ice cream she'd thought about for dessert. She'd ordered a meal fit for a truck driver—a very hefty truck driver.

"You're not eating," Jud commented. "Something wrong?"

"Not hungry," she told him. "I've got to get back to work." She picked her purse up off the floor and took out a ten-dollar bill. "There's my part of the check."

"You can't leave," Kristin said. Greer and Kayla joined in the protest.

But Miranda shook her head. "I need to get things finished here in town and head home. Y'all have a nice afternoon. Hope you feel better, Shelby." The last thing she heard, as she opened the door to the front porch, was the combined laughter from Jud Ritter's table.

She drove home with her stomach growling and her cheeks burning. Jud certainly had won this round.

If only she could convince herself she didn't care.

Jud cursed himself as the screened door slapped shut behind Miranda. He hadn't expected her to run away from her friends and her meal, just because he'd joined them.

Maybe he *had* done something unforgivable.

"Oh, my," Greer said suddenly. When he turned to look, he found that little Shelby had pillowed her head in her arms, folded on the table, and gone to sleep.

He chuckled, and the women laughed with him. "Sweet," Kristin said.

"She should be home in bed." Greer smoothed Shelby's red hair back from her face. "At least she finished her ice cream." After placing a few bills on the table, she put an arm around her daughter and rocked her gently. "Shelby? Honey, let's get you home, okay?"

Shelby opened her eyes about halfway. "'Kay."

"Good to see you all," Greer said, helping Shelby stand. "Especially you, Jud. You'll have to come to dinner so you and Noah can talk over old times."

"Sounds good," he said. "We had some fun when we were in school together, even though he was a preacher's kid."

Greer and Shelby headed for the door. In just a few minutes, it was Kristin's turn to say goodbye.

"I've got a patient at one. And probably some walk-ins, as well, with this virus that's in the air." She walked around the table and laid her hand lightly on Jud's shoulder for a second. "I hope we'll see some more of you, Jud. Ryan and I live in a separate house from his dad, so you don't have to worry about running into Clint if you come see us." She gave him a wink and went on her way.

Jud looked across the table to Kayla, his sister-in-law. "I guess Ryan explained to her how much old man Gallagher hated me, back in the old days."

She tilted her head. "Well, he's not too fond of anyone named Ritter since your father and KC Enterprises bought that big land parcel out from underneath him. Mr. Gallagher thought he'd get another chance when the KC outfit went bust, but the county stepped in first, Miranda got elected and the Home Free plan went into effect."

"So Gallagher's got a reason to dislike all the new people coming into town? They must represent failure, as far as he's concerned."

"I haven't talked much with Mr. Gallagher. I don't think he and Ethan get along."

"Not a surprise," Jud said. Kayla glared at him, eyes bright with indignation, and he realized he'd offended her. "Sorry. Ethan's just always been...reserved."

"He's had a hard time," she said, not appeased. "Things haven't gone well for him since he was a teenager."

"Since I left home, you mean?"

"I don't know when you left home. I only know you haven't come back very often."

Ethan's pretty wife had claws. "Well, I left the summer before he and—" he drew a deep breath "—Angela got into that candy. I didn't know anything about it until months later."

"You could have come home then."

He was surprised by the explosion of anger he had to hold back. "No, I couldn't."

"Why?"

"You'll have to ask your husband." Jud shook his head. "That history's so old it doesn't matter a hill of beans, anyway. Why don't we talk about something more relevant?

Tell me about the vandalism in your vineyard."

She sat for a minute staring down at her empty plate, then looked up. "I moved here last spring and set out six thousand grapevine cuttings. Someone sprayed those seedlings with herbicide—we found the jugs later and traced them to the boy who did the spraying. But he'd been paid by someone else—maybe the man Wade arrested last week, but I don't think we know for sure."

"Anything else happen that might be intended to discourage you from staying in Homestead? Miranda said something about your daughter's asthma?"

"The maintenance man at the school put cat hair into Megan's desk. Her asthma worsened, and she had a life-threatening attack. We borrowed the Gallagher helicopter and got her to the hospital in time." She shivered. "I never want to be that scared again."

"I can imagine."

"And I won't consider Clint Gallagher a bad man. He helped save my daughter's life. Someone else is at the root of these incidents."

"Did the maintenance man give a reason for poisoning your daughter?"

"He's in jail, but he's got a slick lawyer from Austin, and he won't say a word."

"Yeah, I met him this morning." Jud gathered up the cash the other women had left, but when Kayla went for her wallet, he shook his head. "Let me buy your lunch."

"I don't think—"

"It's the least I can do, since I didn't make it to your wedding. You don't have to tell Ethan."

The idea troubled her. "Well, just this once."

"Good." He grinned at her. "I do have hopes of getting on better terms with my brother, and it can't hurt having his wife on my side."

Kayla gave him a level look. "Don't count your chickens before they hatch, Jud Ritter."

And with that warning, she left him at the table by himself.

AN HOUR LATER, Jud found Miranda in the lavender field, pulling weeds despite a chilly drizzle of rain. He stopped his truck on the side of the driveway and got out. "Callie boxed up your lunch," he said, walking to the edge of the field. "I stopped by the house and gave it to Nan."

"Thanks." Miranda kept her eyes on the ground. "You didn't have to do that."

"Since you couldn't eat in my company, I think I did."

Her cheeks flushed, but she didn't look at him. She'd exchanged her business slacks and sweater for jeans and a polo shirt under a blue fleece vest. She looked more natural here than in the mayor's office, though not more comfortable since he'd stopped to talk.

"What is it with lavender, anyway? Why the big field?" Jud snapped off a twig and took a sniff. "Do you really think you can sell all this stuff?"

Miranda knee-walked farther down the row. "Texas is developing a healthy lavender industry. A number of farms in the Hill Country grow and sell, locally and on a commercial level. There's a market right here in Homestead, at Tanner's store. Tourists like inexpensive mementos of where they've been—a bar of lavender soap or a bundle of dried flowers fills the bill."

"You get lots of tourists?"

"I'm planning to."

"What got you started in lavender to begin with?"

Finally, she stopped pulling at the sparse weeds and rested her hands on her knees. "I had a friend who loved herbs, especially lavender. I thought I would grow a few bushes for her, but then I read about other lavender farms in Texas and I got inspired to try a larger scale." She shrugged. "Quixotic, I guess. It's not like I didn't have anything else to do." Her gaze went to the orchard in the distance, separated from where they stood by a wide piece of tilled ground that Martinez had told him would be planted with vegetables for summer sales.

"Has your friend come to see what you've done?"

"No." After a pause and a deep breath, she went on. "Lila was my supervisor when I worked in the bank in Austin. That's where I started, after college. She became my mentor, first, and then my friend. In fact, Lila helped me develop the whole land giveaway concept. Anyway, she died a few years ago—just a month or so after your mom."

Jud was trying to think of the right thing to say when Miranda concluded with, "She gave me Dusty to take care of. Or vice versa." A quick smile. "I've never been sure which."

At the sound of her name, the dog came bounding out of the pine forest behind him. Jud straightened, thinking the Lab would gallop over the lavender plants.

But at the edge of the field she stopped, then walked quietly to where Miranda stood. "I didn't have to teach her that," Miranda said, rubbing the soft ears. "This dog has never put a foot wrong. Sometimes I wonder—" She shook her head and straightened. "Never mind."

"What were you going to say?"

"Nothing." She walked away from him, toward the opposite end of the field, Dusty following right behind.

Jud followed, too. As he walked through the lavender field, the branches of the low bushes brushed his legs. Even though there were no blooms, the sharp fragrance rose around him. He wasn't sure whether he liked it or not.

He was damn sure he shouldn't get any

closer to Miranda Wright. But he needed to hear what she'd started to say.

His limp slowed him down. Still, he caught up with Miranda at the pasture where Flora and Kahlúa stood quietly cropping grass. As he arrived, Miranda closed the gate against him with a chain and thumb latch.

He reached over and caught her wrist before she could leave him behind. "Tell me."

She glared at him for a few seconds. "If you must know, I wonder, sometimes, if Lila is…I don't know…a part of Dusty now."

"Go on."

She glanced around, as if worried someone might overhear them. "Reverend Kelley would be scandalized if he heard me say that, and even Noah might have second thoughts, though he's really relaxed for a priest." With a shrug, she pulled against Jud's grip, but he held fast.

"Sometimes," she said, "when I talk to Dusty, I hear Lila answer. Giving advice, making suggestions." She took a deep breath. "That's all. See, not worth bothering about. And now it's raining. Would you please let me go?"

He freed her hand, but only so he could

unlatch the gate and come through after her. The real downpour started as they reached the middle of the open pasture. A huge live oak in the corner of the fence opposite the gate offered the only shelter.

The green canopy of the tree made a reasonable umbrella, shedding most of the rain to drip around the perimeter. More breathless than he wanted to admit, Jud leaned back against the trunk and eased his leg. Miranda kept her distance, staring out into the darkening twilight like a prisoner behind bars.

This was his moment. He wasn't ready, but somehow he'd get the job done. "Miranda." Jud cleared his throat. "Miranda, I owe you an apology."

She didn't turn to look at him. "For what?"

"What the hell do you think?"

"Oh, that."

"Yes, dammit. That." He couldn't believe how indifferent she sounded when he knew for sure she'd been devastated that night. And shocked and dismayed to see him return on Saturday.

"Don't…." She sighed. "Let's just forget the whole thing."

Jud rolled his eyes. Before he could say

anything else, the pounding of the rain increased, driving Miranda back to the tree trunk, where the density of the leaves gave the most protection.

Taking his chance, he grabbed her wrist again and pulled her around to face him. "Why are you blowing this off? I'm trying to make amends, here. You're refusing even to recognize the problem."

"You can't make amends."

"Why not?"

"What else are you going to do? You apologized, used the right words. But you can't take back what you said that night. You can't undo what…what we did, or turn me into the person I was before."

He opened his mouth to protest, but she held up her hand. "You didn't assault me, Jud. But you used me, then threw me away like I didn't matter. If you feel better having said you're sorry, I'm glad. We've both gone on with our lives, so let's just leave the past where it belongs."

Of all the outcomes he'd expected from this conversation, rejection was not on the list. The response that flared inside him was not anger, however, but something very different.

"Maybe you're right," he said, studying her face. "Maybe an apology was the wrong move entirely."

He brought his hand up and touched her cheek, brushing back a piece of hair that had come loose from her ponytail. Then he cupped his hand around her neck and bent the small distance necessary to put his mouth on hers.

The scent of lavender clung to her, and now he knew he did like it. For a minute, her full lips softened to the kiss, amplified it and returned far more than he'd given.

Then she raised her fists and pushed so hard against his shoulders that he stumbled back, unbalanced by surprise as much as by her strength.

"Oh, no, Jud Ritter. I'm not going this route again."

"I didn't—"

"You appear to think I still spend my time waiting for you, pining until you deign to come back and fling some attention my way. Well, I'm telling you I'm not interested in getting involved with you on any level at all. Stay away from me unless you have some kind of official report to make. I've got better things to do than fool around with you."

She stomped past him while he was still gathering his wits. With Dusty at her heels, she marched through the rain across the pastures to the barn and disappeared inside.

Jud leaned back against the live oak's trunk, feeling very tired. At least he wasn't drunk this time. The cold, wet walk ahead of him would take care of the lust still driving his pulse. And he'd escaped without being slapped...or slugged by Martinez, whom he'd managed to forget about altogether.

What a terrific way to repay the man's hospitality—hit on the woman in his life. At this rate, the moral and upright citizens of Homestead were going to have their every suspicion, past and present, justified.

Brother Ethan was right after all.

The oldest Ritter boy was nothing but trouble.

MIRANDA STOMPED onto the back porch, pulled off her vest and toed her feet out of her sneakers. Cold water from her sopping wet hair dripped down her back, around her ears and over her eyes. She deserved to be miserable, though, so she used the towel on the peg to rub Dusty and get rid of the worst of the rain. That way, the standard doggy shake wouldn't drench the surrounding area.

In the kitchen, Nan stood over a simmering pot of tomato gravy. "About time you showed up," she said. "It's past dark."

"I got caught in the rain and waited it out under the live oak."

Her mom glanced over her shoulder. "I hadn't noticed the rain letting up."

"I…uh…decided I was tired of waiting."

Nan nodded. "Jud brought your lunch by. You've been running all afternoon on one bite of hamburger?"

"I'm okay, Mom. I don't need three meals a day, every day."

"You know how you get when you don't have enough to eat. We worked that out a long time ago."

No sugar or white flour, no dyes, no artificial flavors…yeah, Nan had worked out a healthy diet, all right. Embarrassed to take her oatmeal bread, avocado and sprout sandwiches out of the lunch sack at school, Miranda had eaten pounds of carrot sticks just to fill up until she got home and could eat her meal without the kids' jibes.

"I'm fine," she growled, and jogged up the

back stairs to her bedroom. In the face of all advice to the contrary, Nan hadn't believed in drug treatment for attention deficit disorder—they'd struggled for years with food choices and therapy and exercise to manage the problem. Being elected mayor, Miranda figured, had proved their case.

If the Home Free program failed, though, there would be a reversal of opinion on her competence...and her mental fitness to be mayor. Any kind of personal involvement with Jud Ritter would only add to the evidence against her.

Rather than throw her wet body down on the bed and ruin her sheets, she took a quick shower and dried off properly. She couldn't face herself in the dressing table mirror, so she stood at her window, staring into the dark, as she combed out her hair.

How had she ended up kissing Jud Ritter *again?* Why the hell did she have to enjoy it so much? What was it about him that destroyed her good sense?

How was she ever going to forget about him when he left?

CHAPTER SIX

NAN HELD OUT until Wednesday, only seeing Cruz from a distance across a field or in the corral as they worked with horses. He didn't come to dinner as usual, didn't stop by for morning coffee or a drink late in the evening. They might as well have been simply boss and foreman.

She hated it. So after Miranda left for town that morning, Nan changed her work clothes for a soft, periwinkle-blue sweater and black slacks, traded her muddy boots for soft leather clogs, and walked along the driveway to Cruz's house.

Miranda's lavender field gleamed silver in the morning sunshine, and a crisp breeze carried the fragrance into the piney woods on the other side of the drive. The combination of evergreen and lavender reminded Nan that Christmas was only a few weeks off. Since

Miranda had grown up, their holidays tended to be quiet. They didn't bother much with gifts for each other, but made lots of goodies for friends and neighbors. They would need to start baking soon....

At the sight of Jud's truck pulled up next to the cabin, Nan hesitated and thought about turning back. They needed to talk, she and Cruz, but not with Jud as a witness. Could she hope that he'd hitched a ride into town with Miranda? Since Miranda hadn't said anything about such an arrangement, that was probably wishful thinking. She should just go home.

Nan planted her toe in preparation for an about-face.

"Too late," Cruz called from the porch. "I saw you coming. You can't chicken out now."

Just looking at him made her breathless and achy. His faded work jeans rode low on his hips. A long-sleeved black T-shirt showed off his shoulders. He was barefoot and totally adorable.

Maybe he'd come out because Jud had left for town. "I'm not chickening out," she said, going toward the house. "Good morning."

Cruz toasted her with his coffee mug. "Come in and have a cup. That wind bites."

He held the door for her as she climbed the steps, but didn't offer a kiss, or put his arm around her waist. Nan shivered, suddenly very cold.

Still, the house welcomed her warmly, even if Cruz didn't. They'd chosen some of the blankets, lamps and pictures together, on trips to out-of-the way places to avoid being seen together. Until today, she'd felt more at home in his place than her own.

She stepped closer to the fireplace, soaking up the heat of the flames. "You're right—I didn't realize I'd gotten chilled."

"I'll warm you up."

Though she looked at him hopefully, he only touched her shoulder for a second on his way to the kitchen. She started to follow him, but stopped when she heard footsteps in the hallway.

Damn.

Jud came into the living room. "'Morning," he croaked. "Good to see you."

"You don't sound too good."

He sniffed and shook his head. "Just a cold, probably. Nothing a cup of coffee can't cure." His pale face, red eyes and slumped shoulders made her suspect more than a simple cold.

"There's a new pot on the counter." Cruz returned, carrying two big mugs. "Help yourself."

Jud nodded and shuffled back toward the kitchen. Nan held the mug Cruz offered in both hands and took a small sip. Perfect temperature, perfect flavor—rich, strong coffee with the hazelnut cream she loved and a heaping spoonful of sugar.

"Mmm. Terrific." She drank again. "Nobody does it better." Giving him a wink, she waited for him to respond to the double entendre.

Cruz only grinned. "Thanks."

Nan turned toward the fire. As long as his houseguest could walk in at any moment, Cruz would keep their relationship a secret. That was *her* rule, after all.

Before she could think of something new to say, Jud wandered into the room.

"Good coffee," he said, passing through on his way to the hall. "Two or three more cups and I'll be functional."

"How's your investigation going?" She smiled at him. "You've been here two whole days, after all. I can't believe you don't have the answer yet."

"I work slow." He stopped in the door to the hallway and gave her a weary grin. "I've made phone calls to law enforcement offices around the state, trying to get background on this guy Wade's got in jail. I'm interviewing all of the Home Free participants, as many of the applicants as I can reach, plus anybody people think might have reason to cause problems."

His chest lifted on a deep breath, which ended in a harsh cough. "It's a damn long list of names. I'll let you know when I reach the end." Shaking his head wearily, he shuffled out of sight. A moment later, the door to the guest bedroom closed firmly.

"Did you have something you wanted to talk about?" Cruz asked after a few seconds. "I checked the hay in the cross-creek field this morning and figured we'd be able to bale tomorrow, if the weather holds. The south field should be ready just before Christmas—it's coming along pretty good."

"Great." Nan took a deep breath. "Miranda and I turned the horses out before she left for work. Flora and the foal look good." She cast around in her mind for something important to say about the barn, the farm, the hay…

anything except the issue that took up most of her waking thoughts and all of her dreams. "We should schedule maintenance on the baler and the tractors right after the New Year."

"I already have, and ordered in new parts—belts, plugs, filters."

"Great," she repeated, hiding behind her coffee mug again. "February will be the time to plow under the ground cover on the front field and prepare for seeding."

"We talked about that last week."

She glared at him. "Well, dammit, you know I didn't come here to talk about work!" Cruz glanced at the door to the hallway, and she lowered her voice. "Why are you avoiding me?"

"I'm not—" He stopped and shook his head instead of finishing the denial. "It's easier that way."

"You're making this too complicated. What we have together is nobody's business but our own."

"Don't ask, don't tell? That attitude suggests our relationship is something to be ashamed of."

"You know good and well there are folks

in this town who wouldn't approve of an older woman with a younger man."

"Or a white woman with a Mexican?"

"There's that, too."

"Aren't we strong enough to stand up against stupid people?"

"Yes, but—"

"But maybe the real problem is that *you* are one of those people who doesn't approve."

The shock held her silent for several moments. "Would I be here, practically begging, if I were?"

Finally, he stepped within her reach and cupped her cheek with his hand. "I love you, Nan. I do believe you love me. Somewhere inside of you, though, there's a well of doubt. As long as you draw from that well, the poison will work between us. I've seen this before—my father's bitterness destroyed his marriage, killed my mother. I'd rather live alone than go through that again."

In the back of the house, Jud's door opened and closed again. As his footsteps approached down the hall, Cruz retreated to the other side of the room. "Since things seem pretty stable around here, I'm going to visit my brother and his family for the weekend. You can reach me on my cell phone if there's an emergency."

"You can't just—"

Jud appeared in the doorway. "I'm heading into town," he announced, his voice hoarse. "Can I pick up anything, run errands?"

Nan blinked hard and focused on his pale face. "You should forget town and go back to bed."

"I'm all right." But he winced as he rolled his shoulders.

"Stop in and visit Kristin at the clinic. She's probably got something to make you feel better. Otherwise, I don't think we need anything from town." She gave Cruz a questioning glance.

"No, we're good. Thanks."

"Okay, then." Jud sighed. "I'll see you later."

He'd be gone in five minutes. She could stay and coax Cruz into a better frame of mind. Not necessarily with sex—though that would be wonderful—but with soft words and quiet touches, with the laughter they found together, with his enthusiastic curiosity about the world and her more pragmatic approach.

But that wouldn't resolve the situation. She had already begged for his company and been turned down. A woman did have some pride.

"I guess I'll take off, too." She crossed quickly to the front door and stepped out on the porch. "Jud can give me a ride back to the house." Taking the drop to the ground with a single stride, she jogged over to Jud's truck and hopped up into the passenger seat.

A glance out the rear window as they pulled away showed her Cruz standing barefoot on the cabin porch. Nan had to admit a certain degree of satisfaction as she faced forward in her seat. She could be just as stubborn as anybody else.

But when she walked into her empty house, she realized just how much that stubbornness could hurt.

"I HAVEN'T HAD A COLD in years," Jud complained to Kristin Gallagher, when he finally gave in and showed up at her clinic on Friday. "I don't get sick."

"The fact that you have an elevated temperature and muscle aches indicates that what you have is the flu." The petite blonde flashed her penlight beam into his eyes. "You ought to take it easy for the next few days. Drink plenty of fluids, eat if you feel hungry. Take ibuprofen every six hours for fever."

"Is that the best you can do?" When she turned away to drop the tongue depressor into the trash can, he eased himself off the exam table. "No miracle cures?"

"Antibiotics don't work on viral illnesses like the flu. Unless…" She gazed up at him. "Is this going to interfere with the other healing you're working on?"

"Nah. Those were just bullet holes. All taken care of."

"Of course." Shaking her head, she led him down the hall toward the empty waiting room.

Jud leaned a shoulder against the wall as Kristin finished up his paperwork. "Have you had trouble with vandalism on your property? Any unexplained pranks?"

"No, we've never had any trouble. Since I married Ryan, I've been leasing the land I got through the Home Free program to another family. My son and I moved to the Four Aces Ranch to be with Ryan."

"Clint Gallagher's place." A state senator and the richest rancher in Loveless County, Gallagher had pretty much run things in Homestead when Jud was growing up.

"You're not trying to blame Clint for what's been going on, are you?" When he didn't say anything, Kristin's eyes flashed with anger. "That's ridiculous. He's had enough trouble this last year, without trying to cause trouble for other people."

From what Jud remembered, Clint Gallagher was capable of making trouble whatever his personal situation. "What's wrong with Senator Gallagher's world?"

"All of this is public knowledge, so I don't mind telling you. Clint's going blind, due to macular degeneration. He's got heart trouble. And Lydia, his wife, is fighting cancer." Kristin bit her lip. "She's still with us, thank God. But soon enough…"

That would teach him to be so short on charity. "I am sorry to hear that." Jud put a hand on her shoulder for a second. "Please give Mrs. Gallagher my best."

"I will. But on top of those problems, Clint discovered that Leland Hayward, his attorney, had been embezzling for years. Ryan's still trying to sort out all the records. Leland accused my dad of cheating the Gallaghers, and to cover up the truth, he ordered his nephew to drive my dad's car off the road." She sighed. "It's all just been one big mess."

A lot had happened in Homestead while he'd been gone. "I hope Leland's in jail to stay."

"Yes. But can you understand now why Clint wouldn't be the person you're looking for?"

"He opposed the Home Free plan, didn't he?"

"Yes, because he wanted the land for his ranch. But I don't think he's mean enough to try to run people off with...with violence and intimidation."

"I remember him as a pretty malicious SOB, myself."

"Not anymore, Jud. He's changed. I promise."

"Okay, I'll accept your word, and I'll look elsewhere. Any suggestions?"

Her brows drew together as she thought about it. "I've come to love the people of Homestead like family. But there are a few who make me nervous."

"Who would they be?"

"Max Beltrane opposes the giveaway and just about any other kind of change in this town. He's very critical of Miranda and he's never been the least bit friendly to me or to any other newcomer, that I know of. Of course, that doesn't make him a crim-inal."

"No, it doesn't. Who else?"

"I hate pointing my finger at people."

"You're not. You're just reminding me of some of my oldest acquaintances." He grinned, then coughed, and wound up the moment with a wheez-ing breath.

"I'm reminding you that you should be in bed."

"All the girls say that." This time he settled for a wink.

"I'll bet they do. Well, two other prime complainers I can think of are Rudy Satter-white and Pete McPherson."

"I'll check them out. So that's everybody you can think of?"

Kristin opened her mouth, but before she could speak the front door of the clinic opened. Arlen Enfield stepped in out of the bright sunshine, looking every bit the Southern gentleman in his tan suede jacket, light blue shirt with a black bolo tie and his shiny boots.

"'Morning, Mrs. Gallagher." He aimed a slight bow in Kristin's direction, then turned to shake Jud's hand. "And good morning to you, too, Jud. Feelin' under the weather?"

"A little."

"I hear there's a bug goin' round town, makin' everybody sick. I, fortunately, am here solely for a blood pressure checkup. Mrs. Gallagher keeps after me like a nursemaid after an errant child." Something in his tone implied a certain contempt for Kristin's concern.

"That's right," she said firmly, picking up a medical record. "I've made it my personal crusade to keep you healthy for twenty more years, Mr. Enfield. So let's go back and read that BP of yours."

Enfield preceded her down the hall, where she directed him into the room Jud had occupied a few minutes ago. As he turned to leave, however, Kristin stepped back into the hallway and caught his attention with the wave of her hand. Pointing discreetly at her out-of-sight patient, she mouthed words without sound.

Not sure what she meant, Jud shook his head and raised his eyebrows in question.

Kristin leaned back into the exam room. "I'll be with you in just a second, Mr. Enfield." Then she hurried down the hallway toward Jud.

"It's him," she said, in a near whisper. "He's the other one who gives me the creeps!"

HALFWAY to the Four Aces Ranch, Jud began to regret his stubbornness. A bear of a headache and congestion in his chest and nose would not make interviewing Clint Gallagher any easier. He hadn't mentioned this visit to Kristin—no sense upsetting her. Given her assurances, maybe he was simply wasting time and effort.

But over the years, he'd noticed that people—especially nice people—tended to believe the best of those around them. They made excuses and looked the other way. Kristin would want her father-in-law to be one of the good guys. That didn't automatically make him so.

Four Aces land seemed to stretch all the way across Texas, though in reality Jud knew the holding was about twenty thousand acres. As he got closer to the gate, the livestock appeared—fat, healthy cattle, glossy quarter horses wearing blankets with a fan of cards—aces, of course—on the side. Legend said that a canny Gallagher had won the land from a luckless Ritter in some 1880s poker game.

Jud snorted. Wasn't that just typical of his family's fortunes?

Once he'd turned onto the property itself, the house came into view soon enough. His knock at the front door was answered by an ample Hispanic housekeeper. "Come in, Mr. Ritter. Mr. Clint is waiting for you."

She led him across polished floors, past richly detailed rooms, to the epitome of a wealthy rancher's office, lined with shelves of books and records, filled with leather chairs and a big mahogany desk. The chair behind the desk was empty.

"Over here." Jud turned toward the fireplace end of the room and found Clint Gallagher seated in one of the big armchairs, a blanket over his knees. The shock of the old man's appearance held Jud motionless for a couple of seconds, but he recovered and crossed the Navajo carpet, hand extended.

"Senator." Gallagher's grip was weak. "Good to see you." An outright lie—he would never have imagined the fierce, bull-like man of his youth could look so small, so...frail.

"Even though I look like hell? Sit down," Clint said. Jud took the chair across the hearth. "What do you want, anyway?"

Finesse didn't seem to matter. "I'm looking into some of the vandalism that's been happening on the land giveaway parcels. I hear from a couple of different sources that you opposed the plan. I wondered if you had any ideas about who might be stirring up trouble."

"You think I ordered somebody to commit petty vandalism against those people?"

"I'm looking into all the options. You're just one of them."

"I wouldn't waste my time." The old man spat into the fire. "Sure, I wanted that land. Wanted it years ago, before your dad and his cronies tried to make some kind of communist operation out of it. Went belly-up—I knew they would. Can't run a ranch by committee." He looked at Jud out of the corners of his eyes. "Zeb Ritter would have been a success, if he'd stayed with me. He could be running my operation right now."

"I hear your sons are doing a good job of that."

"Hmmph." Clint squeezed his eyes shut for a few seconds. "Anyway, once the county took over that land, I gave up on it. And I damn sure wouldn't tiptoe around poisoning grapevines or—what was it?—changing trail signs. And it was my helicopter that took the little girl to the hospital when her asthma got bad. Don't blame that on me!"

Jud put up his hands in a gesture of surrender. "Okay, okay. Your daughter-in-law pretty much convinced me you weren't responsible."

"You talked to her? Kristin?" For the first time, the fierce eyes softened. "She's a good girl. Good for Ryan. Kept him home where he belongs."

"You should tell her that to her face," a new voice said. "She'd be glad to know what you think." Lydia Gallagher, Clint's wife, entered the room. Though Jud remembered her as a beautiful, elegant woman, time had taken its toll on her, as well. Lydia's beige sweater draped like a blanket across her thin shoulders and the brown slacks hung as loosely as a skirt around her hips. She wore a panama hat with a colorful band around the crown, but he could see the absence of hair underneath, and his heart ached.

"It's good to see you, Jud." Lydia held out her long-fingered hand. "You've grown into a fine-looking man."

He was afraid to put much pressure on her bones. "Thanks. I—" What could he say? "I'm glad to see you, too."

She smiled at him. "Very tactful. Don't worry about saying the wrong thing. Just be yourself. So you're investigating these pesky incidents on Home Free land parcels?"

"Yes, ma'am."

"Clint does seem to be a likely suspect, doesn't he?" Standing behind the old man's chair, she put her hands on his shoulders. "Senator Gallagher used to be known for his ruthless ways with his opponents. Including me." Her husband tilted his head back and glared up at her. "But he's mellowed in his later years. I think you'll have to look elsewhere for your…what's the word?…perp."

Jud laughed. "Yes, ma'am, I guess I will." He looked at Clint. "Do you have any suggestions about which direction I should look in?"

Gallagher held his gaze. "I'd look outside of the county. There's been some interest from developers over the years—that land could've made a bundle for the builder lucky enough to get his hands on it. Mini-ranches, McMansions...we're not so far from Austin that some of those computer commuters wouldn't set up out this way. And there was enough spacefor commercial development, too. Yeah, I think you might find your 'perp'—" he winked at his wife "—in the Austin business district."

"But you don't have names?"

The senator blew out a wheezing breath. "Haven't heard too many recently. Steve Tilden at Tilden Steel contacted me once about building a plant out this way. Henry Darrow built his fortune with those damn 'planned communities.' Rosa—"

Jud held up a hand. "I'm sorry to interrupt. Did you say Henry Darrow?"

"That's right. He put up a couple of spec houses, and wanted to build more on Clyde Braxton's land, but neither of us got what we wanted." Gallagher slouched a little deeper into his chair.

Time to go. "You've been a real help, Senator. If you think of anything else, give me a call." Jud put a card with his cell phone number on the desk. "I'm glad I had a chance to talk to both of you." He wished he could think of something encouraging to say. But he settled for "Take care of yourselves," as he backed out of the study.

He found Ryan Gallagher waiting in one of the front rooms. "Hey, Jud. Come sit down. Want something to drink? Coffee? Beer?"

The beer tempted him, but he figured his head wasn't on too tight as it was. "No, thanks."

"I wanted to thank you for going easy on the old man. He's not up to much conflict these days."

"I could see that. And I already had Kristin's testimony clearing him. I thought he might send me in the right direction."

Ryan grinned at just the mention of her name. "She called to say she'd seen you."

"You've got yourself a great wife."

"Don't I know it? She's more than I deserve—especially when I think back to some of those stunts we pulled in high school."

"That's for sure. We were lucky to survive, let alone escape jail."

"I never did get my chance to jump that row of cars on the bike, though. The sheriff showed up right as you came down. Zoom!" He made a floating motion with his hand. "Like a pelican coming in for a landing."

"Landed my butt in the doghouse for months," Jud said, grinning. "By the time I got off restriction, Sheriff Montgomery's barn was as clean as my mother's kitchen. You could eat off the stall floors. And then I got to start on my dad's barn."

Ryan shook his head. "Those were the days. Would you have them back again?"

Jud thought about the backbreaking work every afternoon after school—barn chores, horse training, fieldwork, fence repair, house maintenance and then homework. Scraps of the arguments came at him in his head, his dad yelling about jobs left undone, about grades, about a rodeo Jud sneaked off to win.

"No," he said, stuffing the anger back into the deep hole in his soul where it lived. "No, I really don't think I would."

With his truck bed weighted by bags of horse feed, Ethan followed the one-way streets around the courthouse square in Homestead, ready to head back home. As he caught sight of the Christmas decorations on the front of Tanner's General Store, though, he decided to make another stop. He'd been a bear to get along with this week. Kayla deserved something special just for putting up with him. The kids, too.

Tanner's combined old-fashioned style with a selection of basic necessities and specialty items. Toothpaste and gourmet tortellini, a six-pack of beer or a ninety-dollar bottle of champagne—everybody in Homestead could find something they wanted at Tanner's.

For a Wednesday afternoon, the place was busy. Browsing the shelves, Ethan greeted friends from across the county, listened to other conversations, chuckled at jokes told in bona fide Texas twangs. He narrowed his choices for Kayla to three—a picture frame inlaid with different colors of wood in a vine pattern, a hand-thrown ceramic wine cooler glazed in blues and purples or a turquoise pendant hanging from a sterling silver chain.

He knew she'd love the frame so she could put out another picture of the kids, and the wine cooler was pretty as well as practical.

But the necklace would be hers alone. He could imagine her stretched out on their bed, wearing nothing but that glowing blue stone...

"Well, if it isn't the younger Mr. Ritter." Arlen Enfield smoothed his mustache with two fingers. "Good to see you this afternoon, Ethan."

"Mr. Enfield." Apart from Enfield's persistent opposition to the Home Free program, Ethan didn't know anything bad about the man. He seemed to be an honest real estate agent and had been a competent mayor. The Enfield boys spent too much time at the Lone Wolf Tavern, but Arlen couldn't be held responsible for his grown sons' behavior.

Nonetheless, Ethan could barely tolerate being in the same room with him.

"How're things going these days?" Enfield polished his glasses with a white handkerchief. "I talked with your brother at the wedding. Is he planning on settling down in Homestead once again?" The man had a talent for hitting a person where they were weakest.

"I don't know Jud's plans." Ethan grabbed

the box containing the turquoise necklace and turned to walk toward the cash register.

The ex-mayor followed. "He seems to be making himself at home. I saw him at lunch the other day, over at the café."

Ethan could have predicted what was coming next. Kayla had eaten lunch in town on Monday with Greer, Kristin and Miranda.

"Yessiree, Jud made himself quite comfortable at that table full of lovely ladies."

On the toy aisle, Ethan studied the puzzles, hoping Enfield would disappear if he didn't get a reaction.

"Interesting thing was, when most of the ladies left, Jud stayed behind. I have to say, it looked like quite a little tête-à-tête to me…."

Ethan took a five-hundred-piece horse puzzle and hightailed it toward the cash register.

"Your brother and your wife, that is. A nice, intimate little chat."

His hands were full, or he would have turned back and slugged Enfield into next week. By the time he set his purchases on the counter, Ethan had recovered some of his self-control.

"But then, you probably knew that already,

didn't you?" Enfield's voice in his ear was like the buzz of an especially pesky horsefly.

"I did," Ethan lied. "Sorry to ruin your day."

"Not at all, son. Not at all." He put his glasses on his nose and restored the neatly folded handkerchief to his breast pocket. "I'm sure your brother has no designs on your lovely wife. None at all. Although he was quite the wild boy in his younger days, now wasn't he?"

Ethan was saved from answering by the arrival of Ed Tanner. "'Afternoon, Arlen, Ethan." Tall and husky, Ed had taken over running the store from his father, Leroy, who'd expanded his family's dry goods store into a real emporium.

He picked up the necklace and clucked his tongue. "My, my, my. Somebody's gonna be in a good mood tonight." With a wink at Ethan, he pulled out a gift box and placed the piece of jewelry inside. "Or is this in the nature of an apology for past sins?"

"Neither." Ethan managed a grin he was far from feeling. "Call it insurance for the future."

"Sounds good to me." Ed rang up the puzzle. "Say, Arlen, I had a reporter from

Austin in here this morning. Said she was doing a human interest story on Homestead. Know anything about that?"

"A reporter? You don't say?"

Ethan didn't wait to hear the rest of the conversation, but made his escape.

Circling the courthouse again on his way out of town, he saw Miranda standing on the sidewalk with a curvaceous bleached blonde he didn't recognize. The reporter, probably, getting the scoop on Homestead's history, architecture...whatever.

Once free of the town's speed limit, he floored the accelerator. Kayla hadn't said a damn word about talking to Jud. She hadn't even mentioned his presence at the lunch with her friends, let alone that they'd talked together afterward.

About *him,* no doubt. About mending fences, building bridges...as if the gulf between them could be closed with a few words. Or many words, for that matter.

What Jud had done was irreparable. He'd abandoned the family in hard times and refused to come back when things got even worse. He hadn't stayed more than a few days when their sister died. The day after their mother was buried, the sheriff discovered him passed out drunk on a back road out in the county somewhere. And he'd been impossible to contact when their dad blew his brains out.

The problem was, Jud had been justified in running away. An objective observer could even make a case for the idea that he'd been driven away from home by a father who didn't trust his own son to tell the truth.

And by a younger brother whose mistaken version of the facts had blown the Ritter family to pieces.

CHAPTER SEVEN

MIRANDA CAUGHT SIGHT of Ethan's grim face as he headed out of town, but didn't have a chance to wonder about the cause, since the reporter—a candidate for Miss Texas if ever there was one—had yet another question to ask.

"So, is this where all the ranchers and farmers in the area do their shopping?" Deirdre Long's wave took in the stores on the square around the courthouse.

"You can probably find all the basics of life within sight of the courthouse," Miranda said. "Groceries, farm and animal supplies, books, magazines. And you've been into Tanner's—they carry lots of speciality items."

"What about clothes? Shoes?" A glance at Mi-randa's black slacks, gray sweater and boots con-veyed Deirdre's distinct lack of approval.

"We do have a dress shop." Miranda pointed out Elle's Belles across the street. "But Austin's less than an hour away. If you need more than jeans and work shirts, you make the time to go over to the malls." Miranda felt sure the reporter's red leather jacket, tan suede skirt and boots owed their uptown style to a designer showroom.

"And are these the only restaurants? Bertha's Kolaches and Callie's Café?"

"The Lone Wolf Tavern serves burgers and barbecue. There are a couple of fast-food places up by the highway. But, in general, I think most folks around here like to cook for themselves and their friends. If we wanted fancy restaurants and exciting nightlife," she said, forestalling Deirdre's next comment, "we wouldn't choose to live out in the country."

"I guess that's true. So, tell me about this land giveaway program. How ever did you come up with the idea?"

Finally, some meat. "Other towns in various states have developed land giveaway programs to draw new citizens to their areas. I did some research, talked to a few people and decided that the same kind of approach could work for Homestead."

"And have you, indeed, drawn people to the town?"

"We've had twelve parcels taken so far by singles and families, and we have another sixty or so applications to evaluate. I'd say our program has been a real success."

"But there are also some problems with your land giveaway, I understand."

"The application and evaluation process works very well. I think our new residents are quite pleased with their choices." Miranda hadn't realized she had such a talent for political doublespeak.

"I understand some longtime residents are seriously opposed to the Home Free program."

"We live in a free society," Miranda said with a shrug. "One hundred percent agreement never happens. But a majority of Homestead voters elected me specifically because of the Home Free Land Giveaway."

"What about the vandalism and violence that's taken place since the first new residents arrived?"

Stupid, not to have seen that question coming. "We…have had a few minor incidents." God forgive her for playing down

Megan's asthma attack. "Our sheriff is keeping a close eye on the situation."

Deirdre flipped a couple of pages in her notebook. "Yes, I'm supposed to talk to him next. Aren't you worried about luring people to Homestead when there's the possibility of danger for their property—or even their lives?"

Before Miranda could answer, a voice came over her shoulder. "Well, Deirdre, this is a surprise. What are you doing out here in the sticks?"

The reporter gave a delighted squeak. "Jud Ritter! I can't believe this." Miranda stepped out of the way just in time to avoid being squeezed between them as Deirdre gave Jud a fervent, lengthy hug. "What are you doing here?"

"Jud's a hometown boy," Miranda volunteered. "Born and raised right here in Homestead. You two know each other?"

Jud nodded. "We've crossed paths on crime scenes in Austin."

"Among other places." Deirdre propped her hands on her hips and stared up at him—a long way up, since she was only about five-three. "If I'd known you were here, I could have gotten the information I wanted for this article without having to come to the middle of nowhere."

"But you're such a crack reporter, you'd want to see the place anyway, right?" Jud's sarcasm seemed to go over her head. "Why don't you let me give you a tour? Our mayor won't mind." He looked at Miranda. "Right?"

Miranda unlocked her jaw. "Of course. You can show Ms. Long the sites of all your most infamous stunts." She put a hand on Deirdre's shoulder. "Be sure to visit the car junkyard behind Buddy's Gas Station, where our daredevil, here, attempted to jump his motorcycle over a row of rusted Chevys."

Deirdre breathed a long "Ooooooo. Did you really?"

Jud flashed Miranda a grin. "I had my wild days. See you later, Ms. Mayor."

"Thanks," Deirdre called, with a beauty queen wave. Then she clutched Jud's arm with both hands and assumed an awestruck expression as they sauntered away.

"If looks could kill," Wade said, coming up beside her, "I'd be charging you with a double homicide."

"Not at all. Jud did me a favor, since I'd had as much of that b—" Miranda cleared her throat. "I need to get back to work. By the way, she's got you on her list."

"That won't be happening." Wade turned with her as she headed back to her office. "I've left Virgil on duty and I'm going home. Callie's got the flu and I don't want to leave her there without help when the kids get out of school." Callie's younger brother and two younger sisters completed the Montgomery household, along with Wade's dad. Callie and her family had become part of the Home Free Program as refugees from an abusive stepfather, and stayed to be valued members of the Homestead community.

"I'm so sorry. Anything I can do?"

"We're okay." He put an arm around her shoulder and gave her a quick squeeze. "Don't let the turkeys get you down."

"Right." Miranda went into her office, thinking that she'd never liked turkey very much, even for the holidays.

And that Jud Ritter was too…tall…to waste on a short, perky little airhead like Deirdre Long.

ETHAN DIDN'T GET A CHANCE to talk with his wife until after Megan, Brad and Heather had gone to bed. The transition from single bachelor to married father of three had happened almost overnight, but he enjoyed every minute of the kid-generated pandemonium his life now contained. Most of the time.

Kayla finally came into the bedroom about ten o'clock. "Heather's got the sniffles," she said, stroking a brush through her soft auburn hair. "I sure hope she's not coming down with this flu bug."

"Does she have a fever?"

"Not yet." She drew a deep breath and released it in a sigh. "I'm probably worrying for nothing."

"Well, you have to worry about Megan, because of her asthma. So you're just in the habit. Come over here and I'll rub your shoulders. You look tense."

"I knew there was a reason I married you," she said a few minutes later. "This is heaven."

"Just what I was thinking." He kneaded her lovely shoulders and the nape of her neck, stroked softly over her smooth skin, savoring the pleasure of making his wife relax. Then, when she finally sighed in relief, he reached under his pillow, drew out the necklace and slipped the silver chain over her head.

"Oh, Ethan, how beautiful! I love it." Kayla turned and put her arms around his neck. "You are the most wonderful…"

He didn't let her finish. And neither of them had breath to waste on words for quite a while.

When they lay sated and quiet, though, Ethan spoke his mind. "I hear you had lunch with my brother on Monday."

Kayla stiffened. "He joined us at our table at Callie's."

"And stayed with you after everybody else left?"

"Yes. He wanted to ask me about the poisoned vines. He's doing some investigating for Wade and Miranda."

"That's it?"

"Well, no. We talked about you a little."

"And just what did big brother have to say?"

She raised herself up on an elbow.

"Nothing bad, or mean. I think he'd like to make some sort of peace, actually."

"That's not likely to happen."

"Why not? You can let the past go—you know that."

Ethan sat up and swung his feet to the floor, propped his elbows on his knees and rubbed his eyes with the heels of his hands. "I might be able to let go. But Jud's got more to forgive. I don't see how he can."

"I don't understand. You said he left…that he hasn't been at all helpful…."

"Yeah, but I'm the reason he took off to begin with."

"I thought he got a girl pregnant and ran away because your parents expected him to marry her."

"The problem is, Jud didn't have to be involved. Della Bowie—that was the girl's name—wasn't naming the father. She was easy, and everybody knew it."

"So how did Jud get blamed?"

"I did it." After a long silence, he went on. "I was a nosy fourteen-year-old, and I saw them necking a couple of times, down by the creek." He shrugged. "They had most of their clothes off, and it looked like what I'd gleaned from different sources about sex. I was teasing Jud about it while we were working together in the barn one day. My dad overheard and he jumped to the conclusion that the baby was Jud's. The fight between them lasted about a week. Then Jud took off."

Kayla's arms came around him from behind. "That doesn't make it your fault. The news would have come out eventually."

"But—"

"And Jud is talking about reconciliation. Surely that means he's ready to forget the past."

Ethan released a breath he seemed to have been holding for years. "Maybe you're right. Now that he's taken the first step, maybe Jud and I can close the door on our past mistakes and go on from here."

Turning, he took Kayla in his arms as he stretched out on the bed. "And if we do, it'll be because of the miracle you've worked in my life. Thank you, from the bottom of my heart."

She gave him a sweet, sexy smile. "My pleasure."

BY THE TIME JUD GOT BACK to Cruz's house late Friday afternoon, he could truthfully say he felt like hell. Pounding head, burning lungs, muscles as heavy and clumsy as lead pipes...yes, indeed, the flu had taken hold.

Two hours with Deirdre hadn't improved his health. They had dated a couple of times in Austin, and she was pretty in a kind of college cheerleader style. But there wasn't much room in her head for anyone besides her precious self, and even less room in her heart. He'd taken her on this afternoon to rescue Miranda, who'd looked like a deer in the headlights when he'd arrived there. Somehow, he doubted he'd get much gratitude for his effort.

Anyway, all he really wanted at this point was to lie down and die. He took a shower that didn't help, washed down aspirin with cold coffee and collapsed on the couch with the flickering TV screen as his only light in the pitch-black night.

Then, somehow, it was morning again, though he didn't remember being asleep and he sure didn't feel even one degree better. Out of desperation, he swallowed four more aspirin—with plain water this time because the coffee was too rank even for a seasoned professional. Another stretch of semiconsciousness followed, accompanied by Saturday-morning television, which was as bad as the old coffee.

At first, he couldn't separate the pounding of his head from the pounding on the front door. When he did, he wasn't sure he cared or, if he did care, could do anything about it.

In the end, he didn't have to. The door squeaked open, finally. "Jud? Hello?" Miranda called. "Anybody home?"

He wanted to sit up and look well. He really did. "Here," he croaked.

She came to the sofa and stood over him, hands on her hips. "You're sick. How'm I supposed to yell at you when you're sick?"

"Yell away. It's just a cold."

Before he could dodge, her freezing-cold hand rested on his forehead. "You've got the flu."

"Nah." He sat up, away from her touch. "I don't get sick."

"Are you getting plenty to drink? Taking some kind of medicine?"

"Sure."

She surveyed the area around him—the blanket he'd curled up in during chills and thrown off when he got hot, the bottle of aspirin and a glass with an inch of water still left in it. Without saying a word, she stomped into the kitchen and stomped back a second later.

"There's nothing out of place," she said. "You haven't eaten or had anything but water since... when? Last night some time?"

"Not hungry."

"Not thirsty, either?"

He started to shake his head then stopped, wincing at the pain. "No."

Miranda held up one finger in front of his face. "Wait here. I'll be right back." She headed toward the rear of the house. From the particular squeak of the door, Jud could tell she'd entered his bedroom.

"What are you doing?" He wasn't sure the question carried that far, but he had even less confidence in his ability to follow her.

In only a minute, she came down the hallway. "Jeans, socks, shirt, shorts," she said, holding up a folded bundle. "I gather you don't wear pajamas. Now, let's get you on your feet."

"I don't want to." He couldn't believe he was whining like a five-year-old. "I'm doing good right here."

Miranda blew out an exasperated breath.

"You are not doing good. And you're going to get really sick if you don't have somebody making sure you're drinking enough and taking some medicine. Come on, you can do it." She reached around him with one arm and somehow levered him off the couch without his cooperation.

Jud allowed his arm to rest across her shoulders, which were the perfect height for that purpose. "You don't have to do this."

"Mom has a real dislike of having people die on the property. I'm just following the rules." She started a slow walk to the door.

"As long as you're bringing clothes along," he said, "you might want to collect your underwear out of the bathroom."

"My underwear?" Miranda stopped and as a result, so did he. "What are you talking about?"

"Nice lingerie you wear under those sweatshirts." He tried for a grin but had a feeling it failed. "Lavender, to match your plants."

She stared at him, eyebrows drawn together. "In the bathroom?"

Next thing Jud knew, she'd propped him against the wall like a pair of skis and headed for the bathroom at the end of the hall.

"This?" she asked as she returned, swinging the delicate garment from one finger.

He didn't bother to answer. At least he wouldn't have to avoid that end of the shower anymore, wouldn't be tempted to imagine the womanly curves which would shape and fill the soft fabric hanging there.

Without comment, Miranda put her arm around him and took his weight onto her shoulders once more. Out on the porch, she locked the door and then practically carried him down the steps.

"I walked over," she said, aiming him toward the driveway, "so we'll take your truck back to my house."

"I never get sick," Jud protested.

She chuckled. "You mentioned that. Don't worry about it."

In a few easy minutes, he found himself tucked up in a soft bed on the second floor of the farmhouse, with a lightweight comforter over him and a dose of something for fever, aches and pains on his tongue.

Nan tucked him in as Miranda filled a glass with ginger ale. "We'll check on you every so often," the older woman said. "Just go to sleep. You'll feel better in a couple of days."

"Tomorrow," Jud insisted. "I'll be out of your way tomorrow."

"Whatever you say." The light dimmed and the door shut. Jud tried to stay awake, tried to stiffen his body against the urge to melt into the bed. He had no business taking charity from Miranda Wright and her mother. No right at all.

Sleep would not be denied. And when the muscle aches and pounding head returned, he was grateful for the stroke of a cool hand across his forehead and a fresh drink to help him swallow the pills. Smooth pillows and straightened covers felt like heaven at that point. Or maybe he just liked the sense of being looked after.

"Thanks," he mumbled. It was all he could do.

"You're welcome," Miranda said softly. She went to the door, but turned back before she opened it. "Jud?"

"Yeah?"

"That lavender bra isn't mine. I gave it to my mom for her birthday. I'm a white cotton kinda gal, myself." The latch on the door clicked quietly as it closed.

That meant… His fevered brain had trouble following a train of thought. But if Nan had left the bra at Martinez's house, that meant she and Cruz were…

Fading fast, Jud grabbed onto the really important point. The bra belonged to Nan.

Not Miranda. She wasn't involved. Committed. Taken.

Yet.

MIRANDA LOOKED UP from the newspaper as her mother came into the kitchen Sunday morning. "How's our patient?"

"Worse, of course." Nan scraped the contents of the plate she carried into Dusty's bowl. "His throat hurts so bad, he could hardly swallow a couple of spoonfuls of scrambled eggs. Fever is back up to one hundred-two."

"He must be miserable," Miranda said, wincing. "He looked pitiful enough last night."

"I'm glad you checked on him. I'd hate to think of the poor guy lying in the cabin sick as a dog until Cruz got back tonight sometime."

"Speaking of which, this trip to his brother's was kind of sudden, wasn't it? He didn't say a word about it last week, then suddenly he's gone?"

Facing out the window as she washed the plate, her mother shrugged. "He's a free man. He gets time off like any other employee."

"Oh, come on, Mom. Cruz isn't just an employee."

When Nan didn't answer and didn't look her way, Miranda decided the time had come to push the issue. "Look, I'm not blind and I'm not stupid."

"What does that mean?"

"You and Cruz have been sleeping together for at least a year. Knowing you and knowing him, I'm assuming that means you love each other."

"For heaven's sake, Miranda! He's a good fifteen years younger than I am."

"Does that matter?"

"Yes, it does." Her voice shook a little, and she still didn't turn around.

"To Cruz? Or to you?" She didn't get an answer. "Mom, you're going to rub the color off that plate if you dry it one more time. Put it away and come sit down."

But though Nan put the dish away, she didn't sit down. "I've got work to do." The back door slapped closed behind her as she headed outside.

Nan reached the barn and sought immediate comfort from Bailey, who was always glad to see her. He whickered as she pulled a carrot from her pocket and fed it to him through the barred window of his stall.

"Miranda knows, Bailey. How embarrassing is that?" She felt herself blush as she reviewed the implications. Her daughter was aware that she'd been sleeping with a man young enough to be her son, or son-in-law, at least. The whole situation was kind of ridiculous, really. She should be settling into grandmotherhood, not experimenting with whipping cream and massage oil. Not at the same time, of course.

Bailey nosed at her hand, and she gave him more carrot. "At least nobody questions *your* age, or your reaction when a hot filly walks by and flicks her tail at you. That's your job, isn't it? Yes, sir, your whole purpose is making beautiful babies with beautiful ladies. But there are no more babies for me." Nan sighed. "Yet another reason not to hang on to Cruz. He should have kids of his own. I can't give him those."

The stallion snorted in commiseration, then pawed at the floor just in front of his stall door. "No, I don't really have much work to do this afternoon. We could go for a ride, you and me. Sounds good doesn't it?"

In fifteen minutes, she had Bailey groomed and saddled. She was a tall woman, but even for her, mounting the seventeen-hand horse was a challenge. Bailey stood quietly by the mounting block, however, and allowed her to settle on his back.

Once they left the stable yard for the driveway, his spirit took control. He moved into his canter after only a few minutes at the trot. Once they reached open ground beyond the fences, he broke into a gallop.

Nan stayed with him, loving the power of the animal underneath her, the bright, crisp day, the freedom of the wind in her face whipping away her self-consciousness and doubt. Times like this, she wanted to ride forever.

The Hayseed Farm didn't extend quite as far as forever. With his fidgets shaken out, Bailey responded nicely to her request for a down transition, and finally they were walking along the far boundary of her property. She and George had bought this piece of land with their wedding money, thirty-five years ago. They'd expected to live here together, with a passel of kids and a herd of prizewinning thoroughbred horses.

But that dream ended on the day George fell under the tractor and was crushed to death. She'd gone on because of Miranda—when you had a child, you got up in the morning whether you wanted to or not. They'd had a good life, she and her daughter, a busy life. Nan hadn't realized she was lonely until the day Cruz walked onto her farm, looking for work.

A branch of Pecan Creek defined the border between her place and one of the Home Free lots not yet taken. She'd never worried too much about the lack of a neighbor keeping watch over the land…but the recent vandalism did raise some concerns. Maybe she should talk to Miranda and Cruz about fencing off this field, instead of depending on the creek to discourage trespassers—the creek which dried to a trickle most summers and wasn't hard to cross the rest of the year. A wire fence wasn't much of a deterrent, but better than nothing.

She turned Bailey away from the creek, back toward the house and the barn. Before she could ask for a trot, the crack of a rifle shot shattered the afternoon silence.

Her stallion took instant, violent exception to the noise. He stood straight up in the air, then thudded to earth, only to rise again. Nan held on as long as she dared, but when Bailey began to tip backward, she bailed and threw herself out to the side.

CHAPTER EIGHT

THE COLLISION with cold-hardened ground drove the breath out of Nan's chest. She lay motionless, with pain stabbing her side and no air to produce even a whisper.

Once her lungs began to work again, she pushed herself into a crouch and then to her feet. There was nothing to see, of course. Nobody standing at the tree line with a rifle in hand, no sound of boots crashing through the underbrush as the shooter escaped. No sign of her horse, either.

When she started walking, she discovered the bruise on her hip and the wrenched knee that made each stride hurt worse than the one before. The shoulder she'd landed on started to throb. She hadn't fallen off a horse in years. She'd forgotten just how much it hurt.

Where had Bailey run off to? He could

trip over the loose reins and hurt himself. That would be a real disaster.

Hobbling down the driveway, she finally realized she was hearing her name shouted in the distance.

"Nan! Nan, can you hear me?" The voice belonged to Cruz.

She didn't have the breath to yell back. And she didn't have the strength to hurry. So she kept walking, trusting they'd connect eventually.

"Nan!" He approached from her right side, racing through the foot-high hay they'd be cutting this week. "Dear God, are you okay?" His hands gripped her shoulders and his worried gaze searched her face. "What happened?"

"Bailey spooked at a gunshot. He reared and I bailed."

"He showed up at the cabin," Cruz said, brushing her hair out of her face. "He was standing by the porch shivering when I got there."

"Is he okay?"

"He'll be fine. I tied him up and took off trying to find you." That wasn't an answer and they both knew it. Cruz put an arm around her waist. "Let's get you inside, check you over."

But when they reached the cabin, she wanted to examine Bailey first. The slightest glance told her what Cruz hadn't said. A bullet had grazed a path across the big swell of muscle just above the horse's hip—a flesh wound, bleeding sluggishly, which threatened nothing but the stallion's vanity, and that only temporarily.

The thought that someone had deliberately fired a gun at a horse on her property drove her close to collapse.

Cruz got her into the cabin and pushed her to sit down on the couch. At her hiss of pain, he knelt in front of her, taking her hands in his own. "You are hurt."

"Bruised. That's all." She shook her head. "Who would shoot at my horse? Or me?"

"I think that's a question our visiting cop needs to answer. Do you know where Jud is?"

"My house. He's got the flu and Miranda brought him home so we could look after him."

Cruz glanced over his shoulder, as if to confirm Jud's absence. "I'll call Wade. Meanwhile, you can soak in the tub for a while. I've got some bathsalts—"

She wanted nothing so much as to do just that, then curl up in Cruz's bed—in Cruz's arms—and let the world go on without her for a while. But she'd taken advantage of him for too long, as it was.

So she pulled her hands away from his hold. "I'll do that later. I need to get Bailey bandaged up, pull the other horses into the barn. Until I know what's going on, I can't leave them out to graze." Propping a hand on the arm of the couch, she managed to get off the couch and to the door before Cruz could stop her.

"Nan—" he said, coming after her.

"Please, just call Wade. Tell him to meet me at the barn as soon as he can." She looked over her shoulder and smiled. "Thanks."

Then, as she'd done for most of her life, she stepped outside to face trouble on her own.

WADE CAME AND WENT on Sunday afternoon, mak-ing no bones about the seriousness of the shooting incident. Nan climbed into bed without dinner, her aches and pains only foreshadowing the misery she'd feel tomorrow. After helping Miranda gather in all the horses from their pastures, Cruz had locked the main gate and announced he would spend the night in the barn. Tomorrow, he'd go into town for fencing to stretch across the unguarded creek.

Jud had finally fallen into a natural sleep in the middle of the afternoon, and Miranda hated to wake him. But he'd be furious if she left him uninformed any longer than necessary. More than that, she wanted to hear what he had to say about the situation—an impulse that made no sense at all. What could he do, flat on his back with the flu?

Still, she took the precaution of hiding all his pants before she put a hand on his shoulder to shake him gently. "Jud? Hey, Rip Van Winkle, time to wake up."

He didn't move, but his face changed subtly, and she knew he'd heard her. "What time is it?" His voice had regained some of its smooth Texas drawl.

"Nine o'clock Sunday night."

"Not too bad." He moved one shoulder, then the other, and flexed his knees slightly. "Somebody took the razor blades out of my muscles."

"I thought you'd suffered enough."

"Thanks." He slowly opened his eyes. "I'm not sure about that, but I'll take the reprieve." As he focused on her face, his smile faded. "What's wrong?"

"We had some trouble this afternoon." She explained what had happened and what they'd done so far. "I thought you'd want to know."

Muttering, he pushed himself into a sitting position. "Damn right I do. I need to talk to Wade." He glanced around the room. "Where are my clothes?"

"Where you'll never find them without help."

"You woke me up to tell me this so I could do nothing about it? I have to get dressed." He swung his legs out from under the covers...then paused. "I'm wearing my shorts. And a T-shirt."

"Yep."

"You undressed me."

"Don't pretend you've never been undressed by a woman before."

His mouth quirked into a one-sided grin. "I usually like to give them the courtesy of being conscious."

Miranda shrugged. "Wasn't necessary this time. Tonight, you stay in bed. Tomorrow, if you feel like it, you can go into town and talk to Wade." She plumped his pillow before he settled back against it. "I guess you didn't come up with anything helpful this week?"

"I've got some leads, nothing definite. I eliminated Gallagher as a suspect."

"Just like that?"

His turn to shrug. "Kristin and Kayla were both pretty persuasive in his defense. And he was free enough with some information that I feel safe in taking him off the list."

"Who's on the list?"

"This guy in jail, Darrow, is the son of an Austin developer who wanted to build in Loveless County, on the land you're giving away. It might just be that simple."

"You mean nobody local is involved?"

"I can't say one way or the other, right now. I've still got lots of checking to do."

"Maybe taking time out to show Miss Texas around slowed you down. You were looking a little dazed when the two of you walked off together."

"That would have been because my bones were coming unhinged. Nothing to do with Deirdre."

"No big deal. Kind of convenient, though,

to have her come out to do a story at the same time you're in town."

"Dumb luck."

"Exactly." She got to her feet, unhappy with what she'd revealed of her feelings. "Call if you need something. Otherwise, I'll check in on you in the morning."

She couldn't have been more surprised when he lunged to the end of the bed and caught her hand with a grip strong enough to keep her from leaving. Despite spending two days flat on his back, Jud Ritter in just a T-shirt and boxers was a sight which easily shut off her ability to breathe.

"You have no reason to be jealous," he said through clenched teeth.

"I know that." She tugged against his grip. "I'm not. Let me go."

Instead, he pulled her closer, so they stood chest to chest with only the iron bed rail in between them. "I'm here to do a favor for a friend. When I'm done, I'm gone. But if I were staying…"

His other hand came up to frame her face between thumb and forefinger. "Believe me, a flaky reporter would be the last woman on my mind."

With the same suddenness, he let her go. "Get some sleep, Miranda. Tomorrow's going to be a hell of a day."

MIRANDA WAS ALONE in the kitchen Monday morn-ing for breakfast. She'd told Nan to take things easy—she and Cruz could handle the morning chores. Jud was nowhere to be seen, which suited Miranda just fine. As if she didn't have enough to worry about after yesterday's attack on her mother, she'd lost what rest she might have salvaged last night puzzling over Jud's cryptic declaration.

Did he mean he was attracted to her? That thought alone was enough to drive away any possibility of sleep. She could handle having him around as long as they kept their distance.

Thinking about something else—something *more*—with Jud Ritter terrified her nearly as much as the shooting.

On the drive into Homestead, Miranda prepared herself for a difficult day. Millie would want details for a newspaper story. The town gossips would make a point of tracking down the mayor to get a scoop straight from the horse's mouth. Then would come her two o'clock meeting scheduled with Wade and his "investigator." She wasn't sure she could look Jud in the face.

As she walked up the steps into the courthouse, she heard the phone ringing in the town office. Reba looked up as Miranda stepped inside the door, and immediately hung up on the caller.

"Thank God, you're finally here!"

Miranda glanced at her watch, which read eight-thirty, half an hour before she usually arrived. "What's wrong?"

The phone rang again. "Hold, please," Reba ordered, then cut the connection. "This is a disaster, pure and simple. What am I supposed to tell these people? I think I've heard from every household in Loveless County already this morning!"

"Disaster? What are you talking about?"

The assistant stared at her as if she were crazy. "You don't know?"

"Obviously not."

Wordlessly, Reba gathered and folded the newsprint pages spread out on her desk. Then she plopped the paper down so Miranda could see the headline below the fold. The *Austin Chronicle,* Monday edition.

"Land Giveaway Goes Bust," Miranda read

aloud. "Vandalism Gives Voice to Opposition."

The byline above the article read Deirdre Long.

As soon as he stepped into the town office, Jud sensed the volcanic eruption waiting for him behind Miranda's door. He would have waited for Wade's backup, but that meant staying within Reba's predatory reach. Of the two dangers, he'd take his chances with the mayor.

She answered his knock with a terse, "Come in." After he'd closed the door behind his back, she stared at him for a long, silent minute.

"Did you come back specifically to destroy the town, and me along with it?" The newspaper lay open on her desk. "Or was this some kind of lucky accident?"

Martinez had told him about the article. "I had nothing to do with that report."

"Except you spent several hours with dear Deirdre last week. Let me guess…you were 'misquoted.'"

"There isn't a quote from me in the entire piece."

"Just lots of discussion—paraphrased, I admit—on how the vandals are making Homestead unsafe for raising a family. How some of the incidents have been life threatening." She looked down at her hands, pressed flat on the blotter, and shook her head. "Is this your idea of revenge? I gotta tell you, you've hit the jackpot. I expect I'll be out of office in a matter of weeks, if not days, and the Home Free program will be dead."

Jud leaned over the desk, placing his hands fingertip to fingertip with Miranda's. "First off, let me point out that yesterday's attack was, indeed, life threatening. Second, I did not give Deirdre material for the article. She's a friend, we've cooperated in the past, but I don't divulge information about a case to anyone, especially reporters."

After a silent struggle, Miranda raised her desperate gaze to his face. "Who else would have talked to her?"

"I turned her over to Virgil Dunn. Maybe he said too much."

"And she interviewed Ed Tanner, plus God knows who else. All she really had to do was get hold of Arlen Enfield and the damage was done." With a sigh, she covered her face with her hands. "I don't know why the Austin paper would even be interested in the story to begin with. Or who would suggest it."

"But you were ready to blame me right off the bat."

"Not without reason."

"The reason being that I'm fundamentally untrustworthy?"

She dropped her hands, staring up at him as different emotions chased across her face. Surprise, embarrassment—that pink flush again—and regret, followed by an expression he would have labeled hunger, if she hadn't shut it down so fast. Yearning, maybe...the same kind that came over him lately whenever he let himself think about Miranda Wright.

"You want me to trust you?" she said in a low voice.

"Yes." Until that moment, he hadn't realized how much.

Slowly, she came to her feet. "Why should I?"

As they faced each other across the desk, his past rose up between them—not just his stupid stunts as a teenager, his justified reputation for girls and booze and trouble, but the history of these last fifteen years when he'd been everywhere except the one place his family needed him to be. And that night four years ago, when he'd ground her trust into the dirt with the heel of his boot.

"It's asking a lot," Jud admitted. "And I've done nothing to deserve it."

She touched the back of his right hand with the tips of her fingers. "You can't make any kind of case for yourself?"

He shook his head, suddenly short of the air he needed to form words.

"I ought to throw you out of town." Those same fingertips brushed across his cheek, then flicked a shock of hair off his forehead.

"You probably should." Jud caught her hand in his own and placed a kiss on the palm. "I wouldn't blame you."

She drew a deep breath. "If you let the town down…if you let *me* down—"

"I won't." He didn't know how he dared give her such a guarantee. After a week in Homestead, his investigation had turned up exactly *nada*.

"I'll find the bastard behind the sabotage,"

Jud said, with every ounce of conviction he possessed. "If it takes a dozen miracles, you'll have your land giveaway and you'll keep your town."

A knock on the door caused them both to jump. Miranda jerked her hand away and dropped back into her chair. As Wade entered the room, Jud eased himself into the seat he'd occupied last week. He only hoped his cheeks weren't flying the same bright color as the woman's across the desk.

Wade didn't notice. "I've interrogated practically the entire population of the county, trying to find out who gave that reporter all those details." He paced across the office and back. "I can't find a soul who could have expected to benefit from this article."

Miranda tapped a pencil on the desk. "Is there anybody you didn't talk to?"

"Good question." Jud nodded at her, then faced Wade. "Narrow the search. Did you talk to all of the folks who opposed the Home Free Program? Beltrane, McPherson?"

"Got them both at Bertha's this morning."

"Satterwhite, Enfield?"

"Saw Rudy at the gas station. I stopped in at the real estate office and saw Clarice Enfield. She didn't know anything about a reporter in town."

"How about Arlen?"

Wade stood staring for a minute, then shook his head. "How stupid can I get? Arlen's in Austin for the day. He'll be back for the Home Free Board meeting tonight."

Miranda flipped her pencil across the desk.

Grinning at her, Jud slouched down in his chair. "There you go," he said. "Miracle number one."

THE MONTHLY Home Free Board meeting took place in the law library of the courthouse. The board members sat around the big oak table in the center of the room, but there were plenty of chairs for spectators. Since the initial meetings two years ago, public attendance had dropped off. These days only the board members showed up.

Tonight, thanks to Deirdre's article, there was standing room only.

Jud gave up his chair to Bertha, of Bertha's Kolaches fame, and leaned a shoulder against the end of a floor-to-ceiling oak bookcase. The entire room had been paneled with shelves and filled with a valuable collection of gold-tooled law texts. Antique lamps, retrofitted for electricity, cast golden light over the crowd, softening the angry faces.

"Let's get to work," Miranda said, by means of calling the meeting to order. "We've got a number of applications to vote on this evening—"

"First, don't you need to talk about that article?" The question came from Rudy Satterwhite, a small time farmer who supplemented agriculture with construction work. "What's going on with all this vandalism?"

"Yeah, I heard somebody got shot at. Winged with a bullet." Pete McPherson was Rudy's friend and competition. "This is gettin' to be a dangerous place to live."

Arlen Enfield, seated at the table with the other board members, held up a hand. "I don't believe this is the correct venue for such a discussion. Perhaps at the first town council meeting in the new year."

Protest rumbled through the crowd. Wade, also a board member, cleared his throat. "I can assure everyone here that Homestead is as safe a place as it ever was. We've had a few incidents, but we're well on the way to tracking down the culprits."

Jud shifted his weight. Optimism was all well and good, but...

"I don't find anything to be concerned about," Frances Haase said firmly. "This is clearly a case of teenagers playing pranks, and goodness knows we as a community have survived that sort of thing in the past." She looked directly at Jud as she spoke. "We will again."

"That's right." Miranda tapped the papers in her hands on the table. "The problem is now in the hands of law enforcement and I fully expect to see a resolution well before the holidays. Please leave the board alone to consider these applications."

Listening to the board discuss the pros and cons of nameless would-be residents didn't offer as much excitement as vandalism, and the thrill seekers began to leave. The room was still fairly full, however, when a commotion in the library doorway drew everyone's attention.

Jud, taller than almost all of them, could see the top of a woman's head—big hair, tinted bright red—winnowing through the audience. Another head of hair followed, dyed flat black, straight and lanky. Miranda, her back to the new arrivals, gave Jud a searching look. He shrugged, and she turned in her chair to see what was happening.

Fifteen years had changed the town and the people who lived there, but none had changed as much as this woman, Jud thought. At seventeen, she'd been shapely and lithe, with curves the boys craved and the girls coveted. Her honey blond hair had fallen in smooth curves around her heart-shaped face. She hadn't looked like the slut all the kids knew her to be.

Now, her appearance fit the part. The red hair, frizzed and clipped with sequins, didn't match her complexion, or what Jud could see of it under heavy makeup. She'd held on to her curves—too many of them, too ample. Nails an inch past her fingertips, painted bright red, cheap jewelry at her wrists and neck, a short skirt and high heels…

Della Bowie conveyed the perfect stereotype of a fallen woman.

The boy behind her was tall and skinny, with bad skin and a bad slouch. He had to be about fifteen years old. Anybody with a memory could guess who he was.

"Can we help you?" Miranda got to her feet. Her smile was polite—she didn't seem to recognize who she was dealing with.

Della nodded. "I have something to say. To the board." Her twang came out of a Texas soap opera.

Miss Haase's back got even straighter. "This is not a general meeting, I'm afraid. Only the board members are supposed to be here tonight." She glared at the remaining audience. "Everyone else should go home."

Hands on her hips, Della lifted her stubborn chin. "The subject I want to address has to do with this Home Free thing you're running."

Ruth Kelley, Noah's mother, shuffled through her notebook. "If you'd like to make an application, I have a blank one here—"

"Nope, no application for me."

"I'm Mayor Wright." Miranda held out her hand, which Della didn't take. "Why don't you come see me tomorrow? I'll be glad to do whatever I can to settle any—"

Della didn't move, and Wade began to ease his chair back from the table.

"I think we'll just do it tonight. I'm Della

Teague. Della Bowie Teague." A collective gasp went through the crowd. Miranda lost every bit of color in her face.

Della didn't flicker an eyelash as she drew a handful of papers out of her big red purse. "See, these are real important records. I got my marriage certificate." She stepped forward and laid a sheet on the table between Miranda and Miss Haase. "I got birth certificates—for my boy, Sam, and my husband, Braxton. That would be Braxton Teague. I also got Braxton's mama's papers, which show that she was a Braxton by birth. Her great-uncle on her daddy's side was a Braxton. Clyde Braxton, to be exact. Ring a bell?"

Jud studied the faces of the board members, where horror had started to dawn. Nobody said a word.

So he would. "Della, are you claiming that your husband is related to Clyde Braxton of the K Bar C Ranch?"

She shook her head. Someone let loose a sigh. But Della said, "Not is. Was. Poor Braxton died last year in the rodeo. Never could get him to stay away from those bulls. A Brahman named Demon Spawn finally killed him. He made seven seconds, though. Best ride he ever had."

Miranda cleared her throat. "So you're saying your son is Mr. Braxton's heir?"

"I'm saying…" Della hit the pile of papers on the table with the flat of her hand. "I'm saying that Sam Teague, here, should have been the one to inherit the K Bar C Ranch when old Clyde Braxton passed all those years ago.

"This land y'all are having so much fun giving away don't belong to you. It's Braxton land and it belongs to the last of the Braxtons." She put her arm around her son and drew him close to her side. "That land belongs to us."

CHAPTER NINE

MIRANDA REMAINED SEATED at the table in the library long after the rest of the board had gone home. They had managed to eject Della from the meeting by offering to pay for her room—and her son's—at the Rise and Shine Motel. Della had wrangled food expenses, as well. Finally satisfied, she'd requested Wade and Jud escort her to her accommodations. With such juicy gossip to spread, the rest of the crowd had dispersed quickly.

And since the Home Free Board could no longer be sure they had land to give away, they'd adjourned their meeting.

Della Bowie. Homestead's whore, some of the girls had called her back in high school—usually the girls who were jealous of the hive of boys swarming around her. Miranda hadn't tried to be popular. She'd worked too hard, at school and at home, to worry about socializing. There had been only one boy she found interesting enough to talk to, anyway.

That boy had fathered Della's baby and refused to marry her.

Four years ago, the man that boy became had embarrassed Miranda, stripped her of her dignity, her self-respect.

And this afternoon, he'd promised he wouldn't let the town—or her—down.

Could she really afford to give him another chance?

The squeak of the courthouse door opening and the uneven thud of boot heels on the wooden floor spurred Miranda to her feet. Stupid to have stayed this late alone…

"Miranda." The light in the outside hallway threw Jud's shadow into the library before he reached the door. "What are you doing here by yourself?"

The assurance that she was safe from harm did nothing to settle Miranda's nerves. "I…I was thinking. Lost track of time."

He crossed his arms over his chest and leaned against the door frame. "Nobody saw Della coming."

"Not me, that's for sure." Hugging her

briefcase to her chest, she tried to slip through the doorway without touching him. "Time to go."

Jud caught her arm. "I thought you might want to talk about Della."

"No. No, I don't." She pulled against his grip. "I just want to go home to bed."

"You're going to let her march in and stake her claim without a fight?"

"Of course not." When another jerk of her arm failed to set her free, she glared up at him. "Will you let go? Or do I have to scream for Virgil? He'll hear me from the sheriff's office."

"No, he won't." But he loosened his hold. "So what are you planning to do about Mrs. Teague?"

Miranda marched to the door of the courthouse and opened it against a rush of cold wind. "I can't lock up until you leave."

He stepped outside. "Answer the question."

"All we have to do," she said as she wrestled with the heavy lock on the door, "is subpoena a paternity test. Paper records might have been all people had to work with thirty years ago but nowadays we can check Sam's DNA."

"The rest of the Braxtons are dead. How's a paternity test going to help?"

She stood at the top of the steps and looked Jud straight in the eyes. "We don't have to prove Della's son is *not* a Braxton. We only have to prove that he *is* yours."

A harsh gust roared past and Jud swayed on the edge of the step, as if the wind would knock him down. Miranda fought the urge to grab his jacket and keep him from falling.

He held his balance without her, driving his hands deep into the pockets of his jacket. "The past never dies, does it?"

"He looked alive and well to me."

"He's not mine."

"Oh, come on, Jud. After all this time, nobody's going to trap you into marrying Della just because you gave her a baby."

The wind stopped, suddenly, and Jud said, "*I* didn't."

"Then why did you leave? If you could prove you weren't the father—"

"I couldn't prove anything. My own family believed the lie and Della wasn't broadcasting the truth. I'd had as much as I could take of this place anyway."

The fear she'd been staving off broke free.

"Then this Braxton Teague really could be the father? But who was he? Where'd he come from?"

"Maybe he came to visit his great-uncle that summer before senior year. They could have met then and had some kind of long-distance romance."

"Long-distance romance doesn't make babies." She shivered as the wind swept past again. "You dated her, Jud. I saw you making out at school."

"Well, sure." Even in the faint light from the streetlamps on the corners of the courthouse lawn, she could see color in his cheeks. "But she never let me go all the way."

"She never let you?" The idea was so ridiculous, Miranda knew the entire story had to be false. She started down the steps. "Forget it, Jud. I'm not as easy to fool as I used to be, especially where you're concerned."

"She wanted me to marry her," he called after her. "She wouldn't put out without a ring and a wedding date. But I wasn't sticking around this dump to marry anybody. So—" he stretched out his arms "—I never had sex with Della Bowie!"

His voice echoed around the square, but Homestead had closed up for the night. There was no one to hear. Miranda didn't say a word as she walked steadily to her truck.

Despite his limp, Jud reached her and opened the driver's door before she could start the engine. "You'd better figure out how to deal with the facts, Mayor Wright. That boy isn't my child. If he's a Braxton, I'd say you've got a hell of a problem on your hands, because he's got a legitimate claim to the land that belonged to old Clyde. If he's got money to back him up, he might actually be able to take back his property. At that point, your Home Free giveaway will go bust."

He slammed the door with a force that rattled her bones. Miranda set her jaw and sped away without a glance in his direction.

The ride home drove her straight into despair. If Jud was, indeed, the father of Della's son, then the Home Free program would stay safe. They'd have to find the crazy jerk responsible for the vandalism, of course, but the land would be available, free and clear. Jud would have to decide how to deal with the consequences of his own behavior. Sam Teague looked as though he could use a father's attention.

But what if Jud was telling the truth? Suppose he hadn't…had sex…with Della Bowie? The whole town would owe him an apology—they'd scorned him and then banished him for something he didn't do.

This afternoon, he'd asked Miranda to trust him. She wanted to. Oh, how she wanted to.

Believing Jud meant losing everything she'd worked for—her job, her reputation, her town.

If Jud was lying, the life she'd built would be intact.

But her heart would be broken into little pieces.

TUESDAY MORNING, Nan hobbled into the kitchen. "This is worse than yesterday. I haven't hurt like this in decades," she moaned as she lowered herself into a chair at the table. "Man, I'm getting old!"

Miranda set down two bowls of oatmeal, milk and sugar. "Or maybe it has something to do with falling off a seventeen-hand stallion—one who's standing up straight on his rear legs. That's probably a nine-foot drop, Mom. I'd hurt, too."

"Not this long." She played with her cereal for a few minutes. "You came in really late last night. Did the meeting go okay after that newspaper article got everybody mad?"

"Uh, no. We had an unexpected guest. Della Bowie."

Nan's jaw dropped. "She's back?"

"At least temporarily."

"Did she bring the baby with her? Or should I say teenager? It's been fifteen years."

"His name is Sam. And he came along."

"Does he look like Jud?"

Miranda gave that some reluctant thought. "He's dyed his hair that flat black the kids use nowadays. Could be any color underneath. His skin is kinda fair, not tan, like the Ritter brothers. Who knows whether he'll be handsome when he grows up? He isn't at fifteen."

"Jud was handsome when he was five." Nan's smile was warm. "He was a flirt when he was five, too. Always had a way with the girls."

"So glad to hear it." Miranda let her empty

dish clatter in the sink. "Jud says he never went all the way with Della, so the boy isn't his."

"Sounds possible."

"Except the alternative means the kid may well be a relative of Clyde Braxton. A relative who wants the K Bar C ranch back."

"I don't believe that, either." Nan got slowly to her feet. "Jud can be innocent without having the worst-case scenario come true." She put her arm around Miranda's shoulders. "Have a little faith, honey."

"Hmmph." With a glance at the cold drizzle outside the window, Miranda started for the back door. "Don't worry about the barn work today. Cruz and I will take care of everything."

"Sounds good."

Only as she was buttoning her barn jacket did Miranda acknowledge how rarely her mother delegated work to anyone else, especially when it came to the horses. In good health or sick as a dog, Nan was out of the house and checking on her herd before she came back to the house to make breakfast. These last two days, she seemed to be avoiding the barn altogether.

Miranda guessed that might have something to do with the handsome cowboy shoveling manure from Bailey's stall as she walked in. "'Morning, Cruz."

He looked around quickly. "Hey, Miranda." His gaze went beyond her, and his smile vanished. "How's it going?"

"Okay." She took her own pitchfork and began cleaning Flora's stall. Kahlúa barely noticed her entrance, being seriously involved in his breakfast. "Mom's still feeling pretty sore this morning, not up to barn work."

"It was a long way to fall." He paused. "Maybe she ought to go into town and let Kristin look her over. She could really be hurt." Worry threaded through his words.

"My theory is a little different. Move, mare." Using her shoulder and hip, Miranda edged Flora and her baby out of one corner to the opposite, clean side of the stall. "I think she's avoiding something out here."

Cruz didn't comment.

"Or someone."

Still no response. They worked in silence until all sixteen stalls had been freshened up and the waste transferred to the cart behind the tractor. As Cruz got into the driver's seat, Miranda put a hand on his arm.

"This isn't a big secret, my friend. I have no problem with you and Mom being involved."

He fiddled with the key. "She's the one with the problem."

"Because…?"

"Because I'm younger, and Mexican. People in town will cause trouble, she says."

Yesterday, Miranda might have discounted that concern. Today, she could see her mother's point. "Public opinion, especially in a small town, has a way of running people's lives. Or ruining them."

"Only if we allow it to. Which is what she's doing right now, as far as I'm concerned." He jammed the key into the tractor ignition and cranked the engine. In another minute, Cruz and the cartload of manure had rumbled out of the barn.

Nan showed up less than five minutes later. "Everybody okay this morning?"

"Yep. And don't worry, Cruz has driven out to dump manure. Of course," Miranda said, with a pointed glance in her mother's direction, "you probably kept an eye out so you'd be sure to miss him."

"This isn't your business, Miranda." Nan went into Flora's stall to pet Kahlúa, who was nosing at his mother's grain bucket. "You've got a town to worry about."

"I want you to be happy. And I've seen how happy you are with Cruz."

"Drop the subject, Miranda Elayne."

Instead, Miranda dropped the water bucket she'd just washed back into the sink. "I'm not ten years old anymore, Mom. You can't control what I do or don't talk about." Leaving the rest of the buckets undone, she stalked to the door. "I'm having trouble believing that the woman who has always told me to stand up for myself with teachers, with other kids, with professors and employers, is running scared from a few busybodies with nothing better to do than talk trash."

Left alone with her horses, Nan rested her head against Flora's smooth neck. "Believe it, Miranda," she whispered. "Getting older has made a coward out of me."

JUD WALKED into the sheriff's office on Tuesday morning with plenty of righteous anger under his belt.

"I'd like to talk to your prisoners," he told Virgil Dunn, Wade's deputy. "Alone."

"Wade said you might. Right this way." Virgil unlocked the door to the jail and stood back as Jud entered. "Just holler if you need something."

"Right."

Tolly Craddock sat on his cot, elbows on his knees, staring down at the floor between his feet. Hank Darrow might not have moved a muscle since Jud had seen him last. But Wade assured him the food on the guy's trays disappeared.

Jud pulled the one straight-backed chair in the room to the space between the two cells and straddled the seat, resting his arms along the back. Not a comfortable position, but important for his image.

"Mr. Craddock, I want to talk to you about your case." Tolly looked at him through his eyebrows. "See, your lawyer, Mr. Dermody, is making noises about resigning. That's gonna leave you without legal counsel."

The maintenance man sprang to his feet. "He can't do that! I need a lawyer!"

"I understand. But Mr. Dermody seems to be worried about not getting paid." In the other cell, Hank Darrow took his arm away from his face. "Rich lawyers don't do much pro bono work."

"How'm I gonna get out of here?"

"Well, Loveless County will be glad to appoint you a public defender to handle your case." Craddock dropped back onto his cot. "The problem is, we don't have anybody in Homestead who can accommodate us right away. We'll have to call somebody in from out of town. It might take awhile to get the process going again." Jud could hear his drawl taking on a life of its own.

"I already been here awhile! I need a lawyer!"

"Or," Jud said, "you could make a deal with the sheriff."

"What kind of deal?"

"If you have some information that Sheriff Montgomery could use, he might be willing to trade that information for a swift resolution of your case."

"Huh?"

"You tell the sheriff what you know, and he makes a deal that takes care of your crimes."

"I have to stay in jail?"

"He might be willing to settle for limiting the sentence to time served, if—" he held up a hand as Tolly's face changed "—if you give us the details we're looking for."

"What sort of details? What do you want?"

"You know what we want, Mr. Craddock. We want the name of the man who paid you to put cat fur into Megan's desk."

Tolly's glance at his fellow prisoner was as good as evidence. "I said I don't know his name."

"We don't believe you. But if you're comfortable here…" Jud stood up off the chair without wincing, even though the move hurt like hell.

"Wait." Tolly held up a hand. "Let me think."

Hank Darrow swung his feet to the floor and sat up. He was good-looking enough, in his late twenties with black hair worn long, a hawk nose, olive skin and snapping black eyes. The fit of his jeans and his shirt advertised long hours in the gym.

Tolly got to his feet and faced Jud through the bars of his cell, wrapping his hands tightly around the iron. "I'll testify against him. I swear I will."

Darrow got to his feet, as well. "You don't want to do this, fool."

"Not good enough, Mr. Craddock. We need the name. If you don't know it, well, then we don't have much use for you."

"I can't!" Tolly glanced across the aisle again. "He—he said he'd beat me to a pulp."

Jud walked to the door and raised his hand to knock.

"Darrow!" Tolly yelled. "This guy right here. He paid me five hundred to cause trouble for the little girl."

Darrow spat out a stream of cuss words aimed at Jud and Tolly Craddock equally.

Jud glanced at the two men over his shoulder. "Thanks, Tolly. We'll see what we can do with that. And, Mr. Darrow..." He grinned. "I'll be back."

ETHAN DIDN'T HEAR about the article on Homestead in the Austin paper until he stopped in at the feed store late Tuesday afternoon. Max Beltrane saw him come in, dragged him up to the checkout counter where the paper lay open to the relevant page, and made sure he read the whole piece, then followed up with a minute-by-minute account of the Home Free board meeting the night before.

"Della Bowie?" Dread gripped Ethan's windpipe. "She left town years ago. Back when—"

Beltrane nodded and switched his tobacco wad to the other cheek. "That's right, she did. And now she's back, with this boy in tow she claims is related to Clyde Braxton. Got the papers to prove it, so she says."

"But…" Ethan hated to say the words. "Jud was the father of Della's baby. Everybody said so at the time."

"Everybody but Della," Noah Kelley said as he came up behind Max. "Della never identified the father, but folks pretty much unanimously blamed Jud."

Because Zeb Ritter had given them reason to. And Zeb believed it because…

"Excuse me." Ethan turned blindly away from the counter and headed for the exit. He could only hope to find his brother at Hayseed Farm. If not, he guessed he'd just sit and wait until Jud showed up again. There would be no going home to Kayla until this issue was solved once and for all.

Luckily, Jud's black truck was parked by

the cabin Cruz Martinez lived in. Cruz and Jud sat on the porch steps, each with a can of beer in hand.

"Hey, Ethan." Cruz toasted him with the beer. "Let me get you a drink."

"No, thanks." Ethan looked at his brother. "I need to talk to you."

"I think I'll see what's available for dinner," Cruz said, backing up the steps and across the porch. The door to the cabin closed, providing them all the privacy of the great outdoors.

Jud set his beer aside. "What's this about?"

"I just came from town. I read the article in the Austin paper. And I heard Della Bowie is back. She's claiming her son should have inherited Clyde Braxton's ranch? Because his dad was a Braxton?"

"That's right."

Ethan let a minute pass in silence. "The baby was supposed to be yours."

"I denied it, remember? As loud and as often as I could."

"You had sex with her."

"No, I didn't."

"I—" Ethan drew a deep breath, stiffened

his knees. "You told me you had sex with Della Bowie."

"Yeah, well—"

"That day in the barn. We were shoveling stalls. I asked you if you'd done it with Della. You said, 'You bet your ass I have.'"

"I was seventeen. You couldn't expect me to tell anybody—especially my little brother—that the town whore wouldn't put out for me."

"I saw you. Down by the creek. You had her clothes off."

"Sure, I made out with Della. But I never scored."

"Why the hell not?"

"She wanted marriage. I didn't. Or maybe she just enjoyed making fools of everybody in town. God knows, Della never got a break from any of Homestead's self-righteous. Including our parents." He shrugged. "Hell, maybe I was too clumsy, too fast, too inexperienced for her. The fact is, Della Bowie never put out for Jud Ritter."

Ethan dragged in a deep breath. That should be the end. Jud hadn't fathered Della's child. He wasn't the irresponsible jerk he'd appeared to be for the last fifteen years. They could spend some time talking, forgiving, and then put the past behind them. Except for one thing.

"You lied to me." He looked his brother straight in the eyes for the first time in fifteen years. "You let me go on believing you might be the father of that baby."

"Nobody believed me when I told the truth, anyway."

"But they used *me* as proof. Dad heard what you told me, what I said, and used it against you. With Mom, with the rest of the town."

Jud got to his feet. "Let it go. I have."

"This isn't just about you, damn it." Two strides put Ethan within punching distance of his brother. "When you took off, I was the good son, the one our parents could always count on. Sure, I made a mistake, giving Angela the poisoned candy, not to mention eating it myself, but I could be forgiven because I measured up in every other way."

"You're blaming me because you wound up wearing the white hat?"

Ethan shoved at Jud's shoulder with the heel of his hand. His brother staggered back a couple of steps in surprise. "You want to talk cowboy? You left me twisting in the wind, Jud. You headed for the hills, where you've been living like a bandit ever since. Meanwhile, I held down the fort. Because I thought I owed you…because I betrayed my big brother."

He hit out again. This time, Jud hit back. "You never owed me anything."

"That's the lie, damn you." Ethan closed his fists in Jud's shirt and shook him, hard. "My whole life was a lie, because you never told me the truth. Not a month later, or six, or a year. Not when Angela died, or Mom, or Dad. You never cared that I was living with the guilt."

The explosion inside of him was part rage, part hurt. He released his hold, but only so he could draw back his arm and slug his brother with every ounce of his strength.

Jud took the first hit, because Ethan was right—he deserved it. But he ducked the second and came up swinging. His fist connected with his brother's gut. He grinned in satisfaction as Ethan groaned.

They'd scrabbled as boys, but these were men, fighting. Kicking, punching, swearing, they drove each other across the clearing and back again. Ethan aimed a kick at Jud's groin, but Jud came in with a knee first and they both went down. Blood and sweat smeared their faces and hands as they rolled over the hard December ground, struggling for the upper hand.

Other hands interfered, then. Jud registered the grip of fists on the shoulders of his shirt, found himself being dragged backward. Ethan came after him, only to be jerked to the side. Miranda held him on his back with her knee pressing into his chest.

Jud got an extra shove before being released. Martinez stepped in front of him. "Are you *crazy?*"

"Yeah. Get out of the way." But he didn't have the strength to enforce the order. He could barely scrabble to his feet.

Miranda gave Ethan a hand up. Both his eyes had already swollen almost shut. Jud noticed a similar limit to his own vision. From the fire in his shoulder, he had a feeling he might have torn some stitches loose. Terrific.

"You can't drive," Miranda told Ethan. "You can't see."

"I'll be okay." Ethan staggered toward his truck, then stopped and turned again. He came at Jud so fast, neither Miranda nor Cruz could stop him.

"I don't want to see you again," he said, his voice shaking just as his finger shook in front of Jud's face. "Don't come near me or my family. If I find out you've been talking to my wife, I'll chase you down and—" He shook his head. "Just don't."

Miranda had climbed behind the wheel of Ethan's truck and refused to budge, so Ethan allowed himself to be driven home. When their dust cleared, Martinez tapped Jud on the shoulder.

"You'd better get some ice on your face. And your shoulder is bleeding. Should we call Kristin?"

"Nah." Jud climbed the porch steps, using the handrail for lift. He kicked his beer over in the process.

"Figures," he muttered. "It's been that kind of afternoon."

CHAPTER TEN

ETHAN DIDN'T VOLUNTEER conversation on the drive to his place, and Miranda didn't ask questions. She had a pretty good idea of what they'd fought about.

Kayla was not nearly so tranquil in her response to Ethan's condition. Miranda left her fussing and muttering over her husband's battle wounds and begged a ride home from Charlie, Ethan's ranch hand. At her request, he let her out at the cabin, where she walked in without knocking.

Cruz came to stand in the kitchen doorway. "He's in the bathroom. Didn't want any help."

"Surprise, surprise." At the end of the hallway, she rapped her knuckles on the door panel. "You'd better be decent, because I'm coming in." Before he could protest, she did just that.

Jud stood at a sink full of pink water, wearing jeans. Period. Suddenly, Miranda felt as if she were the one who'd been punched in the stomach.

He glared at her through the mirror. "Make yourself at home."

"Thanks." She took the washcloth out of his fingers and pulled the plug on the sink. "You look like hell."

"That's about the way I feel. Why don't you let me take care of myself?"

Miranda didn't want to answer that question. "Sit," she said instead, pushing him down onto the side of the tub with a hand on his bare shoulder. The fact that he cooperated revealed exactly how much he was hurting.

Cruz's medicine cabinet behind the mirror contained gauze sponges, peroxide and bandages. With those supplies, she started working on Jud's cuts and scrapes for real. He closed his eyes and sat quietly under her touch. After last night, just about everybody seemed to be too tired—too stressed, too worried?—for words.

Despite the bruise and the swollen eye, he had a beautiful face, and she took full advantage of the opportunity to stare at it. Dabbing peroxide with a square of gauze wasn't as satisfying as using her fingertips on his skin, but Miranda enjoyed the process. His dark brown hair contained more gold and red strands than she would have predicted, and there wasn't much hair at all on his chest. Fortunately, she found a few grazes there she could treat, as well.

"What's this?" A line of puckered skin, raised and red, ran over his pectoral muscle, disappearing under his arm. Stitch marks remained, like bird tracks along the skin, but in between there were leaks of blood, as if the wound had broken open. "Is this why you're on medical leave?"

Jud drew a deep breath and blew it out slowly. "Part of the reason." After a pause, he said, "And in case you feel the urge to strip me down, I'll confess I have a couple of bullet holes in my right leg, too." He opened his eyes. "They're fine. I checked."

"Too bad. I was looking forward to wrestling you out of your pants."

His mouth quirked into a half smile. "That can be arranged."

Miranda felt her cheeks heat up. "So how'd you get shot?"

"The usual. Bad guy with a gun."

"Brag a little, why don't you?"

"Nothing to brag about." He shrugged, and winced. "I caught a crack dealer on a street corner right across from the high school. He ran, I chased, he shot first and hit me three times."

"Did he get away?"

Jud shook his head. "I fired as I fell and he went down, too."

She took a step back. "So you really are a hero."

"No, I'm a police officer doing his duty." He squinted down at the scar. "Are you done yet?"

"Let me see your hands."

"I'm okay. Really."

Holding out her own hand, palm up, she said, "Hand, please."

And then couldn't repress a gasp when she saw the damage he'd done. "Your poor knuckles."

"Ethan's got a hard skull."

"I expect he could say the same of you."

"No doubt."

Turning to the sink, she ran warm water into the bowl. "Put your hands in here. We'll wash them off, then get you some ice." Jud switched his seat to the toilet lid and did as ordered. Miranda plunged her hands into the water and began to massage the swollen joints. "Let me know if this hurts."

"Sure." Jud closed his eyes again, in the hopes that eliminating the visual of Miranda stroking and massaging his hands would help him keep control.

Instead, blocking one sense only heightened the others. Her fingers on his skin jangled his nerves and crimped his breath. She stood between his knees, and he wanted nothing so much as to pull her close, hold her tight against the ache building in his body. His bruised and battered cheek was level with her sweet, rounded rear end, adding fuel to the fire in his imagination.

"Okay." She draped a towel over her palms and held it out. "Put your hands here."

He did as instructed, and she wrapped the soft cloth around his aching bones, pressing gently. When she looked into his face, Jud realized he was staring. Her golden eyes widened, and darkened. Still holding his hands, Miranda bent and touched her lips to his.

Different from any kiss they'd shared, he held back and let Miranda set the pace. No expertise involved, no experience, just a straightforward expression of curiosity, of need. The way she explored him was a turn-on by itself, leaving him free to discover the shape of her mouth as defined by his, the texture of skin against sensitive skin, the richness of the taste they became together. His hands shook with the need to touch, but he didn't move. Didn't want to break the spell.

"Supper's ready." Cruz's voice came from somewhere in the front of the house. "There's plenty for three, Miranda. You're welcome to stay."

Miranda straightened up slowly, and her mouth clung to Jud's until the last moment. When they were far enough apart to see each other, he smiled at the rosy color in her cheeks, the heaviness of her eyelids, the fullness of her lips.

"I should go," she said in low voice. "Mom will wonder where I am."

He nodded and, as she backed away, forced himself to stand. "Thanks for the doctoring." Surprisingly, his aches and pains had faded. The curative power of pheromones? "I think I'll live."

"Good." Miranda backed all the way out the bathroom door, her gaze still locked with his. She turned around just as Cruz came into the hallway.

He waved a spatula. "Did you hear? We've got food."

"I can't stay. But it smells good." A second later, she was on the outside of the door.

"I don't want to know," Martinez said, putting up a hand in a gesture of surrender. "One Wright woman is all I can handle."

Jud grabbed a shirt, then limped down the hall and followed Cruz to the kitchen. "You're a stronger man than I am. I think even one is likely to kill me."

"Yeah." Cruz grinned. "But what a way to go!"

DELLA APPEARED to have no qualms about reacquainting herself with her hometown. On Wednesday morning, as Miranda moved her ladder from streetlamp to streetlamp, hanging wreaths and wrapping white lights around the poles, Mrs. Teague visited the different businesses surrounding the courthouse square.

Her first—and longest—visit was to the beauty shop. She emerged after an hour, hair newly curled and nails painted a glowing red, and crossed the street to enter Tanner's General Store. Miranda persevered with her decorating, wishing she could be a fly on Ed Tanner's wall.

"It's about time we had some holiday cheer around this town." Arlen Enfield approached from her blind side. "Christmas is only two weeks away. In my time, those wreaths went up the first day of December."

"In your time, nobody came downtown to see the decorations," Miranda told him. "We've got businesses here now, and customers. I'd say that's more important than timely hall-decking."

She backed down the ladder and moved the box of wreaths and lights to the next lamppost. Arlen stood watching, offering helpful comments but no actual assistance, as she fought with the stiff hinges to get the ladder folded.

He waited until she got to the top rung again before asking his question. "What are your plans regarding Miss Della? Have you spoken to her about her demands? Are all these poor victims—er, beneficiaries—of your land giveaway simply out of luck?"

"I spent hours on the phone yesterday with the Texas attorney general's office. I consulted an attorney in Austin. The property was seized by the county for nonpayment of taxes. Since Della didn't step forward when the original notice was filed, she may have lost her chance."

"But then, the law is such a slippery creature. A crafty attorney can make black look white."

"Thanks so much for the encouragement, Arlen."

"I call it as I see it, my dear." He walked past her ladder, and Miranda considered dropping her hammer on the former mayor's head. That would be one less snake in the grass for Texas.

Arlen crossed the street at the corner and arrived at the sidewalk just as Della came out of Tanner's store. Their voices didn't carry as far as the courthouse, but Della backed up as the former mayor advanced on her until her back was against Tanner's Christmas window. After a minute of intense conversation, she sidestepped and put distance between herself and Arlen, just as fast as her snakeskin boots would take her. Miranda expected her to stop in at the new women's clothing store opened by a recent "victim" of the Home Free program, but Della hurried on with barely a glance at the display. At the end of the block, she unlocked a shiny white car, gunned the engine and drove off.

Miranda climbed down, moved the ladder and climbed up twice more before she'd finished the eight streetlamps on the courthouse square. Getting the ladder back into the building was difficult, and she was struggling to keep the door open while maneuvering the extra-long, stainless steel monster when the burden suddenly lightened.

She looked down the steps, and saw that Jud had picked up the end of the ladder. He looked like hell, all bruised and scraped up.

"Thanks," was all she said, until they got the ladder stored in the equipment room. After locking the door, she turned to face him. "Did you come for a reason? Or are you just passing through?"

"We need to talk about what happens next. I'm not crazy about coming face-to-face with Reba, though. Is there a back entrance to your office?"

"No, but we can use one of the other rooms." She led him down the hall to the end of the building opposite the town offices, unlocked the last door and flipped on the lights. "You'll be safe here."

Jud chuckled as he stepped inside, then stopped in his tracks to gaze around the courtroom. "I know we came here on school trips," he said. "But I don't remember being so impressed."

"You probably weren't paying attention. I know I wasn't." Miranda sat down on one of the wooden spectators' benches which faced the elaborately carved judge's podium. On the plaster walls above the oak wainscot, brightly painted murals depicted the advance of settlers across Texas. The windows on this side of the building faced south, and sunlight flooded the huge space most of the year, so the windows remained shuttered at all times. With electric light for illumination, however, the artwork came brilliantly to life.

"There's Hildegard and hubby," Jud said, pointing to a depiction of Homestead's founding. He dropped down beside Miranda. "You'd think one memorial would be enough. I guess it's like shoes, though—a woman can never have too many."

He grinned at her, teasing, but Miranda's concentration had taken a hit when he sat so close. "So…um…what did you want to talk about?"

"I've finally gotten some results from my phone calls, and come up with a few connections. Hank Darrow is the son of Henry Darrow, a contractor and developer who's had his eye on property in Homestead off and on."

"He sent his son to sabotage the land giveaway?"

"I'm still working on all the details, but it's possible. Henry might believe he could buy the property if the program failed. The only way I'm going to get a feel for what he thinks is by talking to him. That means going to Austin."

"Okay." She nodded, trying to look as if it didn't matter to her where he went, or when. "What about Della?"

"That's another puzzle that might have pieces in Austin. I want to look for her Braxton connections, her previous address, any details that will give us leverage against her. Basically, that means a lot of time in the state records archives. In Austin."

"Sounds like you've got a lot of work to do."

"But—" He swiped a hand over his face. "Austin has some good times to offer, too."

"Well, sure." Miranda got to her feet, hoping she didn't look as desperate as she felt. "Have fun." She walked away from him, along the bench to the aisle. This was no more than she'd expected, right?

Jud cleared his throat. "I was wondering if you wanted to come with me."

She stopped. "I beg your pardon?"

He came up behind her, put his hands over her shoulders. "I would really like a chance to be with Miranda, instead of Mayor Wright. I figured if we got away from here, we might both feel…more relaxed." He twisted a strand of hair around one finger. "Was I wrong?"

Speechless, she shook her head.

"No strings," Jud continued. "I'm not pressuring you for anything you don't want to give. Understood?"

Miranda swallowed hard, then nodded.

"Do you have commitments tomorrow?"

She finally found her voice. "Nothing I can't reschedule."

His hands turned her gently to face him.

"Great." He punctuated the word with a soft kiss. "We'll plan to leave about eight. I'll see you then."

Alone in the gorgeous courtroom, Miranda sank onto the bench again. She'd agreed to go away with Jud Ritter. No strings, of course. Only this incredible craving he stirred in her, just by saying her name. Would she return to Homestead the same person she was when she left?

Miranda decided she wouldn't bet on it.

WHEN JUD LEFT the sheriff's office late that afternoon after a long consultation with Wade, he noticed Della heading toward the Lone Wolf Tavern. In high school, she'd been a cheap drunk—a couple of beers and she'd do anything. Well, anything except go all the way with him. But maybe a few drinks would at least get her talking.

The heavy air inside the Lone Wolf might have been hanging around for the last fifteen years, a concoction of cigarette and cigar smoke, whiskey fumes and spilled beer. The jukebox in the corner played CDs now, instead of the 45s they'd listened to in high school, but the tables and chairs were the same. Jud wondered if the same peanut shells littered the floor, or if someone had swept at least once since he graduated from high school.

After asking a waitress to bring him a beer—he knew she hadn't been there since his time, because she wasn't old enough—Jud made his way to the table in the far corner where Della nursed her longneck. She glanced up as he approached and started to smile. Then her eyes narrowed as she recognized him.

"Jud Ritter?" Her tone could be called discouraging or, more accurately, hostile.

"Hey, Della." He didn't ask for permission to sit down.

She frowned at him. "What are you doing here? You left town same time as I did."

"And for the same reason. Talk about coincidence." He gave the waitress a smile as she set down his beer. "You really screwed things up for me, refusing to tell the truth."

"It's not my fault people believed you'd get a poor girl pregnant, then abandon her." Della fluffed her hair. "Even your parents believed it, which doesn't say much for you."

Jud ignored the goad. Della had always known how to stick her knife into the most vulnerable spot. "Your son looks like a good kid."

"Well, you know how teenage boys can be…." She smiled, but her tone was worried. "He was his dad's pride and joy."

"You and Braxton were together a long time, weren't you?"

Della downed the dregs of her beer. "Oh, sure. A marriage made in heaven, that was us."

"Did you get married before you had your baby?" Jud signaled the waitress for two more drinks.

"Uh…no. No, see, Braxton was in the army. Over there in Desert Storm. I had to wait for him to come back."

"Where'd you go, when you left town?"

As soon as the bottle hit the table, she took a drink. "My folks went to Lampasas, where my mama's sister lived."

"Near Fort Hood?"

"Right. That's where Braxton was stationed. And when he got back from the war, I married him."

"So you've been living up in Lampasas all this time? You didn't go too far from Homestead."

"Well, we moved around a lot, actually, Braxton liking the rodeo and all." She shook her head. "Too bad he wasn't any good."

"And when old Clyde Braxton died? Why didn't you and your husband show up to claim the property then?"

"Well, see, we didn't hear about it. Nobody from here knew I'd married Braxton, and nobody told my mama or daddy about Uncle Clyde. Then, when we finally did find out, no way did we have the money to pay all those taxes. Braxton just blew it off. He didn't want to be a rancher, anyway."

"But you're here now?"

"I'm here 'cause my son and I need a place to live. And that land is rightfully his. My lawyer says I can get it back, 'cause the county never should've given it away in the first place."

"You went to a lawyer?" He signaled for more beer.

"Well, he came to me. Same thing."

"What's this lawyer's name?"

"Why?"

"I could check him out for you, make sure he's legitimate."

"I know he's legitimate. I don't need your help." She got to her feet, swayed from side to side and sat down again.

"Dermody," Della said. "Raoul Dermody." Then she put her head down on the table and moaned. "I feel sick."

"Three was always your limit, Della." Jud got to his feet and put cash on the table for the drinks. "I'm taking you home to bed."

Her head popped up. "Well, it's about time—"

He held her elbow as she lurched to her feet. "To sleep it off, Della." She leaned heavily against him as they crossed the floor. "You blew your chance with me fifteen years ago."

"I know." She staggered as the cold outside air hit her in the face. "He told me he wouldn't pay me if I screwed around with anyone else."

Finally. "Who told you that?"

"Ar…Braxton, of course." She stood up straight and let go of his arm. "Braxton Teague was a jealous man."

"Right." Now Jud was the one reeling, thanks to the revelation she'd just given him. He opened the truck door for her. "Who wouldn't be, with a woman like you?"

Della settled herself in the passenger seat, then smiled as she laid her palm along his jawline. "You're so sweet." A minute later, her head tilted to the side and she started to snore.

At the Rise and Shine Motel, Jud parked in the space next to Della's brand-new white Lexus and left her sleeping in his truck while he went to rap on the pink door of room 15. After a second, harder knock, the door swung back. When he saw Jud, Sam Teague did a double take and took off his earphones.

"Where's my mom?" He'd slicked his black hair back from his face. In this light, standing this close, Jud saw that Sam's eyes were green. A thick crop of freckles sprinkled his fair skin. Reddish-blond hair dusted his skinny arms.

"In my truck." Jud went back to the truck and got Della awake enough to stay on her feet as he guided her into the room with his arm around her waist. She curled up on the bed as soon as he released her, and was instantly asleep.

"Thanks." Sam slipped his mom's shoes off her feet and pulled the bedspread over her. "She's not a very good drinker."

"She never was."

"You went to school with my mom, didn't you?"

"Yeah, I did."

"Did you know her real good?"

"We...dated...some."

The boy stared hard at Jud's face, then surveyed him from head to toe. "She says you're a cop down in Austin."

"That's right."

"You going to arrest her?"

"Has she done something wrong?"

Sam glanced at his mother. "She's just looking out for me."

"I always knew her heart was in the right place." He put a hand on the kid's shoulder for a second. "I'll try to keep her out of trouble as much as I can."

"Thanks."

Jud backed out and the pink door shut in his face.

He'd just made another promise he wasn't sure he could keep.

"YOU'RE GOING WHERE?" Nan stood in the doorway of Miranda's room late Tuesday night, watching her daughter pack. "With who?"

"Austin. Jud."

"When?"

"Tomorrow morning."

"Why?"

Miranda blew an impatient breath. "He made an appointment with somebody he thinks might be funding the vandalism. And he's got friends in the bureaucracy who can help verify or contradict Della's claim on the K Bar C land."

"He needs you to check this out? He can't go by himself?"

"Yes, he could go by himself. But he asked me to come and I said I would."

Nan sat down on the edge of the bed. "Are you sure this is a good idea?"

"Not at all." Miranda sat down on the other side. "But I have to know if there's anything…real… between Jud and me. Or else I'll never get him off my mind."

"He's not the hellion he used to be," her mother conceded. "But he could break your heart. His life is in Austin."

"And mine is definitely here in Homestead." She put her hand over Nan's and squeezed. "I'll be back, don't worry about that. I don't know if anything will happen. I just have to find out." She grinned. "And I don't want the entire population of Homestead looking on while I do!"

Nan didn't smile back. "Amen to that," she said somberly, and went to her own empty bed.

CHAPTER ELEVEN

AFTER SPENDING several hours at the Texas Bureau of Vital Statistics, Jud and Miranda ate their fast-food lunch sitting in his truck, parked outside the Darrow, Inc. building in Austin. Along with their burgers, they digested the message sent by twenty floors of marble, glass and bronze.

"Money," Jud concluded. "Lots and lots of money."

"Power, too." Miranda sighed. "This is not a man who'll be intimidated by the mayor of a yokel town."

"I doubt he'd be intimidated by the governor. Or the U.S. president, for that matter."

"Are we chickening out?"

"Hell, no." Grinning, he got out of the truck and came around to open Miranda's door. "We just use bigger, sharper weapons, that's all."

"That's all? I didn't know we had weapons to begin with."

Henry Darrow's personal office occupied the top floor of his building. Once Jud informed the receptionist that Henry Jr. sat in a cell in Loveless County, she treated them respectfully, bringing coffee and cookies while they waited for Darrow's two o'clock meeting to end.

Three cookies later, the massive double doors behind the reception desk opened and a stream of business types poured out. "I wore a suit to work five days a week for six years," Miranda told Jud in an undertone.

"I can't believe you survived that long." He gave her a wink. "You must have really wanted the job."

"I really wanted to prove I could do it."

"I could have told you that."

Before she'd recovered enough to reply, the receptionist picked up her phone, then got to her feet. "Officer Ritter, Mayor Wright? This way, please."

They followed her across the charcoal-gray carpet, through those big doors, into a room with floor-to-ceiling windows on three sides. The desk in the center of the space would have filled Miranda's courthouse office wall to wall.

Henry Darrow finished signing a multi-page document on the blotter in front of him before acknowledging their presence. Everything about the man screamed "power," from the expensive suit, French-cuffed shirt and gold links to the perfect cut of his black hair, the hawkish nose and manicured hands. He capped his gold fountain pen, carefully placed it in the penholder and, finally, challenged Jud with a steady black stare.

"Officer Ritter?" His voice indicated a childhood spent in Mexico and a real contempt for ordinary mortals like Jud. "How can I help you?"

Miranda's blood began to boil.

"Mayor Wright and I are here to talk with you about your son, Hank Darrow."

"Yes?" Darrow finally gave Miranda a moment of his attention. "I understand you have him under arrest in...where is it? Homestead, Loveless County?"

"That's right." Without being invited, Jud pulled a chair over for Miranda, and then one for himself. "He's been charged with soliciting vandalism."

"Well, I am sorry, Officer Ritter, Ms. Wright." Darrow bowed in Miranda's general direction. "But my son and I have been estranged for quite some time. I really can't be held responsible for his transgressions."

"When did you see him last?" Elbows propped on the arms of the chair, fingers loosely laced together, Jud appeared completely relaxed, while Miranda could barely keep her hands from twisting against each other with nervous tension.

"Months ago." He waved a hand. "Maybe as much as a year."

"Does he have a job?"

"I doubt it. Hank has...problems."

"What kind of problems, Mr. Darrow?"

"I would rather not—"

Jud shook his head. "You don't have that choice. I can come back with a subpoena, but this will go easier if you just give me the answers I need."

Darrow rubbed his eyes with the fingers of one hand. "Hank drinks, does hard drugs, drives too fast, fights too much and hasn't got a loyal bone in his body, for women or anyone else."

"So you aren't surprised that he's involved in causing trouble for people in Loveless County?"

"Hank causes trouble wherever he goes."

Miranda sat forward. "But why Homestead? What would draw him to such a backwater town?"

Darrow opened his hands outward in a helpless gesture. "I've no idea. I would expect someone asked him to come for reasons of their own."

Jud shifted in his chair. "You had interests in Loveless County at one time, didn't you?"

"I had hoped to buy the K Bar C land, yes. I wanted to develop the area."

"What happened?"

"Senator Gallagher also wanted the land, and I needed his support with other projects too much to antagonize him by ruining his plans. Besides…"

Miranda prompted him. "Besides what?"

"I didn't trust the man I was dealing with."

"And who would that be?"

"The real estate agent. Very smooth, but dangerous underneath. Enfield was his name."

Miranda's throat closed on a gasp.

Jud took over again. "Did Mr. Enfield meet your son?"

Darrow thought a moment. "Yes, he did. This was some years ago, and at the time I wanted to interest Hank in my business. Unfortunately, he lacked the discipline needed for success. But I took him with me on several visits to different properties."

"Do you know Raoul Dermody?"

"The attorney? Yes, he worked for me at one time."

"No longer?"

"No. He was cheating me. I don't stand for that."

"One more question—is there a chance that Dermody and Enfield know each other?"

"Oh, I think it's quite likely. Enfield would have worked with Dermody while I was considering the K Bar C deal."

Jud nodded and stretched to his feet. "We really appreciate your cooperation, Mr. Darrow. You've been a tremendous help."

"I don't like betraying my own son."

"I understand. In the long run, I think what you've told us will probably spare your son most of the punishment he deserves."

Darrow blew out a deep breath. "Yes, Hank has always had a talent for avoiding penalties. That may be the source of his problems."

After saying goodbye, they made the trip down the elevator and out of the building in silence.

"So," Miranda said, once Jud climbed into the driver's seat of the truck, "You've connected Arlen to Hank Darrow."

"Circumstantially, at least. I need hard evidence."

"Is this all about money?"

"No, it's about you."

"You think...? No."

"Yes." Jud dropped his head back against the seat. "He wanted to make money on the land deal. He expected to be mayor forever. And you're standing in the way of both those goals."

She thought for a few minutes, as Jud started the engine and they left the Darrow building parking lot. "Then why hasn't there been more trouble on the farm?"

"A gunshot is pretty big trouble."

"That's very recent."

"A sign of growing desperation, maybe. Your favorite mare getting pregnant could be considered trouble. Or maybe just a warning you didn't understand."

"You think Arlen paid somebody to let Bailey loose? Who?"

"Maybe one of your hands. Or maybe Hank walked onto the place one night and took care of it."

Miranda shivered. "Still, most of the damage has been done to other people."

"Because, I suspect, Enfield knows that having the Home Free program fail, having your friends injured, would be more of a defeat for you than getting hurt yourself. He's watched you grow up—he knows how responsible you feel, how much you want this plan to succeed. How devastated you'd be if people suffered because of your ideas."

She looked out the window and blinked back tears. "I guess I'm pretty transparent."

"I'd call you honest." Jud's hand closed around hers, tightened, then let go. "What do you say we get away from this place?"

Miranda took a deep breath. "I think that's a terrific idea."

JUD DROVE TO HIS APARTMENT complex first, just to pick up mail. "Won't take but a second," he promised. "The mailbox is at the front of the parking area."

He unlocked the small door, pulled out a sheaf of envelopes, then got back into the truck. "Mostly bills. Now, where shall we eat?"

Miranda lifted an eyebrow. "You're not going to show me your place?"

"Not worth the effort." He avoided her gaze by turning to look out the rear window as he backed up. "It's just a place."

"I could use a chance to freshen up."

His glance flicked over her. "You look great."

"Are we coming back tonight? I could drop off my bag."

"I made hotel reservations. Your bag is fine in the backseat."

She blew out an irritated breath. "I want to see your home, Jud."

"Why?" His hands tightened around the steering wheel.

"I don't know, because…because it's you, your life. Because I'm nosy. Because I plan to spread the word around town what a decadent lifestyle you lead. Humor me, please."

He heaved a big sigh. "What the hell."

After parking the truck in front of a building at the rear of the complex, he led her up three flights of stairs to a unit on the top floor.

"For what it's worth," he said, unlocking the dead bolt, "this is my place." He pushed the door open and ushered Miranda inside.

The first room—a dining area, judging by the chandelier hanging from the ceiling—was empty, the beige carpet free of even footprints. The kitchen came next, counters bare of dishes, cookbooks, crumbs.

Miranda opened the refrigerator. "You weren't kidding, were you?" Two beers, a box of butter and a jar of strawberry jam were the only contents.

"I don't cook," Jud said tightly. "And I haven't been here for a while, you know."

She patted his arm. "It's okay." The next room contained a long, square leather couch in front of a state-of-the-art TV. Sound components occupied the built-in bookshelves. Miranda spent a few minutes examining the hundreds of CD cases arranged in rotating storage units nearby.

"You've got everything from sixties rock to folk to funk." She looked up at him from her position kneeling on the floor. "Do you like all of it?"

"Depends on the mood. What do you like?"

Running her finger down the ends of the cases, she smiled and drew out one recording. "How about this?"

He winced, but put in the disc and turned up the volume. "She Thinks My Tractor's Sexy," played as Miranda visited the bathroom, and then, finally, Jud's bedroom.

"A bed." She looked at him as he leaned against the door frame. "Books. A dresser, no mirror. What are you, a monk?"

"Not at all. I just don't have much…stuff."

Striding to his closet, she pulled back the door. "Nothing here to indicate what you do." For a moment she shielded her face with one hand. "Where's your life?"

"I play basketball on the department team. Go for a run most days, take a bike ride, work out. In summer I coach youth baseball, most winters I'm coaching b-ball for the YMCA. I missed out this year because of the injury."

When she looked at him again, her hazel eyes held a world of regret. "Sounds to me like you stay on the move so you won't have to think."

Jud walked back into his living room and stood staring out the window overlooking an open field of tall grass and short cedar trees. After a minute, he heard Miranda come in.

"I moved around a lot for several years, in the rodeo. Then I lived in a dorm at UT while I got my degree. Since then, I've been busy with training, work. I don't…need much."

"I understand." Her palm settled on his shoulder. "I'm sorry I pestered you. Let's find somewhere to eat."

THEY DECIDED on supper at Threadgill's, an Austin landmark famous for live music and Texas-style cooking. Miranda silently promised herself she'd order a salad and maybe, if Jud wanted some, dessert.

"Chicken-fried steak, right?" Jud looked at her over the menu. "Mashed potatoes, gravy, biscuits?"

She clenched her fists in her lap. "I think I'll just have a big salad. With grilled chicken."

He slapped his menu on the table. "Why would you do that?"

"Well, I—"

"This is like that day at Callie's, when you didn't eat your burger. Do you lose your appetite around me?" He thought for a second. "Is that a good thing—you're so crazed with lust you can't think about food? Or a bad thing—I'm so repulsive you'll toss your cookies if you try to eat?"

Miranda laughed. "Not repulsive, no. But—"

"So you're pulling the 'I can't eat anything because I'm female' stunt."

"It's not a stunt."

"It's not necessary, either. You're gorgeous. Just be yourself and have a good time."

Luckily, she hadn't taken a drink, or she'd have spewed margarita all over him.

"I think I'll go to the restroom," she said, hoping her voice didn't sound as breathless to him as it did to her. "Be right back."

Out of sight behind the restroom door, Miranda leaned back against the wall and closed her eyes. The day had been all business, and she'd begun to believe the night would be, too.

But now... Did he really think she was gorgeous? Did she owe him sex for that? Was he just being nice, or did he really want her?

Should she get roaring drunk to make the experience easier? Why hadn't she thought this through before she agreed to...ahem...come?

"You all right, missy?"

Miranda opened her eyes to see a big-haired blonde with a worried expression on her heavily made-up face. "You look like you're gonna pass out. Too much tequila?" The turquoise camisole and short leather skirt the woman wore exposed lots of tanned skin which, unfortunately, revealed too much about her age.

"No. No, I'm fine, thanks. Just thinking."

"Well, good. You get yourself pulled together, then go out and enjoy the night with that handsome cowboy you got in tow. Even if he does look like he went six rounds with a buckin' bronc and lost, I can tell he's a hot one." She patted Miranda's shoulder and returned to the restaurant.

A few minutes later, Miranda followed. When she got to the table, she found Jud had ordered in her absence.

"I took a chance on what you'd like." He gave her his sexy half smile. "If you want something else, we'll order that, too."

In a few minutes their table was laden with

chicken-fried steak and all the fixings. Miranda didn't need to order anything else. She declined dessert, though she did take a bite of Jud's peach cobbler before he polished it off.

They sat over coffee for awhile, reviewing the day's discoveries. "I guess Arlen could have hired Hank Darrow," Miranda said, taking a sip of the strong, black brew.

Jud stirred cream and sugar into his mug. "Unless Hank agrees to testify against Enfield, though, we don't have any leverage with that information. So far, he's not talking."

"Since none of the birth or death records help us prove who fathered Della's baby, we may not be able to stop her from taking over the K Bar C land."

"They'd have to pay the back taxes," he reminded her. "Plus a penalty. And they'd have to convince a judge that the land should have been transferred to Sam in the first place."

She didn't want to be humored, or comforted. "A case like that could be tied up for years in the court system. Meanwhile, we can't in good conscience give away land that might not belong to us. Arlen put himself to the trouble of paying for sabotage, when all he really had to do was find Della and bring her home." Tears pricked her eyes, and for the first time in her life, she wished she carried a pack of tissues in her purse.

"Come on." Jud grabbed her wrist and pulled until she came up out of her chair. "I'm not going to let you sit here feeling sorry for yourself."

In the truck again, she asked, "Where are we going now?"

"You'll see."

He drove down 6th Street with its clubs and bars. "I'm kinda tired, Jud. I don't want to go line dancing."

"Me, neither." Soon enough they had reached the suburbs west of town, subdivision after subdivision, with malls large and small in between.

"Do you suppose this is what Henry Darrow wanted to do to the K Bar C land?" Miranda gazed out the window. "Maybe we should be glad Arlen is such a weasel."

"I'll be sure to thank him when I arrest him." Jud grinned and turned into a parking lot. "Here we go."

"Here we go, what?" She took a look

around, then returned his grin with a big one of her own. "Batting cages? Yes!"

Fitted with helmets and bats, they stepped into one of the net enclosures and spent the first twenty minutes pretending the various balls coming at them were Arlen, Darrow and other troublesome folks.

"Tolly Craddock," Miranda called, hitting a high fly into the ceiling net.

"Ethan," Jud said, sending a grounder to the back corner.

Miranda frowned at him, then muttered, "Deirdre Long." The pitch came fast, and she hit it hard, ignoring Jud's grin.

Settling into a rhythm, they took turns hitting, all the while talking, mostly about the past. "I can't believe we were both at UT for three years and never saw each other."

"You were a business major, I was in criminal studies. Not much overlap."

"Did you pledge a fraternity?"

He shook his head. "I was working nights and weekends at a grocery store. No time and no money for a frat."

She stood still for a minute. "I hadn't thought about it, but your dad didn't put you through school, did he?

Jud swung and missed. "Nope." Rubbing his shoulder, he stepped out of the batter's zone. "I'm going to take a rest and watch you for awhile. You're pretty good for a girl."

"Four years hitting for the University of Texas fast-pitch softball team says I oughta be." Taking her stance, Miranda began some serious batting practice.

Jud enjoyed the display, as he'd known he would. He liked watching Miranda move, liked her control and coordination. As a kid, she'd horned in on the boys' games—football, baseball, running, swim-ming, anything they were up to. Most of the time, she played better than any of the guys, including Jud, which was one reason he'd teased her so much. What ten-year-old wanted to be beaten by a girl?

She handled a bat better than he did now, even when he wasn't sore as hell from his brother's punches and still healing from gunshot wounds. But tonight, Jud didn't resent that physical superiority at all.

He watched the twist of her body as she stepped into the ball, the strength of her legs driving the hit. He appreciated the pull of her shirt over her breasts, the way her rear end rounded out the seat of her pants. When she concentrated, she closed her lips between her teeth, which made them even plumper when she relaxed. Jud thought about the taste of those lips, and his breathing got a little tight.

"I think that's it," she announced finally. "I'm going to be sore as the dickens tomorrow. But it felt so good." She gave him a carefree, beautiful smile. "Thanks—this was a terrific idea."

"You're welcome." He didn't dare touch her as they walked to the truck. His own control was precarious right now.

When they checked into the hotel, he discovered they had not been given adjoining rooms, as he'd requested. The bar was open, but the music blaring out the open doors was nothing they could dance to, or even make conversation over. He'd blown his chance with Miranda, anyway. His churlish attitude about the apartment had probably already warned her off.

Until today, he hadn't realized his life was so sterile.

Anyway, he'd come back down in a few minutes and drink a couple of beers. Or maybe he'd just splurge and open the minibar. Then he could drink his beer underneath the cold shower.

A crowded elevator dumped them at the twelfth floor, where they realized their rooms faced each other across the hall.

Miranda unlocked her door, then turned to face Jud from within the doorway. "Thanks for all your work today. And for dinner, and the batting practice." Talking to his blank face and distant gaze was like talking to a wall. "I'll see you…in the morning."

"Sleep tight." He closed the door between them, but he'd already shut her out.

NAN HAD NEVER DONE ANYTHING like this in her whole life. She couldn't believe she was doing it now.

Wrapped in her heavy flannel robe, with a pair of black velvet house slippers on her feet, Nan eased out the back porch door and ran toward the barn. Dusty, pining for Miranda, stayed on the sofa in the house.

The barn lights were off, but she moved along the dark aisle between the stalls with confidence—there wasn't an inch of this place she didn't know as well as she knew her own bedroom. Even without a visual clue, her hand found the handle for the pocket door to the tack room. Cruz had left the panel open slightly, so he could hear any disturbance among the horses.

But he hadn't heard her silent approach, and he didn't hear her slide the door open far enough to squeeze inside. She could hear his even breathing—he slept soundly on the cot in the far corner of the room.

Nan stood still for a moment, listening, gathering her courage. She'd tried to stay aloof, struggled with all her might to cut the connection between them.

Tonight, alone in the house, she'd lost the fight. She couldn't bear his absence any longer.

The cot squeaked. "Nan?" His whisper wel-comed her.

She stepped out of the slippers, untied the belt at her waist and let the robe fall to the floor. Cruz gasped as she went into his arms and he realized she wore nothing at all.

Sometime later, Nan resigned herself to getting up in the cold for a trip to the bathroom. Shivering, she pulled on her robe and slippers, then headed back to the house—she'd been meaning to put a bathroom with a shower in the barn, but there never seemed to be extra money lying around for luxuries. Maybe this summer...

Outside, she hunched into her robe and scurried as fast as she could for the porch. Halfway across the yard, though, she stopped and stared at the golden glow flickering on the white siding. No moon cast that kind of light.

Inside the house, Dusty barked without breaking for breath. Nan turned to look beyond the barn.

"Cruz!" She screamed his name. "Cruz!" Her feet had frozen in place. "Cruz!"

He ran out of the barn, pulling on a sweatshirt as he raced toward her. "What's wrong?"

Wordless, Nan pointed toward the rich yellow glow beyond the trees in the curve of the driveway.

The cabin was on fire.

JUD HEARD THE CLOCK click 2:00 a.m. He rolled over and squinted in that direction to be sure—maybe he'd fallen asleep and it was actually morning. He could get up and go to the hotel gym, work up a good sweat.

But, no. Two o'clock it was. What was another four miserable hours, anyway?

When a knock sounded on the door, he thought he'd imagined it. The second time, though, she spoke. "Jud? Jud, are you awake?"

He got up as fast as his body would allow and pulled on a T-shirt over his jeans as he went to the door.

Miranda stood in the hallway, barefoot, wearing a terry cloth robe with the hotel insignia on the pocket.

"What's wrong?" He glanced down the hallway to the right, then left. "Why aren't you asleep?"

She looked both ways, too. "Can I come in?"

He raked his hand through his hair. "Not a good idea, Miranda. We can talk tomorrow."

"I…" She swallowed hard. "I don't want to talk."

Which was fortunate because, at that moment, Jud couldn't think of a word to say. He stepped back and let her into his room, then shut the door.

Miranda walked to the window. "You have a good view from this side, too." Before he could answer, she turned to face him. "This is really hard. But I want to be with you. I—I always have."

A blow straight to the solar plexus. He couldn't possibly return the compliment... Or could he?

"Even when I called you Miserable Miranda in the eighth grade?"

She smiled a little. "Maybe not that part of always. And for the record, you started that trash in the fifth grade."

"I was a mean little cuss, wasn't I? How about when I put superglue on your desk chair just before you sat down?"

"Definitely not that part of always. I had to take off my skirt to get up. Jerk."

"But you were wearing shorts underneath. I always thought that was weird." He crossed the room and took her hand.

"Us tomboys had to take drastic measures." She came easily when he pulled her to sit down on the end of the bed.

"I do remember you hanging upside down on the monkey bars a lot." Her hands were cold, so he linked their fingers together.

"I thought it would make me smarter. More blood to the brain, you know."

"Must've worked. You're a smart lady today."

"I bet you say that to all the girls."

The collar of her robe had loosened a little. Jud bent his head and set a kiss on the pulse at her throat. "You think too much about 'all the girls.'"

"Your love life was never much of a secret, as long as you were in town."

"But you're the only one here now." Using the leverage of their joined hands, he eased her backward to lie on the bed. "I'll think only about you and…" He kissed those full, sweet lips. "…and you think only about me."

"Okay," she whispered. In the next second, though, she looked anxious again. "Tell me what you like. I…um…"

"I think you'll figure it out, honey. Speaking from my vast experience, I'd say you have a natural aptitude."

The smile she beamed at him stole his breath away.

Lying beside her on the bed, Jud drew her slowly down the garden path, with plenty of stops along the way for exploring, enjoying. Miranda responded to his touch with shivers and sighs and moans, and she learned quickly how to draw the same sounds from him. The scent of lavender surrounded them, but he thought that might be his imagination. Then he smoothed the robe away and saw what she wore underneath.

"I was expecting white cotton," he said raggedly, trailing his fingertips from the silk of her skin to the black silk she wore. Again and again.

"I know." Her arms twined around his neck. "I wanted to surprise you."

"You've been surprising me since the day we met."

Whatever confidence problems Miranda might have had pretty much disappeared at that point. Desire blazed the trail—they took their pleasure as equals, demanding, giving, receiving in turn. They came together as halves of the same whole, and the explosion of relief left both of them stunned.

Miranda didn't remember falling asleep, but she drifted awake to find that Jud had pulled the covers up and wrapped his arms around her, pillowing her head on his shoulder. Smiling, she snuggled closer. She couldn't think of a nicer way to spend the night.

When a metallic tune cracked the darkness a few minutes later, she wasn't sure where it came from or how to make it stop. Radio? Alarm? Finally, she recognized the ring of Jud's cell phone.

"Wake up," she said, shaking his shoulder. "Wake up and answer the phone!"

"Yeah, yeah." Groaning, he rolled away from her and felt around on the table. "Got it." A green glow lit his face as he put the open phone to his ear. "Jud Ritter. No problem." His voice sharpened, and he sat up away from the pillows. "Miranda? She... uh... probably turned her phone off when she went to bed. I can go get—"

In the midst of rubbing his hand over his face, he froze. "What did you say? All of it? Everybody all right? Damn. Damn, damn, damn. Okay, sure. We'll be there before sunrise."

He closed the phone and looked at Miranda. "That was your mom. Somebody put used motor oil on the hay bales."

Holding the sheet to her chest, she sat up. "How many?"

"All of them. But—" He took hold of both her hands. "It gets worse."

The sheet dropped as she held on tight. "Is everyone okay? The horses?"

"Horses and people are fine. But someone set fire to your lavender field. Doused it with gasoline and sent it up in flames. There's nothing left but ash."

CHAPTER TWELVE

As DAWN BROKE in the clear winter sky, Nan sat on the steps of the cabin, her hands wrapped around an empty mug, her gaze on the smoking debris that had been Miranda's lavender crop. To her far right, across the pasture, stood the shed containing hundreds of bales of hay—her entire fall crop—doused with paint, used engine oil, and who knew what else.

Wade Montgomery had been there since 4:00 a.m., along with the volunteer firefighters. As word spread through town, other folks began to show up, like spectators at a circus. Jud and Miranda should arrive any time now. Nan wondered if she ought to cook them all a big breakfast.

Ed Tanner, the fire chief, came over. "They didn't bother to hide the evidence." He held up two five-gallon gasoline containers.

"Found these on the other side. Whoever did this simply poured gas on the plants and threw a match. Whoosh."

Nan winced at the image. She glanced at Dusty, walking a sentry line along the charred edge of the field. Nan could almost feel the dog's concern.

"We can try for fingerprints," Wade said, his breath white in the chilly air. "Although anybody with half a brain would have worn gloves." He and Ed took the containers to his truck.

Hiram and Millie Neibauer had both come out to write a report. "I'm real sorry," Hiram told her. "This isn't the kind of news I like printing."

Millie opened her notepad. "What happened last night? When did the fire start?"

"I'm not sure." Nan pushed her hair off her forehead with one hand. "About two o'clock, maybe."

"But Cruz didn't see anyone?" The reporter glanced at the cabin. "I mean, he's right here by the field."

"I wasn't here last night." Cruz took Nan's empty cup and handed her a new mug filled with hot coffee. "I've been sleeping in the barn."

"In the barn?" Millie's eyebrows climbed toward her hairline. "Really?"

"We're keeping the horses in at night," Nan explained. "And Cruz stays with them to keep an eye out for intruders."

"Of course. And no one heard a truck in the middle of the night? These guys made no noise as they ruined the hay?"

Praying she didn't blush, Nan shook her head. "The hay shed is a quarter of a mile away from the house and barn. I didn't hear anything." If she'd been more alert, if she hadn't been preoccupied with a man young enough to be her son, maybe the outcome would have been different.

Flipping to the next page, Millie clucked her tongue and shook her head at the same time. "That's too bad. We sure could stand to catch these creeps. Do you have any hay in reserve?"

"Just what's growing in the fields. Most of it won't be ready to bale until January."

"In other words, horse folk in Loveless County will have to go somewhere else to buy hay for their animals over the winter."

Nan tightened her hold on the coffee mug. "I guess so."

"And they'll probably have to pay more for it, right?"

"That's right," Cruz said, moving to stand between Nan and Millie. "Nan's always given the local ranchers a good deal."

The reporter scribbled furiously. "So the loss of this hay will have an economic impact on the entire county?"

"I'd certainly say so," a new voice answered. Arlen Enfield stood by Hiram, surveying the charred field. "This rampage has got to be stopped. Somebody obviously has a vendetta connected to the Home Free land giveaway, and he's punishing anybody involved."

Cruz took another step forward. "And who do you think would do something like that?"

Arlen gave an open-handed shrug. "I can't imagine. Our sheriff has kept two men incarcerated for weeks now, and yet..." He gestured toward the field.

"Looks like they hooked the wrong fish," Pete McPherson said, with a harsh laugh.

Before Nan could reply, Cruz pushed Pete back a stride, then another. "Get off the property, McPherson. You're not welcome."

"That so?" McPherson said. "You the boss around here these days, Martinez? Now, that would almost make that trip back and forth across the border worthwhile, I guess."

Nan surged to her feet and stepped between the two men. "This is *my* land. I say who stays and who leaves." Pete started to snigger, and she threw him a glance. "Go home. Mind your own business."

"Now, isn't that interesting?" Arlen crossed his arms over his chest. "It occurs to me that this reign of terror began not long after Mr. Martinez, here, arrived in town. I could be wrong about the source of the vendetta. Maybe there's somebody in town these days who makes trouble for trouble's sake."

The rumble of a truck engine distracted them all from Arlen's vile insinuation. Jud's truck stopped on the side of the driveway, the passenger door flew open and Miranda jumped out. A second later, she had her arms wrapped around Nan's shoulders.

"Are you all right? Did anyone try to hurt you?"

Nan laughed and cried at the same time. "I'm fine, except for the coffee you just spilled all over my jeans and coat."

"Oh, damn. I'm sorry." Miranda backed up. "I'm a mess, too. We match." As she turned, Dusty charged through the crowd and nearly took her down. Dropping to her knees, Miranda accepted her dog's wet welcome. "I missed you, too. Yes, I did."

Finally, she faced the lavender field. The crowd standing in front of her silently melted away so she could see the mess someone had made of her tribute to Lila.

Ugly. Mean. Evil. With all her will, she resisted turning to face Arlen Enfield and screaming out her accusations, her rage. She and Jud had talked about keeping their suspicions quiet until they had irrefutable proof.

She turned away from the ruins to face her mom again. "Well, there's nothing else to do out here, let's go to the house."

Arm in arm, with Dusty following, they passed through the crowd like ground mist on a summer day. As they passed Jud, he put a hand on Miranda's arm.

"We'll talk." His face displayed no emotion, unless you were close enough to see the dark fury in his eyes.

Miranda nodded. "I'll be in the office later today."

Then she walked her mother home so they could take care of each other.

W‍HEN J‍UD RETURNED to the Loveless County jail on Thursday afternoon, Raoul Dermody greeted him from inside Tolly Craddock's cell.

"I believe you've misled my client, Officer Ritter."

"Me?"

"You told me he dropped the case!" Tolly's face turned red as he clung to the bars between them. "You said I'd need a new lawyer."

"That's what I heard," Jud said with a shrug. "I guess rumor was mistaken this time."

"And for the record, Mr. Darrow has also engaged me as his attorney." Dermody crossed one knee over the other.

"That's good, because he will need one." Hands in his jeans pockets, Jud leaned back against the wall. "Henry Darrow Sr. has given us plenty of information concerning his son's less civic-minded activities."

Hank swung his feet to the floor, stood up and walked to the front of his cell. "My old man doesn't know anything. I don't believe you."

"That's your prerogative. But by the time we've presented your record, which includes drug charges and a hit-and-run arrest, I think a judge will be persuaded that we're on the right track when we accuse these two."

Dermody cleared his throat. "Now, how can you say that, when the worst episode yet occurred just last night while my clients were tucked up safely in their cells?"

Jud deliberately loosened his jaw. "These two aren't the only tools in the box. We'll get the others soon enough, though, and then… snap!" He snapped his fingers. "Your lucky break will be shot."

"What's he talking about," Tolly demanded of the attorney. "What lucky break?"

"Explain, Officer Ritter."

"The name of the bastard who thought up this scheme would be very valuable to me, and to the sheriff. So valuable that we might persuade the judge to consider a suspended sentence, time served, community service… instead of a long stretch in a state penitentiary."

Dermody stared straight ahead for a long minute. "A tempting offer for my clients," he agreed. "But I think we'll take our chances."

"I suggest you encourage them to accept the offer. That way, you don't go to jail as an accessory to attempted murder, either. And we don't probe too deeply into your tax returns, your accounting methods, your offshore bank business." Jud smiled. "Quid pro quo, we call it."

"Bullshit is what I call it." Dermody sighed. "But get the sheriff in here and let's hear what y'all have to offer."

MIRANDA WENT INTO TOWN after lunch and returned as many calls as she could manage in two hours. Some were genuine expressions of concern—from Greer, Kristin, Callie. Many callers demanded an end to the "reign of terror," as someone put it. She got several lectures on what her job description entailed, including, of course, the prevention of property damage and personal injury.

But the worst calls came from six people in different areas of the country, all of whom had been accepted by the Home Free Program and all of whom had now decided to withdraw their applications. Those six people represented twenty-two new citizens for Homestead, Texas. Miranda knew this was only the beginning.

After making sure nothing urgent needed her attention, she closed her office, said good-night to Reba and left the building. She would go home, build a fire and sit on the sofa with Nan until they fell asleep with Dusty curled up between them.

On the way to her truck, she saw lights still burning in the office of Enfield Realty Company. Without any purpose in mind, Miranda walked toward the building. Someone had used fake snow and stencils to spray Happy Holidays across the plate glass window. Full of the Christmas spirit, that Arlen.

Bells tied to the knob jangled as she opened the door. Clarice Enfield looked up from her computer keyboard, clearly startled.

"Oh, Miranda. It's you." She giggled, and put her hand to her throat. "I'm always a little nervous staying here after dark. But Arlen doesn't like to close the office until six."

"You never know when a last-minute house sale will come in." Miranda sat down in the client chair in front of Arlen's cluttered but organized desk. She didn't know why she was here, didn't know what to say.

"Can I do something for you?" Clarice saved whatever she'd been working on and closed the program. "Arlen won't be back in the office tonight—he had meetings in Austin."

"How are your sons doing these days?" A guaranteed conversation gambit for most mothers.

Clarice smiled, a little sadly. "Some days I hardly see them—they wake up late, after I've gone to the office, and stay out very late with their friends." A frown flitted across her face. "But they're well, and they seem happy."

Miranda examined the framed photograph of the two boys displayed on Arlen's desk. "They graduated from high school a couple of years ago, didn't they? Are they planning to go to college?"

"Not—not right away. They both want some time off, first."

"But they're not working." The big December calendar page serving as Arlen's desk blotter was covered with his small, square printing, almost impossible to read upside down.

"Arlen doesn't see a need for the boys to

get jobs right now." Clarice fluffed the back of her perm, and Miranda noticed she needed her roots touched up where a dull brown and gray showed through.

"You must be so busy, working all day and taking care of three men at home." Miranda smiled with real sympathy. "I don't know how you do it."

"I like the office. I enjoy getting out, seeing people."

Miranda nodded. "Did you see that Della Bowie is back?"

A cattle prod at maximum power would have had the same effect on Clarice as that simple question. She straightened her back, lifted her chin and gritted her teeth. "I heard she had come back. I haven't seen her, thank goodness."

"You don't like Della?"

"It's not a question of liking or disliking. The girl is simply…trouble."

"She's thirty-two years old," Miranda pointed out gently. "Not a girl anymore."

"She still behaves like the slut…like the wildcat she was in high school."

"Has Della been raising hell? I hadn't heard."

"Well, I saw her myself Tuesday evening, as drunk as could be at barely five o'clock. She came out of the Lone Wolf Tavern with her arms around Jud Ritter like he was the Rock of Gibraltar in the midst of a hurricane."

Miranda felt as if a stone had sunk to the bottom of her belly. "What happened?"

Clarice shrugged one shoulder. "He loaded the little tramp into his truck and they took off." She glared at Miranda as if she could have stopped them. "I mean, really. She'd been in town less than a day. Of course, everybody knew they were running together, back in high school. The boy is his baby, I'm sure of it. Maybe they're trying for another one."

Clarice's giggle set Miranda's teeth on edge. Before she could generate a civil answer, Clarice's phone rang.

She made an apologetic face and picked up the earpiece. "Enfield Realty. May we help you?"

What would Arlen's December calendar reveal? Miranda glanced around the office, and used the water dispenser on the back wall as an excuse to get up. She made a motion to Clarice and walked back to draw several servings of water, which she realized she actually did need.

Then, seeing a trash can conveniently placed close to Arlen's desk chair, she went to throw her paper cup away.

Arlen's printing wasn't much easier to read right side up. Luckily Clarice had turned to the computer, which kept her facing away from Miranda.

Bending close, Miranda's quick scan of the page showed events she would expect to see—the Home Free board meeting, the Homestead Historical Society holiday party coming up this weekend, and a big X over Christmas Day. Most of the names he'd written in were local—lunch with Myron Guthrie and Max Beltrane, breakfast with the bank president, haircuts scheduled with Rae Jean Barker on the third and the seventeenth at ten in the morning.

On Monday the fifth, he'd written simply, "D.L. Austin. 2 p.m."

Clarice hung up her phone with a final, "Thanks so much for calling." She turned just as Miranda straightened up. "That was Mr. Fremont. He and his wife planned to retire here from Houston and open a health food store, because they were convinced Homestead would be growing by leaps and bounds." She drew in a deep breath, and exhaled loudly. "They saw that article in the Austin paper and decided this wasn't the place for them, after all."

That made eight for the day. "We'll get past this," Miranda said. "I'm not giving up."

Arlen's wife looked at her doubtfully. "I'm glad you're the mayor now. I wouldn't want Arlen being responsible for this mess."

"Yes, well..." Miranda said, retreating toward the door. "I'll let you get back to work."

"It's six o'clock." Clarice sighed yet again. "Time to close up, go home and fix dinner."

"Better you than me, sister," Miranda said to herself as she slipped outside. She waved at Clarice through the window as she hurried to her truck. "Better you than me."

"THERE SHE IS, FINALLY."

Miranda heard her mother's comment as she and Dusty came through the back door into the kitchen, so she was prepared to find a man in the house. Just not *this* man.

Jud got to his feet as she entered the

living room. "You've had a long day." He motioned to the chair he'd just left by the fire. "Have a seat."

She was too surprised to argue with his order. "What are you doing here?"

He grinned. "I'm staying just down the drive-way, remember? I came to see how you two are doing." His nod indicated Nan, wrapped in a quilt on the sofa.

"I offered him tea, if he made it, and cookies from a box." Her mother's eyes were dark with fatigue, circled by shadows.

"Great cookies," Jud affirmed, sitting on the other end of the couch.

They stared at each other during the awkward silence that followed. "Dinner's not going to be much more complicated," Nan said, at last. "Soup from the freezer, biscuits from a can. Thank God for the microwave." She left the quilt behind on the sofa and walked toward the kitchen, hugging her arms around her as if she were still cold.

Jud sat forward, his elbows braced on his knees. "I'm sorry about…"

She shook her head. "Not your fault."

"I'd hoped to get to the bottom of this case before something like this happened again."

Remembering what she'd discovered, she sat up with more enthusiasm. "I was in Arlen's office, a little while ago, and I saw his calendar. He'd written down an appointment on the fifth—the Monday after Greer's wedding. Guess who?"

Smiling, Jud shook his head.

"The initials were D. L. Deirdre Long! Arlen's the one who brought her down here. I bet, if you talked to her, you could get her to admit that he suggested the article, and told her to slant it against the Home Free program. Maybe he paid her, as well. You could subpoena his bank account, look through his records—"

He held up a hand. "I don't think we're quite there yet, but close. I've got some news, too. Hank Darrow is willing to admit he met Arlen when he traveled with his father."

"That's great! And he'll say Arlen masterminded the vandalism—"

Jud shook his head. "No, he won't go that far. His attorney—a sleaze, but a smart one—won't let him incriminate himself."

Miranda dropped back into the chair. "We need him to confess."

"In time, we might persuade him. He also

dated Della that spring, by the way. So she can corroborate that he knew Enfield."

"Will she?"

"I don't know yet."

"You mean you haven't brought it up, in all the time you've spent together." *Jealous cat,* she told herself.

You're damn right I am.

"What do you mean?" His body had tensed, and his hands clenched on his knees.

"I hear you and Della did some partying. At the Lone Wolf."

Grinning, he relaxed again. "We talked. She got drunk, I took her to her room, left her in her son's charge."

The simple explanation made her feel like a fool. "Oh."

"Yeah. Oh." Getting to his feet, he pulled her to stand up. "Can I stay for dinner?" His arms slipped around her waist.

Miranda snuggled into his arms. "Only if you kiss me first."

"Bribery will get you everything." She closed her eyes in anticipation as he lowered his head. Suddenly, he stopped. "What the hell…?"

Miranda staggered as he let go to approach

the bookcase behind her. With one long finger, he pulled a volume off the shelf and flipped open the back cover.

"How did you get this?"

"Get what?" She held out her hand to take the book, but he moved it away.

"I checked this book out of the library years ago." Jud showed her the spine. *"Lady Chatterley's Lover.* Miss Haase said I never turned it in, and she expects me to replace it." He glared at Miranda. "How did it get here?"

As she thought back, she started to laugh. "I remember. You'd done something obnoxious, as usual, and I took the book as a hostage. I think I meant to ask for ransom." Miranda shook her head. "But I was so scatterbrained, I guess I forgot I had it. Isn't that hysterical?"

"I'm not laughing," he said sternly, but his eyes twinkled. "I'm not paying ransom, either. And I just might charge you with kidnapping. Booknapping, that is."

"Supper's ready," Nan called from the kitchen.

So much for that kiss she'd been promised. "And what's the sentence for this terrible crime?"

Jud set his palm against the side of her neck, and she leaned into his touch.

"Life," he said quietly. "Without possibility of parole."

FRIDAY MORNING, Jud knocked on the pink door at the Rise and Shine and waited for Della to answer. Her scowl warned him he was in for a hard battle. "What do you want?"

"Ah, Della, I knew you'd be glad to see me. We need to talk."

"I don't think so." She glanced over her shoulder. "Sammy's still asleep."

"We don't have to wake him. I could take you next door and buy you a steak biscuit."

The bribe reached her. "You go ahead. I'll be there in a few minutes."

A few turned into twenty, but she finally arrived and he bought her the food he'd promised, even waited until she'd downed half a cup of coffee.

"Okay, Della, here's the deal. You and I both know your son wasn't fathered by Braxton Teague." He held up his hand when she started to protest. "I'm not saying he couldn't inherit Teague's property. If

Braxton is listed on the birth certificate as Sam's legal father, then you do have a case."

She relaxed back into the seat. "So?"

"Who was Sam's biological father?"

"What difference does that make?"

"I think you know very well. I need some leverage, Della. And you can give it to me."

"Why should I?"

"You owe me. You used me, that spring, as a diversion. You didn't want people to know what you were doing, so you made them look somewhere else."

Della's pout could still bring a guy to his knees. "I didn't have a choice. If people found out, I wouldn't get the money."

Jud kept his face blank, but that one surprised him. "He paid you?"

"Well, first it was about the rent. He wouldn't raise the rent on my folks if I..." She shook her head. "When I got pregnant, he paid me to keep quiet. Paid for us to move, got us a house in Lampasas, free and clear. He kept sending money over the years, but Braxton pissed most of it away. I manage a lot better these days."

That explained the new Lexus. "But now you're here for a bigger prize."

"We need a place to live!" The red streaks of her nails fanned out over her forehead as Della pressed her fingers into her eyes. "Sammy's in with a bad crowd, out in Amarillo where we've been living. I want him to be safe."

"Safe is relative, Della. You can help make Homestead the kind of place you want your son to live."

She put her hands flat on the table. "What do I have to do?"

MIRANDA DRAGGED HERSELF into the office Friday morning at ten, poured a cup of coffee and snagged two of the boxed doughnuts Reba had left by the coffee machine. Her assistant extended a thick stack of message slips, which Miranda waved away.

"Give me half an hour." Juggling food, coffee and her briefcase, she unlocked her office and backed inside, waiting for Dusty to come through before closing the door. Turning toward the desk, she found Arlen Enfield sitting in one of the visitors' chairs.

He glanced at her over his shoulder. "Good morning, Ms. Mayor."

She dropped a doughnut. "How did you

get in here? No, wait, let me guess. You copied the keys to the building before you handed them over."

"Clever girl."

Leaving the pastry for Dusty to consume, Miranda walked around to her chair, set down her breakfast and her briefcase. "What do you want?"

"You visited my wife last night."

"I stopped in at your office to say hello."

"You upset her."

"*I* did nothing of the kind."

"She was overcome by a migraine headache and retired to bed as soon as she got home."

"I'm sorry Clarice had a headache. But it's not my fault."

Arlen sat forward, and for the first time she recognized the hate behind his handsome face. "You have interfered with me time and time again, missy." He pointed a shaking finger at her. "I'm not going to stand for it any longer. You better mind your own business from now on, or there will be consequences."

"Is that a threat?" She tried to laugh, not very successfully. "I think you're crazy."

"Oh, no. I'm quite sane. And I will get my

way." Suddenly his anger evaporated. "You, unfortunately, can't say the same. This little scheme of yours is going to disintegrate. Your white knight from the big city has already found other ways—other women—to amuse himself."

Jud had erased her doubts on that issue last night. Still, she could feel Arlen's poison working on her mind. Her heart.

"You never could pay attention for any length of time," Arlen told her. "I guess it's no surprise you can't hold a man's attention, either. How you fooled this town into electing you mayor is one of the great scam stories of all times."

"You should know." Miranda struggled to keep her voice from shaking. "You've pulled off plenty yourself."

"I'll look forward to your memoirs." He got to his feet. "If you can sit still long enough to write them."

Miranda looked at the door as Enfield turned to exit. There stood Jud, arms crossed as he leaned back against the panel.

"Interesting discussion you're having. Mind if I join in?"

"I'm just leaving," Arlen said coldly.

"That's the best news I've heard all day."

But as the older man approached, Jud made no move to get out of the way.

"Excuse me." The chill in Enfield's voice lowered the room temperature ten degrees.

"Not a chance," Jud said. Then he straightened. Though Arlen was a tall man, Jud was taller. Some-how, at that moment, he made the difference in inches seem significant.

"If you ever threaten Mayor Wright, her friends or family or property again," he said, "I'll make sure you go to jail. After I've beaten the crap out of you."

Stepping to the side, he opened the door and, with a flourish, motioned the ex-mayor through. "Have a nice day."

CHAPTER THIRTEEN

THE REPERCUSSIONS from the encounter with Arlen Enfield commenced almost immediately. Barely an hour later, Myron Guthrie stomped into the office and gave Miranda an earful on the respect due a former town mayor and the duties of the current mayor to act on behalf of all the voters. Max Beltrane sent a terse e-mail. You're headed for trouble, he wrote. Quit while you still can.

Miranda wasn't sure whether he wanted her to quit running the Home Free program, or quit being mayor altogether. She wouldn't resign, of course. And the only way the malcontents could push her out of office would be to demand a recall vote.

That happened at 1:30 Friday afternoon.

Reba called Miranda to the outer office, where she found Arlen handing her assistant a sheaf of papers.

Miranda leaned against the door frame, hoping for at least the appearance of nonchalance. "What's going on?"

Arlen gave her what passed for his charming smile. "A petition, Ms. Wright. Signed by two hundred seventy of Homestead's concerned voters."

By Reba's expression, she knew this would be bad news. "And what does this petition say?"

Reba took a deep breath.

"We, the undersigned voters of Homestead Township, Loveless County, Texas, do hereby petition and request a special election for the purpose of reconsidering the election of Miranda Elayne Wright to the office of Mayor."

Ice water poured through Miranda's body, followed immediately by a hot flood of anger. "You're petitioning a recall vote? On what grounds?"

Her assistant continued to read.

"It is the contention of the undersigned voters, that Mayor Wright has endangered the financial well-being of the town of Homestead. Morever, the safety of the citizens has been compromised through her incompetence. Pursuant to section 32.B.42 of the Homestead Township constitution—"

Reba looked into Miranda's eyes. "They have the right to do this?"

Enfield jabbed a finger at the recall papers. "Damn right, we do. We have much more than the fifteen percent of eligible voters required to implement this petition."

"Could I see the petition?" Miranda reached out with a hand that, thankfully, didn't tremble. Reba reluctantly gave her the papers.

Three hundred seventy-three voters had signed the list, complete with addresses and phone numbers. Using black ink, blue, red, orange and green, they'd come down on Arlen Enfield's side. Not just those people who'd always supported the former mayor, but many of the folks she saw every week— whose children she'd grown up with, whose hands she shook on a regular basis—had signed this form. Farmers she sold hay to, grandmothers who bought her peaches and tomatoes in the summer, teachers she'd had in school...well, maybe that wasn't such a big surprise.

None of the Home Free members were on the list, of course. Cruz hadn't signed, nor had any of the hired hands who worked for her.

She took a deep breath and dropped the petition onto Reba's desk. "Well, okay. This is democracy in progress. We can schedule the recall vote for January—"

"No," Arlen said harshly. "This vote will take place before Christmas. On December twentieth, to be precise."

"Come on, Arlen. That doesn't give either of us enough time to make our case with the people."

"I'm calling a town meeting for next Monday night, so we each have a time to present evidence to the public. The voters of Homestead are well aware of what's going on, of course, because many of them have suffered as a consequence of your rash policies. What they haven't experienced, or heard about from their neighbors, has been amply reported by the newspapers." He drew a rolled-up copy of the *Homestead Herald* out from underneath his arm and threw it on Reba's desk. "I believe this makes my position perfectly clear." Pivoting on his heel, he stalked to the outside door, threw it open, and marched out of the building.

Miranda picked up the newspaper and looked at the front page. Photographs of the ruined hay, the burned lavender and Nan sitting alone on the cabin steps illustrated the story headlined, "Wronged Wrights: Homestead Vandals Strike Again." Millie and Hiram hadn't made much effort to moderate their prose.

"I'm going to lunch." Miranda went back to her office for her wallet and Dusty. "If I were you, Reba, I'd take the rest of the afternoon off."

When she looked at her assistant, however, Reba wore a look of stubborn resistance. "I'm staying here. And these people who call to give us a hard time are gonna get a piece of my mind back in their faces."

That simple word, *us,* kept Miranda warm as she walked through the cold, dreary day.

WITH THEIR SUPPLY RUINED, Nan had to go elsewhere to buy hay for her own horses.

Friday afternoon, she drove two counties over to pick up a hundred bales on her flatbed trailer, then drove back so the bales could be hoisted into the loft of the barn.

"We haven't stored hay up here for ten years or more," she commented to Cruz as he and the other hands rigged the pulley that would lift the bales from the trailer to the door of the loft. "I don't like the potential for a barn fire."

"You're careful," he assured her. "It's winter, so heat won't be as big an issue. By the time warm weather rolls around, you'll have the ruined hay out of the shed and your own bales back where they belong."

His comment stirred up butterflies in her stomach, which she decided to ignore. "I hope our luck has bottomed out, and will start turning up again. Until these stupid criminals get put away, I can't feel comfortable on my own land."

The two of them stood on top of the load of hay as he worked. "This morning in town, I picked up supplies to build that fence along the back line." He hesitated, tying a knot, then looked into her face. "Arlen Enfield was passing a petition around. He wants a recall vote on Miranda's job."

"That miserable SOB. Nobody's going to listen to such nonsense. He's just making a stink."

Cruz shook his head. "The sheet I saw in Guthrie's hardware store had almost a hundred names on it."

Nan stood dumbfounded, unable to believe that folks she'd known for thirty years would turn on her daughter like this.

"Damn." She never cried. But now her eyes stung and her nose was stuffy.

"Don't worry too much." Cruz put a hand on her shoulder. "Enfield might get his petition signed. But those are all the votes he'll get. You know Miranda beat him five to one in the last election. Same thing will happen again."

She smiled at him. "Thank you. You're the calm in the middle of the storm. What would I do without you?"

His face hardened, and he stepped back. "You set up there?" he called to the guys in the loft. When they shouted back an affirmative, he fastened the hooks of the pulley into the first bale. "Take 'er up!"

As the bales transferred from the trailer into the loft, Nan went into the house to make a big pot of hot chocolate. She tried to call Miranda, but she'd stepped out of the office. Reba assured Nan that they had the situation under control. But the edge of desperation in her voice couldn't be disguised.

Once the last bales were hoisted into the barn, Nan took her pot of hot chocolate outside, along with a ladle and mugs. The men grinned at her and talked to each other in quick Spanish that she only half followed. Cruz had been her interpreter for a long time now. She'd stopped struggling to learn another language in her spare time.

His rebuff worried her. She gazed at him for a minute, trying to catch his eyes, read his mood, but Cruz managed to evade her.

Cruz followed when she went back to the house, carrying the empty pot and mugs. In the kitchen, he washed, dried and put away the dishes. They didn't talk, but that had been one of the good things about their relationship—the silences didn't have to be filled with words.

As he folded the dishtowel, he turned toward the table where she sat and leaned his hips back against the edge of the sink. His hair was rumpled from a day under his hat, and he looked like a little boy just up from his nap.

Nan frowned at herself. Cruz was not a little boy.

"I hate to pile trouble on trouble," he started, "but I want to give you as much time as possible.'

"Time for—?"

He gazed at her with sad eyes. "I'm moving on, Nan. I'll be resigning as foreman of Hayseed Farm, effective January first."

All the customary reactions wouldn't work. She knew why—she'd driven him to this. And she'd done it deliberately, out of cowardice, maybe, but also because she wanted the best for him.

Somehow, though, she'd never gotten around to imagining the actual process of saying goodbye. She hadn't anticipated the shrieking pain that came with the thought of never seeing Cruz Martinez again.

Being right had never felt so wrong.

"Well," she said, but no sound emerged. She cleared her throat and tried again. "Well, I understand why you'd make this decision. You're a great manager, and there are bigger, richer operations that can use your skills."

"That doesn't have anything to do with my decision. You know it."

She needed to pretend. "I'll be glad to write you glowing reference letters. Just give me the addresses." After a few seconds, she said, "Have you thought about where you'll go?"

"Away," he said, with a shrug. "Maybe to Mexico. I might try to teach, work with farmers to improve their crop systems, that kind of thing. I'd like to be doing good for somebody."

"That sounds terrific." As long as she didn't listen to her heart, or her brain telling her what an idiot she'd been. "I know you'll be a success."

"Thanks. Jud tells me he expects to get this vandalism problem cleared up very soon. He needs some hard evidence on Enfield, which he thinks he can get with a subpoena from the attorney general's office in Austin. I won't leave until I'm sure that it's safe for you and the horses here alone."

"Kahlúa will miss you."

"Horses forget." His smile held heartbreak. "He'll find someone else to rub his ears."

"Okay, then. Thanks for letting me know."

"Sure. You're welcome. I'll take care of

the horses tonight. Miranda might not feel so good when she gets home."

"I appreciate it. 'Night."

He nodded, and left. Nan held herself very still for quite a long time. Then she posted a note on the refrigerator for her daughter, explaining she'd gone to bed early, and climbed the stairs. Cocooned in blankets, she lay shivering upon her bed until the room got dark enough for her to fall asleep.

BY THE TIME HE ARRIVED at Miranda's office, about five o'clock on Friday, Jud had heard all the bad news. He'd read the *Homestead Herald* and been offered a chance to sign the petition, which he refused. He'd consulted with friends in the attorney general's office and been told his evidence was too circumstantial. They said that he'd never be able to convince a judge to issue a subpoena, especially during the holiday season. Wait until after the new year, they advised him. The system will be more efficient once the holidays have passed.

All well and good, except he was running out of time. A judge might not want to start up a legal wrangle during the season of peace and goodwill, but for the same reason, a judge might frown on holding two men in jail indefinitely, waiting for some kind of nebulous charges to be filed.

Arlen had forced the issue, with his town meeting and recall petition. Homestead citizens would want evidence that their ex-mayor had solicited criminal acts and deserved prosecution. Even with Della and Hank's statements, his case was a long way from real evidence.

He explained this to Miranda as they faced each other across her desk. She stared at him as he spoke, and she looked...well, beaten was the word. The corners of her mouth tilted down, her hunched shoulders and unfocused gaze accepted defeat.

And he didn't have any way to give her hope.

"I heard from my lieutenant this morning," he said. "He asked when I was coming back to work. I can probably hold him off until the first of the year, but no longer. They're short on manpower, as is."

She sat silent for a long time. "Suppose we just arrest Arlen now?"

He shook his head. "He'll find a lawyer

even smarter than Dermody, and be out again in a matter of days, if not hours."

"But if he's under indictment, he can't become mayor. The town constitution prevents felons from serving in town offices."

"The U.S. constitution has this pesky requirement…innocent until proven guilty. Until we convict Enfield of something, he's not a felon."

"The voters would think twice, though."

"Maybe. They could still vote you out of office, however, and appoint an interim mayor."

"If—"

"Also consider the fact that whoever is working for Enfield is still on the loose. We can put him in jail till Judgment Day, but his thugs will remain a threat to you and the Home Free program."

Miranda muttered a curse, then repeated it as she clenched her fists in front of her face. "Sounds like what you want is a signed, itemized receipt. 'Burned, one dormant lavender field. Poisoned, one hundred round bales of hay, estimated value, fifteen thousand dollars. Delivered to Arlen Enfield,

December thirteenth. Paid by check number six-six-six.'"

"Have you got one of those?" He thought he could make her chuckle, at least.

"I sure as hell don't." She exploded, instead. "I don't have a way to keep my job, I don't have a way to save this town, and I don't know why you bothered to come in the first place if this is all you can do."

"Wait a minute…"

"You haven't accomplished anything that Wade couldn't have done by himself. He asked you to help because he thought you'd get this mess taken care of. If we wanted to wait until January or—or, hell, July, if we wanted to be nibbled to death by pranks and vandalism, we wouldn't have asked for the big-city cop to step in and make us all look like fools."

Jud leaned back in his chair, stretched out his legs and crossed his arms over his chest. "Go on. Have your say."

"Things have deteriorated since you arrived. The violence has escalated. Did you notice that? My mother is now nervous about staying at her own house, on her own land, alone at night. I'm waiting for bomb threats to arrive at the mayor's office. Some technique you've got there, Officer."

"I guess you expected some kind of hero? The Lone Ranger, maybe, riding in to solve all your problems? I didn't make that kind of promise, Miranda. I said I'd do what I could."

"You told me to trust you! You said you'd save this town if it took a dozen miracles."

A man should never promise the impossible under the influence of a woman he loves. "I did what I could."

"You've made things worse, just like I knew you would. You're squiring your ex-girlfriends around town, beating up your brother—"

"He started it."

"Oh, yes, let's go back to grade school. All these years, you've made a fool out of Ethan. And your dad. Now, you're making a fool out of Wade, because he believed you could help. And you've made a grade-A, number one fool out of me. Tell me, did you plan this, back in high school? Did you decide that sometime, somewhere, you were going to figure out a way to get in my pants? Was I simply a challenge to you?"

"That's enough." Jud got to his feet. "If you think—"

She cut him off with a karate chop through the air. "Well, congratulations, Jud. You win. You convinced me I mattered. But your old life is waiting for you, so just say goodbye and get gone. Good riddance."

He stood for a minute, stone-cold with anger and a hurt he'd never imagined, not when his dad kicked him out, not when his mom turned away, not even when he watched his little sister's casket lowered into the ground. Turning on his heel, he strode quickly through the outer office to the courthouse door, and then jogged down the steps.

He'd parked his truck at the end of the block, next to Miranda's. The nearest streetlight was dark, which meant she'd be dragging that ladder out again, replacing the bulb in her never-ending effort to please everybody....

Blocking the thought, Jud rounded the bumper on the driver's side. As he pressed the remote key to unlock the door, he heard the scuff of footsteps on concrete. Before he could look around, somebody tackled him from the back. His face smashed into the asphalt and gravel pavement. A pair of hands on his neck held him down.

"Hit him," somebody said.

Jud got one second to think, *No*...

HE DIDN'T SLAM THE DOOR. She would have felt better if he had.

Slowly, her bones creaking, Miranda stood up from her chair. Nan would be waiting to serve dinner. They needed to talk about this recall business, figure out how to respond. Her mother was still her closest friend.

Her closest *human* friend. Miranda looked over to the corner where Lila's dog sat on her pillow, her tail thumping against the floor. If ever Miranda had needed something warm to hold onto, tonight was it.

She sat down on the floor beside the dog and placed a hand on the soft golden fur. "This is bad, Dusty girl. Really, really bad." Again, the thump of that tail.

"I was so completely out of control. I threw everything I could think of at him. Why? What the hell was I doing?"

Dusty inched her paws forward until her elbows and belly touched the floor. Miranda ran the fingernails on both hands gently up and down the dog's sides.

"He's going to leave me, Dusty. He's going

back to Austin, back to his job, back to the women he sees there. Back to baseball and basketball and dope dealers who shoot at him."

With a sigh, Dusty lowered her chin to rest on her front paws.

"Maybe I was trying to make it easy for him. Was that it?" Miranda laughed at herself. "Oh, sure, you're such a martyr. Make him hate you so he won't feel bad about leaving? Please!"

Closing her eyes, she scooted her hips away from the pillow until her head came to rest on Dusty's hip. As she allowed the full weight of her head to rest on the dog, Dusty thumped her tail twice, as if to say, "Okay."

"How does this sound? I wanted to hurt him before he hurt me. Self-defense is a legitimate excuse, right?"

In the quiet office, she seemed to hear a whisper.

"You don't think so, do you? You think I was just being a bitch? Thank you so much."

Smoothing Dusty's soft fur, she called up the memory of Jud as he'd stood before her. Stiff, unyielding, a little sulky, the way he'd often been all those years ago. Shoulders square, spine straight, as if bracing himself for a harsh wind. He'd withstood plenty of storms in his life, and had turned out to be a decent, honorable man. A man who could make love with tenderness and laughter. A man strong enough to defend himself against attack, physical or emotional.

Except with her. He had never offered her an excuse for any of his mistakes, never tried to evade responsibility. Over and over again, Jud had made himself completely vulnerable to her scorn, her insults, her disapproval.

He's what you want, whispered the voice. *He's what you love.*

"And I sent him away."

Before she got to her feet, Miranda spent an extra minute on her knees, praying she'd get the chance to apologize, to make amends. What mattered in life were the people she loved, the people who loved her. The job, the land giveaway, even the town, would go on without her. Other people would come up with other plans. If they didn't, that might mean that no one in Homestead cared enough to save their town. In that case, they deserved to see it die.

She was careful to lock the office and the

courthouse doors, even though she knew now that Arlen could enter at will. Next week, she would try to get a locksmith to change the keys. This weekend, she had more important issues on her mind.

Coming down the courthouse steps, she noticed the streetlight on the corner had gone out. She'd replaced all these bulbs the day she'd put up decorations—how could the light blow so quickly?

Another ladder excursion lay ahead—one more mayoral perk. But not until Monday. She didn't intend to come into town again until the Historical Society party. Miranda sent a quick prayer heavenward. *Please let Jud forgive me and come along. Please.*

As she unlocked the doors of her truck, her attention caught on a flash of silver under the left front wheel. Once again down on her knees, she fished for the object and dragged it into view.

A flashlight, one of the heavy-duty models, with a ribbed aluminum casing. She flicked the switch, but the light didn't work. Jud carried a full toolbox in the back of his truck. Had he pulled out the flashlight for some reason, then left it behind?

Shrugging, she tossed the heavy torch into the backseat of her truck. Dusty jumped into the front passenger seat and Miranda climbed in after her.

She would call Jud when she got home. The flashlight gave her a good excuse. Somehow, she'd convince him to talk, and they'd make peace. Maybe they would never be lovers again—she'd accept that outcome, though her heart ached at the prospect.

But at least they could be friends.

CHAPTER FOURTEEN

JUD WOKE UP the first time in the backseat of his own truck. His hands and ankles had been duct-taped together, but his attackers hadn't taped his mouth. The credit he gave them for that small mercy was canceled by the penalty he assigned for the loud, lousy rap music on the radio. Every bone in his head throbbed separately with the bass vibes coming through the floor, and with every bump in the road. He threw up the food he'd eaten during the day, then passed out again.

The next time, consciousness crept over him like a mouse. He sat on the floor, in a corner, in frigid, pitch-black darkness. Hands and feet still bound, he rested with his cheek against a wall and spit running down his chin. He'd never before realized what a luxury the ability to wipe his face could be.

Somewhere outside of wherever he was,

the same rap music fouled the air. He could hear the truck engine running, so whoever had brought him hadn't abandoned him. Though his head still hurt, he could think around the pain. Until he knew more about his surroundings, though, he didn't have much to think about.

His mind shied away from all references to Miranda. The anguish in that direction would incapacitate him. He'd save Miranda for the next hospital visit, when the nurses would monitor his heartbeat and make sure he stayed alive.

His captors joined him after a while, smelling of cigarette smoke and whiskey, making use of every foul word they knew as often as possible and sounding like the hicks they probably were.

"Sure wish we hadn't lost the damn flashlight."

"Not we, you. You're the one who dropped it."

The voices were similar in quality, and familiar. He'd heard them before, recently. He knew these guys. If he could remember…

"Think he's awake?"

"Kick him and find out."

Jud refused to respond. So they kicked him in the groin.

"I thought he was waking up."

One of them squatted down beside him and turned his head with a steel-claw grip. Jud kept his eyes closed.

"We're gonna kill you." The breath in his face was strong enough to use for anesthetic. "Just so you know. First, though, we're gonna have a good ol' time. Soon as daylight comes."

Great, he thought. *A deadline.* The pun made him want to laugh.

MIRANDA READ NAN'S NOTE and immediately went upstairs. Her mother was sound asleep...or pretending to be.

In her own room, she picked up the phone and dialed Cruz's number.

"Hello? Nan?" He sounded...cautious.

"No, Cruz. It's me."

"Hey, Miranda." A different tone of voice entirely. "What's going on?"

"Besides the end of the world? Listen, can I talk to Jud a minute?"

"He's not here."

She sat down on the bed. "Not there. Are

you sure? He left the courthouse a good long time ago."

"Haven't seen him. His truck's not parked out front."

There wasn't much she could do to change reality. "If he comes in, ask him to call me, please."

"Sure. Uh…is Nan okay?"

"She's asleep." When he didn't say anything, Miranda put the pieces together for herself. "What's going on? What did you do?"

"I told her I'd be leaving, come January."

She guessed the rest. "You bastard."

"Don't give me that. You know—"

Miranda hung up before he could finish.

DAWN BROUGHT recognition of who held him.

"The Enfield boys," Jud said, with as much contempt as he could manage. "I should've guessed."

The one standing by the door grinned. "Yeah, you shoulda."

The one standing close to him, flipping a knife from hand to hand, wasn't in such a good mood. "You caused a heap of trouble, son. You're gonna have to pay."

Jud rolled his eyes. "Oh, come on. Can we

step out of the B-class blood-and-guts movie? What's this about, anyway? Your daddy?"

"Like I said, you caused trouble."

"Killing me won't change much. The sheriff knows everything I do. And you two will rot in jail." He surveyed them through half-shut eyelids. "I think you'll go over big with the guys in the pen."

"Oops." The knife flipped, but wasn't caught, and landed point down in Jud's thigh. "Sorry 'bout that." Enfield leaned close and pulled the blade free, which hurt more than when it went in.

When they tired of tormenting him, they went out for breakfast. Jud decided he could hope for rescue, or he could goad them into killing him quick. He wasn't sure which choice to make.

Miranda watched the clock until noon, then called Cruz again. "Didn't you tell him to call me?"

"I would have," he said, his irritation as blatant as hers. "But he didn't come home. Didn't call, didn't write. I haven't seen or heard from Jud Ritter. Got it?" The line went dead.

She'd never seen Cruz lose his temper. Another time, she might have cared.

Grabbing up a jacket and her keys, she went to find Nan in the barn. "I'm going to town to look for Jud." She'd filled her mother in this morning on the gist of last night's argument. But not even to her mom could she reveal how badly she'd behaved.

"What about the Christmas party?"

"I don't think I'll make it."

"But—" Nan shook her head. "No, I guess you won't. Good luck."

"Thanks." She kissed the smooth cheek offered to her, then jogged to her truck. "Yes, come on," she told Dusty, as the dog hesitated. "You'll help me find him…I hope," she muttered under her breath.

The speed limit signs she passed on the road might not have existed for all the attention she paid. Only when the Rise and Shine Motel came into sight did Miranda slow down.

Trip Dooley told her the room number without protest, and then she was standing at Della's pink door. This could be the biggest mistake she'd ever made in her entire life.

Sam Teague answered her knock. "Hey," he said.

"Hey," she returned. "Is your mom around?"

"In the shower."

How did she ask a teenager if his mom was in the shower *alone?*

She looked at Della's son, really looked at him for the first time. The lanky black hair had lighter roots, the skin was fair and freckled. His green eyes looked familiar. Who did she know with green eyes?

The answer blew her away.

"Uh, Sam? Have you seen Jud Ritter recently? Last night, or this morning?"

He shook his head. "Not for a couple of days. He took my mom to breakfast, and they brought some back for me. He hasn't been back since. I've been here the whole time."

She put a hand on his arm for a second. "Thanks. Tell your mom I said hello."

On the way into downtown she called Wade at home. "Do you know where Jud is?" She could hear the sound of kids playing in the background.

"Haven't seen him since yesterday. What's wrong?"

What was right? "Nothing new. If you see him, ask him to please call me."

"Sure."

She parked in the same space she'd used last night, and walked the entire square, stopping in any business she could tenuously connect with Jud. Including Arlen's.

The man himself sat at his desk. "Can I help you?" The look in his green eyes chilled her like a winter sea.

"Have you seen Jud Ritter today?" Not that he would tell the truth if he had a chance to lie.

"No."

"Last night?"

"No."

"Thanks." Miranda turned on her heel and walked out.

No one in town had seen him, and she returned to her truck with equal parts dread and despair churning in her stomach. Had Jud returned to Austin without his clothes, or a goodbye to anyone? Had he driven into a ditch on some isolated backwoods road? Was he drunk, or dead?

As she unlocked the truck door, the flashlight she'd found last night caught her eye. She picked it up for closer examination, turning it between her hands. What she saw in the afternoon sunlight, what she hadn't seen in the dark, was the band of blue electrical tape around the neck of the torch, just below the bulb....

And the dried blood in the crevices of the bulb cover and the head of the flashlight. Dried blood and dark brown hair.

HOMESTEAD'S HISTORICAL Society held its annual holiday party in the public library, housed in an 1890s Victorian house on a street right behind the courthouse square. Most folks in town had been attending these parties all their lives and kept up the tradition with their own kids—donning red or green church clothes in the middle of a Saturday afternoon to drink cranberry ginger ale punch and eat sugar cookies and Texas pecan kisses. Miss Helena Stein, the only piano teacher in town, played carols as mood music.

Flashlight in hand, Miranda stalked into the gathering at about three o'clock, wearing jeans, boots and a barn coat. She bypassed the receiving line and went straight to the refreshment table, set up in the nonfiction section. The men always congregated near the cookies.

She hesitated for a moment when she saw

the sheriff talking with Ethan, then went up to him and grabbed his coat sleeve.

"I've got to talk to you. I think something's happened to Jud."

Wade's brows lifted when she showed him the flashlight, the blood, the hair. "Where'd you get this?"

"I found it in a parking space at the courthouse."

Ethan snorted his disbelief. "What makes you think this has anything to do with Jud?" Still bruised around the eyes and with a cut on his lip scabbed over, he didn't look quite as smooth and controlled as usual.

"He's gone. Nobody's seen or heard from him since last night."

"Maybe he went back to Austin." Ethan shrugged. "He does have a history of taking off without warning."

A crowd was gathering around them. Kayla heard her husband's comment and came to stand beside him. "Don't be mean, Ethan. Miranda, have you tried calling his cell phone?"

She nodded. "No answer. He didn't come back to Cruz's cabin last night, and all his clothes are still there."

"He might have made a trip to Austin," Wade suggested.

"Or New York, Rome, Singapore...who knows where my wild card brother would take it in his head to go?"

Nan had come to stand behind Miranda. "I think he would have come by to say thank you," she said quietly. "And given some of the things going on here lately..."

"We need to get search parties going." Wade glanced around the room. "If folks pair up—"

"What's all the commotion about?" Arlen Enfield strolled across the foyer to join them, with Clarice following a couple of steps behind. "This looks more like a posse than a party."

No one wanted to explain what was going on. While they hesitated, Clarice eased through the crowd. "Are y'all playing spin the bottle over here?" Her gaze fell on the flashlight, and her eyes widened. "How in the world did that get here?"

Wade flashed Miranda a warning glance. "You recognize this flashlight, Mrs. Enfield?"

"Of course. It belongs to Allen. Remember Arlen, we marked one of them with red tape for Abel, and one with blue for Allen."

She looked from Wade to Miranda and back. "What's wrong?"

The tilt of Wade's head gave Miranda permission to speak. "Clarice, where are your boys this afternoon?"

Arlen stirred. "I fail to see what that has to do with anything."

Clarice looked at her husband, then Miranda. "They...they said something about going hunting."

"Do you know where they might choose to hunt?"

"Clint Gallagher's place," Arlen said quickly. "I asked him about it last week."

"I don't think so." His wife twisted her hands together, thinking hard. "Abel said something about their hideout. I—I think they spend a lot of time somewhere out on K Bar C land. I'm afraid I didn't pay close attention. They're always running off—"

"That's enough, Clarice." Arlen turned to Wade. "I can't believe you would even consider the possibility that my sons are connected in any way with the hypothetical disappearance of Jud Ritter. For my part, I think the man has deserted the town again, just like he did fifteen years ago."

Though he'd said the same thing himself, not ten minutes past, Ethan would not let that insult stand. "Fifteen years ago, Jud was a kid with reasons to be angry and a strong drive for survival. Now he's an honorable man who would not abandon his responsibilities." He looked at Wade. "I'm going with Miranda."

"Right." Wade divided the willing volunteers—most of the men in the room—into pairs with assigned territories. As the searchers began to leave, the sheriff saw Nan. "Where's Cruz? We could use his help."

"He stayed to keep an eye on the farm." She exchanged glances with her daughter. "I'll call him, and we'll start looking at the back border of our place on horseback."

"Good."

Ethan handed the truck keys to Kayla, then pulled her into his arms. "I'll be home as soon as I can get there." He kissed her hair, her forehead, her lips. "Be careful driving home."

"You be careful," she said fiercely. "Supper will be waiting."

After a hug for each of the kids, he and Miranda headed for the library door, where Frances Haase caught his arm. "I always had a soft spot in my heart for that boy," she said quietly. "I'll be praying for all of you."

"Thanks."

In Miranda's truck, Dusty surrendered the passenger seat to Ethan as they headed out of town.

Miranda turned on the windshield wipers against the mist. "I'm sure this isn't the way the Historical Society ladies expected their party to end."

"They'll have something to talk about for decades," Ethan said, staring out the side window. "Remember the year all our guests left to search for bandits out in the hills?"

She laughed at his mimicry. "Stories do change, don't they?"

"Always." Ethan blew out a deep breath. "Especially Jud's. He deserves for people to know he's not the father of Della's son."

"We'll work that out," she promised. "Right now, we just have to find him. Got any ideas?"

"I do, as a matter of fact. Remember that abandoned oil well at the back end of the ranch?"

"Tell me which way to go."

"Be sure you've got your seat belt on. It's a bumpy ride."

Nan reached home in record time, parked with a screech of her truck's brakes, then changed into jeans and boots faster than she'd ever done in her life. By the time she got to the barn, Cruz had Bailey ready to go and was just about finished saddling his own horse, a showy pinto gelding named Pancho.

Bailey sensed tension in the air. He danced around as she mounted until she felt like a trick rider, balancing with one foot in the stirrup, one leg in the air.

"Rodeo auditions are next weekend," Cruz said, as she settled on the saddle.

She couldn't stifle her smile. "A little practice never hurts. Ready?"

"Let's shake the fidgets out of these guys for a start."

The first time they'd ever "gone out" together had been a long ride through a gorgeous autumn afternoon. Before dark, Nan had fallen deeply, irrevocably in love with the quiet, intelligent man who'd hired on as her foreman.

Despite today's dire situation, she couldn't help remembering those moments as she and Cruz rode toward Pecan Creek and the boundary line between Hayseed Farm and the K Bar C Ranch.

When they got to the creek, her stallion balked at stepping into the cold water. Finally, Cruz grabbed the cheek strap of Bailey's bridle. Pancho, the rock-steady gelding, pulled the bigger horse across the stream and up the steep bank onto pastureland again.

"Silly boy." Nan stroked her hand along Bailey's quivering neck. "I guess we need to do some water work with you."

"You know this place better than I do. Which way do we go?" Standing in his stirrups, Cruz scanned the horizon. "There's not much here besides grass, and more grass."

"Let's cut the pasture into thirds—you ride along one line, I'll take the other and we'll scan for anything unusual till we meet up at the far corner."

Cruz nodded. "Good plan."

The misty rain diminished visibility, but Nan thought she would have seen something moving in the high grass, or under the trees bordering the field.

"We started at the point of a diagonal," she told Cruz when they reconnected, with no results. "The K Bar C land widens, then narrows again. It's a lot of ground to cover."

"We're heading along the western side, right?"

She opened her mouth to agree and, with a frightening feeling of déjà vu, heard the crack of a gunshot in the distance. Then another, and then two more. Underneath her, Bailey's muscles clenched. Nan crouched over his neck, trying to be ready.

Cruz was faster than both of them. At his urging, Pancho shouldered into the stallion's chest. Cruz grabbed Bailey's reins just behind the bit, holding tight. Wide-eyed, sweating, Bailey attempted to rise but the three of them—Nan, Cruz and Pancho—kept those huge front hooves on the ground.

"Thanks," Nan said, breathless.

"You're welcome." Cruz glanced away. "Where did that shot come from?"

"The left?"

He nodded. "Let's get over there."

ETHAN SAID, "Stop here."

Miranda followed instructions, though all she could see was rolling grassland. "Where are we?"

"The well sits on the other side of that big rise," Ethan said. "If we go over in the truck, the engine noise will carry. We might want surprise on our side."

With the door open, Miranda jumped down into the knee-high grass, then let Dusty out of the backseat. "Guns under here," she told Ethan, lifting the seat cushion to reveal a shotgun, two rifles, and several hand weapons, plus the necessary ammunition.

"This one's mine." She picked up the Remington and a box of shells. "Feel free to bring along whatever suits you."

Ethan nodded. "A nice selection. I didn't know our peaceful mayor was such a gun-totin' mama!"

Miranda grinned. "I have my secrets. And my permits."

The hill in front of them was steeper than it looked, and the three of them were panting hard by the time they reached the top. Just over the rim, a convenient clump of stunted cedar trees provided cover from which to observe the rusted oil "grasshopper" pump and the dilapidated trailers nearby.

"That's Jud's truck," Miranda said quietly.

"Parked on the left. The red one belongs to the Enfield boys."

Ethan nodded. "Nobody's moving around. Let's get closer."

They moved by stages until they crouched behind a boulder only a hundred yards or so from Jud's tailgate. Just as Miranda ducked down, a door on the farthest trailer slammed open. One of Enfield's sons stepped out and paced across the ground, holding a cell phone to his ear.

"I know, Daddy." His voice carried easily in the still air. "You don't have to worry, we already took care of the problem. That's right, we killed him last night, soon as we got here. Just like you told us to."

Miranda crammed her hand into her mouth to keep from crying out. Ethan pressed his forehead against the cold rock that sheltered them.

Dusty started to whine.

"Shh." Miranda patted the dog's head and briefly, gently closed the circle of her fingers around Dusty's mouth. "Hush."

"We'll clear out right now," the twin told his dad. "We already drove his truck into thick woods down in Real County. Nobody's gonna find it. Or him."

He listened for a minute. "Right. We been hangin' out huntin', drinkin', sleepin'. No problem." He snapped the phone closed. "Abel! Abel, get out here!"

The other twin emerged from the same trailer. Even at that distance, the knife in his hand was easy to see.

"Daddy's gone crazy. The sheriff's on his way, looking for Ritter. We gotta get him gone. Now."

"We ain't finished yet," Abel whined.

Ethan grabbed Miranda's wrist, gave her a glance both fierce and hopeful. Dusty whined again.

"We'll finish someplace else. Tape him up good."

Swearing, Abel went back into the trailer. Allen, the one with the phone, got into Jud's truck and moved it closer to the trailer door, then followed his brother inside.

"If they take off, we won't be able to follow," Miranda whispered.

Ethan nodded. "How good a shot are you with that thing?"

"What do you want to hit?"

"The tires."

Miranda grinned. "I'm good enough for that."

AWARENESS RETURNED with the Enfield twins screaming at each other, their nasal twangs bouncing off the metal shell of the trailer.

"What are we gonna do? How are we gettin' out of this?" Abel was the one prone to hysteria. Jud had learned to tell them apart by the freckles on their faces.

Allen put his hands over his ears. "Stop yellin' and let me think."

"They're out there, man, and they got guns. We step outside this door and we're dead."

Jud nearly smiled, despite the pain. Maybe the posse was on its way. Or the Lone Ranger.

"Could we go out the back? Make a run for it in the woods?" Allen went to the high, narrow window openings. "We could get through these holes, I know we could."

"Yeah, right. We leave a dead body in here waiting for them to find, tracks all through the woods, you think they won't find us? Besides, that would leave Daddy taking the blame."

Abel's eyes widened. "We can't do that."

"No, we can't. So…" He turned to Jud. "We're goin' to use the leverage we got on hand. Get him on his feet."

"I get it. A hostage." Abel hooked his hands under Jud's arms and dragged him upright. Jud made himself dead weight, but what Abel lacked in brains he made up with muscle.

"What they don't know out there is that I've got a gun, too." He pulled the weapon out of the waistband of his jeans. "So we'll just give 'em a choice. They can let us go, or they can bury this pig."

Abel hesitated. "But we're supposed to kill him, anyway."

"And we will. We will. Later."

"What about his truck? You told Daddy we'd get rid of it."

"If we get away, Daddy can deny knowing anything about this mess, and they'll believe him. The truck won't matter. Now," Allen said, drawing a deep breath, "let's go."

Abel went first, stepping out backward, pulling Jud after. Then Allen hopped to the ground, walked up to Jud and jammed the muzzle of the gun between his eyes.

"Your friend ain't dead," he yelled. "Yet. You let us drive out of here, you can have him back. We'll drop him off on the side of the road."

Though his vision was blurred, Jud noticed a pair of horses off to his right about a hundred yards. He could hear engines, and sirens getting closer. None of them seemed likely to reach him in time. If he struggled, the Enfields would probably shoot him and take their chances. Death looked like a sure bet no matter what.

Too bad, because he'd really wanted to settle things with Ethan, first. And he'd have liked to kiss Miranda one more time.

If wishes were horses…

He heard a dog's agitated barking before he saw Dusty streak through the high grass.

Allen turned in that direction. "What the hell…?" The gun moved with him.

Jud grunted, drew his knees up and kicked out as fast as he could, connecting solidly with the back of Allen's knees. The gun went flying. Both Enfields hit the dirt, with Jud underneath them.

Dusty darted in to take a bite of an exposed arm or leg, then retreated, barking and snarling. Allen yelled, "Get the gun. Get the gun. Get the gun!"

Abel threw himself on the weapon and rolled to sit up, shifting his hands for the proper grip.

But he had run out of time. Martinez cornered Allen, who refused to go down easy until Cruz proceeded to kick him around the yard. Miranda ran toward Jud, coming from out of nowhere, he thought. Then Dusty got in her way and sent her tripping to her knees.

So Ethan was the one who reached Jud first, the one who slipped an arm under his shoulders and braced him to sit, then stand.

"Come on," he said, breathing hard. "Let's get out of the action."

Jud did his best to limp along, to take some of his own weight, though without much success. Now that the worst was over, a black curtain seem to be falling across his vision.

Above all the noise, he heard Miranda yell, "No!"

The handgun fired.

Beside him, Ethan sagged to the ground.

CHAPTER FIFTEEN

JUD PLAYED THE ROLE of cooperative patient for a full twelve hours before he started breaking the rules.

First, he persuaded an orderly to bring him a set of scrubs and shoe covers to wear on his bare feet. Then he left his hospital room on the regular ward and walked down two flights of stairs to the surgical intensive care unit.

Ethan's room was dark, except for a small fluorescent light by the bed. Jud closed the door without making a sound, only to jump like a bullfrog when his brother spoke.

"You make a lousy Lone Ranger."

Breathing fast, he turned into the room. "I was Tonto, you jerk, tricking the bandits into betraying themselves. You were supposed to be the Ranger, coming to my rescue."

"I guess somebody mixed up the cue cards."

"Yeah, but we caught the bad guys. Two of them, anyway." He eased into the chair by the bed. "The noose is cinching around Arlen's neck, and he knows it."

"Drinks all around." They toasted with imaginary shot glasses, then sat for a couple of minutes in silence.

"I appreciate what you did," Jud said. "You risked your life for me—that means a lot."

Ethan waved his gratitude away. "Kayla's seriously pissed, though. I'd stay out of range for a while if I were you."

"You think Austin's far enough?"

"If you leave quietly."

"Right."

The next silence lasted so long, Jud thought his brother had fallen asleep. He edged forward, intending to leave.

"Something weird happened," Ethan said. "I'm supposed to tell you about it."

Jud sat back. "What kind of weird?"

"In the helicopter, I could tell things weren't going too well. Losing blood and all that. By the time we landed, I was watching the whole scene from *outside*. You understand what I mean?"

"Yeah, I do." He stared at his clasped hands for a moment. "You were watching the doctors and nurses working on you, right?"

"Exactly."

"You heard what they said to each other, saw them wheel you down the hall."

"Yeah. They didn't sound too optimistic."

"A spleen is a terrible thing to lose. I know—I lost mine a couple of years ago."

"Gunshot?"

"Car accident."

"You always did drive too fast."

"Not my fault this time. A suspect rammed me with his SUV."

"I never heard about that."

"You were going through your own stuff at home."

His brother's silence demanded an explanation.

"Ethan, I was...in the hospital when Dad...died." Would he ever be able to say *suicide?* "I didn't know anything until I got home about two weeks afterward. By then, I figured it was too late."

"Ah." After a minute spent filing that information away, Ethan stirred on the bed.

"Anyway, I'm standing in the operating room, watching them stitch me back together and—"

"Let me guess. Dad stepped up beside you?"

His brother did a double take. "You believe that?"

Jud nodded. "He came to see me a couple of months ago, when I got shot."

"What'd he say?"

"Nothing. We stood around for awhile, made sure everything would be okay." Jud took a deep breath. "But I knew, without a doubt, what I was supposed to do."

"Which was?"

"Go home…to Homestead. Sort out the mess I'd left there. Make a fresh start. Especially with you."

Ethan nodded. "I got pretty much the same message. 'Stop being such a pain in the ass,' basically."

Jud laughed, even though laughing still hurt. "I second that motion."

"He looked good, didn't he?"

"Better than I remember seeing him since…I don't know. Since before the ranch fiasco, at least."

"Yeah. I like knowing he's waiting for me."

"*They're* waiting. He and Mom and Angela. They'll be glad to see us." Jud closed his hand over his brother's. "But not yet, thank God."

Smiling, Ethan closed his eyes. "Not yet."

JUD VIOLATED another hospital rule when he checked out early Sunday morning, against medical advice. He couldn't lie in that bed any longer with his brain running like a hamster on a wheel. A thousand details had to be pulled together before the town meeting tomorrow night. Those details were his responsibility.

Since his truck was still out of action with three flat tires, he called Ryan Gallagher and asked for the loan of a Four Aces Ranch vehicle. Ryan sent a ranch hand to the hospital to pick Jud up, and Jud drove the man home. A little while later, he knocked on the door of Frances Haase's small bungalow.

"Jud Ritter!" She looked past him to the vehicle, then into his face. "I saw that truck in my drive and couldn't imagine who would want to visit me on a Sunday morning. Come in."

"Thank you." He followed her inside, keeping one hand behind his back.

He'd never visited Miss Haase's house before but, just as he'd expected, neat and clean didn't begin to describe it.

"You look terrible," she told him. "Sit down in that soft chair right there and let me brew you some tea."

Jud put out his free hand. "I appreciate the thought, but I can only stay a minute." Then he brought the item he carried out from behind his back. "You asked for this."

Gently, she took the ancient copy of *Lady Chatterley's Lover* from him and opened the back cover. There was the library card she'd stamped all those years ago. "Due September 10," she read aloud. "Nineteen eighty-five." Her gaze, a little misty, met his. "You've kept this book since then?"

He shook his head. "I can't lie. Miranda stole the book from me and didn't give it back. I found it on her shelf."

Frances tilted her head. "Did you ever actually read the story?"

"Uh...no, ma'am."

She nodded. "That's what I thought." Then she smiled. "I wonder if Miranda did."

Walking him to the door, she said, "Shouldn't you still be in the hospital?"

"I'm okay. I have things to do before the meeting tomorrow."

"And then what?"

He shrugged one shoulder. "I go back to work. In Austin."

"You're saying goodbye, then?"

He knew she referred to Miranda. "I have to…think."

"Ah." She nodded once. "Then you should definitely go. Back to Austin."

Jud stepped outside and she shut the screen door between them. "Thomas Wolfe was wrong, you know."

He frowned, trying to remember the reference.

Miss Haase waited until he looked at her for help.

"You *can* go home again," she said. "Merry Christmas, Jud."

A TOWN MEETING held the Monday before Christmas would not ordinarily get much of a crowd. But as Miranda looked over the courtroom from the floor in front of the judge's bench, she thought almost every resident of Homestead who was eligible to vote had turned out for this particular meeting.

Arlen Enfield had marshaled his supporters and seated them in the front pews on the left side of the room. Solid men, they were, dependable, fairly easy to get along with most of the time. Now they glared at her as if they wanted to try her for witchcraft. Maybe they did.

Clarice Enfield, however, was notably absent. When informed that her sons had been arrested for kidnapping and attempted murder, including the shot at Nan and Cruz, Clarice had collapsed. She remained in the hospital today, under treatment for an unspecified condition. Miranda thought Arlen had probably ordered his wife to stay out of sight.

Nan sat on the right side of the courtroom with their friends from the Home Free program—Noah and Greer, the Hubbells and the Garners and Elle from the clothing shop. Kayla and Callie sat together—Ethan hadn't yet been released from the hospital and Wade was acting as sergeant at arms. Miranda stopped in shock when she saw Kristin and

Ryan Gallagher seated with the senator and his wife. She'd never dreamed Clint Gallagher would offer his support.

Of Jud, she'd had no word. He'd checked out of the hospital yesterday before she'd arrived to visit him. Though his clothes remained in the closet at the cabin, the man himself was, again, nowhere to be found. She reassured herself with the knowledge that Arlen had been under twenty-four-hour surveillance since Sunday, so the chances of another kidnapping were slim.

As she rose to begin the meeting, Della Teague and her son entered the courtroom. Della took a seat on the second pew, but Sam sat in the rear of the room, on the far end of the bench, almost completely hidden by a column supporting the balcony. Then Wade took up his post in front of the door. He nodded, and gave her an encouraging wink. *Showtime.*

Miranda cleared her throat, and the conversation in the room died immediately. "As mayor of Homestead, I call this town meeting to order. Since this meeting has been requested by Arlen Enfield for a specific purpose, I will give him the floor to proceed with his agenda." She took her seat on the front row bench.

Arlen didn't bother with the false courtesy of acknowledging her introduction. He gazed across the audience, with his hand placed over his heart, making eye contact with as many as possible.

"Ladies and gentlemen," he began in a husky voice. "Despite the tragedy which has befallen my beloved family these last few days, I am here tonight because I have a sincere and abiding love for my hometown of Homestead, Texas, and for the people who live here. I truly believe, deep in my heart, that our town has fallen prey to a most dangerous swindler. Therefore, I have come to propose a recall vote for the position of Homestead's mayor.

"I have talked to most of you in recent days, and I believe there is a consensus that the present occupant of this office, Ms. Miranda Wright, has demonstrated such incompetence and dereliction of duty as to render her unfit to serve the people of this fine town as dogcatcher, let alone mayor!"

Miranda shifted in her seat. She'd expected the insults, but that didn't lessen the sting.

"As evidence of Ms. Wright's malfeasance, I offer the sheriff's accounts of the violence our community has endured since the mayor's misbegotten Home Free program went into effect." He slapped a thick folder down on the prosecutor's table. "Copies of these reports will be available for every citizen to peruse at their leisure."

Somehow, Arlen Enfield was making this charade work, despite the fact that everyone present knew about Allen's and Abel's arrests. But the boys weren't talking, and Arlen insisted he knew nothing of their intentions for Jud or their reasons for the crime. He had his audience mesmerized. Folks on both sides of the aisle were nodding their heads.

Polishing his glasses with a white handkerchief, Arlen surveyed the crowd with a pained, yet fatherly, smile. "I know many of you feel you have benefited from the Home Free program. I submit, however, that a more traditional approach to development would have produced far greater profit. The land currently being given away might have been sold at substantial prices. Instead of sparse settlement, Loveless County could have experienced intense growth, including the arrival of retail and manufacturing concerns. Homestead has lost thousands of dollars—tens of thousands—by instituting Ms. Wright's nonsensical plan." He paused for effect, or maybe to take a breath.

Della Bowie Teague stood up and faced the audience. "Are you really going to let this old geezer lie his way back into the mayor's office?"

A collective gasp swept across the room.

"I mean, he was pulling dirty deals back when I still lived here. He owned the house my family lived in, and he raised the rent every six months, even though the contract said no more than once a year. If my daddy tried to refuse, ol' Arlen here started talking about eviction. And he threatened to take us to court if we didn't pay." She shook her head. "Sam Bowie was too proud a man to let his family get thrown out in the street, so he let this snake have his way."

"Outrageous. Simply outrageous." Arlen stood with his fists clenched at his sides. "That woman has no business at this meeting, and certainly no right to speak.

Sheriff, I suggest you escort her out of the building right now."

Wade shook his head. "I don't think so."

While Arlen searched for a response, Della continued. "For years, he's been looking for a way to sell you people out. Hank Darrow—that's right, the guy downstairs in jail—told me how good ol' Mayor Arlen brought Hank's dad to town and showed him the K Bar C land, wined and dined him in Austin, promised he'd get the property for pennies on the dollar." She looked around the room, her chin lifted, inviting a challenge. "That was back just before old Clyde passed. I dated Hank while he was here with his dad. And I've seen him since I came back. He told me, two days ago, that Arlen Enfield had paid him twenty thousand dollars to make trouble for the Home Free program."

Arlen's friends in the front rows frowned at each other. Almost to a man, they crossed their arms over their chests, waiting for Enfield's reaction.

"Lies, all lies." Arlen blotted his forehead and mustache with his handkerchief. "Is there any reason we should believe a woman who left town under such…such *tawdry* circumstances?"

The reaction to this question contained a strong female current.

Della lifted her chin. "Good word, Mr. Ex-Mayor. You think I don't know what it means? Tawdry, as in tarnished, cheap, no good? Maybe that's what these people believe I am. I liked the boys when I was young. Still do," she said with a grin and a flirtatious glance that got some laughs. "But I never asked for money, never expected presents or anything else, except a little love. Until a man came after me, taking me to fancy restaurants, buying me jewelry, letting me drive his big car. I refused him. I thought he was…*old*.

"But this man had me anyway. You know how?"

"Sheriff, this is completely beside the point." Enfield's voice cracked, and the smooth coating fell away, leaving a high, shrill tone. "I must insist—"

"He threatened my family," Della said. "He said he would throw them out into the street if I didn't sleep with him. He would get my daddy fired from his job, ruin my mother's reputation around town. Unless I gave him sex."

She shrugged. "So I did what he asked. And when I got pregnant with his baby, I did what he told me to—I moved away, took my family with me. We had a pretty easy time, up in Lampasas, with the checks he…" Della paused dramatically. "With the checks Arlen Enfield sent me each month."

She paused, but no one spoke, no one moved. "I might not be a college graduate, but I'm a pretty smart girl. I decided early on that I should have some insurance. And so when those checks came, to my little box in Lampasas, I opened the envelope right away. And before I left that post office, I stopped by the copy machine and I copied those checks, front and back. Fifteen years' worth of checks." She picked up an envelope from the pew beside her and held it above her head. "Right here."

Pandemonium broke loose. Arlen made a dash for the judge's chambers behind him, but Rudy Satterwhite and Myron Guthrie cornered him and brought him back to the courtroom.

Miranda stayed in her seat, accepting hugs

and congratulations, fighting back tears. Finally, finally, an end to the threats.

Just to be safe, she wanted to formally close the meeting. She couldn't possibly make her voice heard over the crowd, so she climbed up behind the judge's bench and made use of the antique gavel.

"Order, order," she called. "Order in the court."

With laughter, the town complied. "At this time, I'd like to ask if anyone else wants to address this meeting concerning a mayoral recall election."

Max Beltrane raised his hand. Heart sinking, Miranda nodded. "Go ahead, Mr. Beltrane." Frances Haase, taking notes, shook her head.

"Ms. Mayor, citizens of Homestead. I would like to propose...I would like to propose that the petition for a recall vote be invalidated and the motion to hold the election be denied."

A chorus of "second" rang from every bench in the room.

"A-All those in favor?" Miranda asked.

The "ayes" rattled the windows.

"All opposed?"

Nary a one.

Miranda was crying as she picked up the gavel again. "I declare this meeting—"

"One more thing."

Jud was standing there in the center aisle, grinning. He exhibited a stack of papers wrapped in a blue legal folder. "This is an arrest warrant and an indictment of Arlen Enfield for too many crimes to be listed. He'll be taking up residence in the Loveless County jail, Sheriff."

Wade shook his head. "I'm running out of jail cells for all these prisoners. I might just have to let a couple of them go. Come on, boys." He motioned to Satterwhite and Guthrie. "Let's get this garbage downstairs."

After that, Miranda couldn't have said anything else if she'd tried.

THE DAYS BEFORE Christmas Eve raced by, crammed with all the holiday preparations Nan had so far ignored. Miranda spent a couple of hours in town each morning, but they filled most of their hours baking cookies, pies, cakes and sweet rolls they would give as gifts. They took a day trip to Fredericksburg to buy toys for the children on their list—

Ethan's three, Greer's daughter and Kristin's son, plus Callie Montgomery's sisters and brother. They found a nice tree to cut from the small patch of firs they'd once planted with fond hopes of developing a Christmas tree business before the drought moved in. Decorations appeared as if by magic—bows and stars, candles and twinkling lights.

What Nan and her daughter didn't do was talk about the men in their lives. Work got done around the barn and the fields, but Cruz kept to himself. Jud had surrendered to familial pressure and moved into Ethan's guest room for a few days before his return to Austin. He sent a huge basket of fruit, wine, pasta and chocolate, with a beautifully written thank-you note. And that seemed to be that.

Christmas Eve dawned warmer than the days before, almost springlike, between the sunshine and soft breeze. The church held a potluck dinner before the Christmas Eve service, so Nan made up deviled eggs and potato salad in honor of the weather.

Darkness came early—it was, after all, still winter. When they arrived in town for the dinner, Homestead looked its very best.

"We need a photographer," Nan declared,

"to take a picture and make a postcard. Wouldn't this be a terrific scene to say 'Merry Christmas'?"

Miranda gave her the sad smile she had come to expect. "We can talk to Millie about that. She'd probably do a good job. And then find a company to print them up in sets. Callie could sell them in the café. If we ever get a bookstore, that would be another good outlet."

"Don't you have somebody in that stack of applications who wants to sell books?"

Staring out the window, Miranda shook her head. "The stack has dwindled considerably." She sighed. "But we'll do some publicity, after the new year, and make people aware that this is a terrific place to live. We could use the photograph in a brochure for that, too."

The St. Mark's parking lot overflowed with trucks, vans and cars, so they parked in Miranda's usual spot by the courthouse and walked around the block to the church. The gymnasium, which doubled as their fellowship hall, was crowded with children fueled by excitement and sugar, adults all talking at once, and the heavenly aroma of home-cooked food. Shortly after the Wright women arrived, Noah Kelley tapped on the microphone.

"Let's have a moment of prayer," he said.

Simple but profound, his prayer gave thanks for the season, and especially for the birth they celebrated. He went on to express gratitude for the town leadership, for the courage and dedication that had given Homestead back its honor, its self-respect. Asking that the food be blessed, he also asked for a peaceful, prosperous and safe new year, in which all the families of Homestead could grow.

"Amen."

"Well," Nan said, leaning close to Miranda. "All except for the Enfield family."

"Let's bless poor Clarice," Miranda suggested. "And just leave out the men."

"Done."

The noise level lowered as people filled their plates and found places at the long tables to sit down and eat. Coming away from the serving tables in front of her daughter, Nan surveyed the empty chairs, wondering who would make a congenial dinner partner.

Her gaze found Cruz on the other side of the hall, at the end of the table farthest from where she stood. He sat alone, with an empty chair to his left and two empty chairs across from him.

He looked up as she set her tray down next to his.

"Merry Christmas," Nan said, softly.

"Merry Christmas to you, too." He smiled, and she thought she would cry.

Miranda joined them. "I'm starved," she announced. "So nobody comment on how full my plate is."

"I've got at least a pound more on my plate than you do," Cruz said. "You're an amateur at this game."

"That's because I plan on seconds." She stuck out her tongue as she sat down.

"This is seconds," Cruz said. "You lose."

The tension eased as they ate, and soon enough Nan felt as if nothing had changed between her and Cruz. They were partners. They worked together, laughed together, worried together.

No, she decided, as he smiled at a kid running by. Not partners. *Mates*.

Miranda had volunteered for cleanup duty,

so Nan and Cruz stayed behind to help. The hall returned to normal just in time for all of them to slip through the back door of the sanctuary.

On Christmas Eve, everybody in town came to church, whether they showed up any other day of the year or not. And they started filling in from the back, so the preacher wouldn't see them, Nan supposed.

As a result, the only empty seats were on the front pews. That meant walking the length of the aisle, observed by every eye in the building.

Without a second thought, Nan stepped forward, with Miranda beside her.

Cruz hung back. When Nan turned to look at him, he shook his head. "See you later," he mouthed.

"No," she said, quite loudly, then walked back to where he still stood and took him by the hand. "You," she said, in a voice audible over the organ prelude, "are sitting with me."

Miranda moved over as they reached the pew, and Nan slid in without letting go of her man. She could hear the whispers starting behind them. *I don't give a damn,* she thought. Then said a prayer of apology.

When Noah came to the pulpit, he looked down and gave her a wink.

Children's cards, words of peace and goodwill—the beautiful service offered all the blessings of Christmas. After the last "Hallelujah," Nan turned to her daughter first. "Merry Christmas, sweetie. I love you."

"Merry Christmas, Mom." Miranda returned the hug. "And a Happy New Year," she whispered wickedly in Nan's ear.

Then Nan faced Cruz. "Merry Christmas," she said softly. "Marry me?"

He stared so long, she expected the church to be empty by the time he got around to answering.

Then his eyes warmed, softened, blazed with joy. "Yes, ma'am," Cruz said. "Wherever, however, whenever you want."

"Here," she said. "With all our friends watching."

He grinned.

"Next Saturday," she told him.

She wasn't sure which of them moved first but suddenly they were holding each other tight, sealing their engagement with a kiss.

Around them, the family and friends

who'd waited so long to hear this news applauded.

Above them, in the steeple, the bells played "Joy to the World."

CHAPTER SIXTEEN

MIRANDA HEARD through the grapevine that Jud had been recalled to duty in Austin, and given a twelve-hour shift on Christmas Eve. She figured he hadn't yet had time to replace his cell phone, which the Enfields had thrown away. And maybe the phone in his apartment had been disconnected for non-payment of bills. His cable service was down, making e-mail impossible. He'd broken his arm, so he couldn't write.

Those excuses got her through New Year's Eve, with the help of the bottle of champagne she consumed while she and Dusty watched a killer-robot movie. Nan and Cruz had gone to Mexico after their wedding to meet his family and then spend a couple of weeks alone at the beach. When they returned, Nan intended to move into the cabin so Miranda would have the house to herself.

Whoopee.

When she went back to the office on January second, Reba met her with a smile and a hug. "Coffee's made." She turned Miranda toward the table with the percolator. "And I brought Cowboy Cookies."

"Mmmm…my favorites. What's the occasion?" Miranda balanced a stack of three chocolate chip treats on top of a steaming mug.

"Happy New Year." Reba shrugged. "Gotta be better than the last one, right?" As Miranda headed to the door, her assistant said, "There's somebody waiting in your office."

Miranda froze. Stupid heart, leaping into her throat like that. "Who?"

"Della Bowie…uh, Teague. She was here when I arrived."

"Oh. Okay. Thanks for the warning." Miranda opened the door and plastered a smile on her face. "Hey, Della. Good to see you. Happy New Year!"

"Back at ya'." She'd chosen a different look today—plain jeans, sneakers and a sheepskin jacket over a deep blue sweater. The red of her hair seemed more subdued than Miranda had last seen it, with all the curls brushed smooth and gathered in a ponytail at the nape of her neck.

"What can I do for you this morning?" Miranda set her mug on the desk. "Did you get some coffee and cookies?"

"No, thanks. Gotta watch my figure." Della tented her fingers in front of her. Her nails were still long, but now gleamed a pale rose. "I wanted to talk about this whole K Bar C thing."

"Sure." Jud had taken off without settling this issue. But then, saving Homestead wasn't part of his job description anymore, was it?

"I came back to town determined to get what's rightfully Sam's by inheritance. My lawyer—not that snake Dermody, by the way—still thinks I should go for it."

"Do I hear a 'but'?" Miranda gripped her hands together on the desk.

Della nodded. "I've been here for a few weeks, and it's given me a chance to remember things. I really liked this town, even though some people were mean to me. Lots of people weren't. You never gave me a hard time."

"I was one of the problem kids, too. Why add to somebody else's troubles?"

"Anyway, taking back the K Bar C would hurt the people who have started living there. And what am I gonna do with that much land? I'm not a rancher. Don't even ride."

Miranda cursed her own sense of fairness. "You could sell the land for a lot of money. And then do whatever you want. If—and it's a big if—a judge decided you deserved to get it back."

"Yeah. I've seen how well kids with lots of money turn out. What I'm thinking is that I'll just leave the arrangement as it is, not try to make trouble."

"Della, that's terrific."

She held up a hand. "As payback, I want to apply for the Home Free program, and I want to be accepted. That way Sam and I can live here, where he's got a chance of straightening up and turning out right. I don't suppose everybody will welcome us to town." Her grin was full of mischief. "But what's life without a little arguing to spice it up?"

Another knot in Miranda's stomach unraveled.

The first meeting of the Home Free Board was scheduled for Monday, January 9. The agenda included discussing who would serve in Arlen's place. Maybe they should bring two people on board—that way the mayor could be a nonvoting board member. Miranda had decided she should begin to delegate authority. She wouldn't be mayor of Homestead forever.

At least, she hoped not. There had to be more to life. Right?

Just before 7:00 p.m., she unlocked the courthouse library, turned on the lights and sat down in her usual seat at the table. Ruth Holden came in a few minutes later, followed by Frances Haase. Wade hurried in at the last second, grinning.

"More dirt came down on Arlen today," he announced. "The judge decided—"

Miranda held up a hand. "Let's not get into that mess right now, okay? I'd like to get home early for a change."

He shrugged and took his seat. Once they'd all arranged their papers, the process of evaluating applications began. After an hour, they'd almost reached the bottom of the bundle.

"I thought this one was interesting," Wade commented, holding up a form. "Sounds like someone we could use in this town."

"What's the app' number?" They avoided names in these sessions, to keep the process fair and impersonal.

"610."

Miranda looked through her remaining pages. "I don't have a copy of 610. Anybody besides Wade have this one?"

Frances and Ruth both nodded yes.

"That's weird. Why wouldn't I give myself a copy?" She shrugged and gave up searching. "So, anyway, what's good about this application?" Miranda leaned back in her chair. "Tell me about it."

Wade cleared his throat. "A single male, it says."

"That's not so great. Families support the schools."

"But he's got a fat savings account, a good bank balance, solid investments. College-educated, born and raised in Texas."

"So-so. References?"

"Let's see…" The sheriff flipped through the pages. "He's got a minister, his current boss, a schoolteacher and a friend who's in law enforcement. All really positive about his personality, his goals, his commitment and perseverance."

"He sounds perfect to me," Frances commented.

Ruth closed her notebook. "I agree."

Miranda had her doubts. "But what does he want to do? What makes him special? How can he contribute to the community?"

"Says here, he wants to get one of the larger land parcels and establish a cattle ranch. He's still researching the breed, but leaning toward longhorns, of course."

"As if we don't have enough of those around here."

"He's also interested in growing things. Wants orchards, vegetables, lavender."

She sat up straight. "What did you say?"

"Lavender," repeated a man standing behind her. "Purple plant, nice smell. Lavender and kids."

Miranda put her burning face in her hands. She heard the door to the library open, heard people enter, talking, laughing.

"Did he ask her yet?" they wanted to know. "Did she say yes?"

"He said he'd be willing to act as a deputy, too." Wade chuckled. "Virgil's thrilled. I could use a vacation, myself. I vote yes."

"Yes," Ruth said, sounding teary.

"Yes." Frances blew her nose.

Opening her eyes, Miranda saw her friends first—Kayla and Ethan, Callie, Kristin and Ryan, Noah, Greer, and even Nan and Cruz, plus half the rest of the town.

She stood up and turned. There he was, right behind her, grinning and waiting. His eyes were anxious.

In his hands, he held a giant bouquet of lavender spikes. How she'd missed that crisp scent.

How she'd missed this man!

Miranda swallowed hard. "This guy does have some…um…points in his favor," she said, dismayed to hear her voice shake. "Sheriff, does the candidate indicate how long he's prepared to live here in Homestead?"

"A lifetime," Jud said simply. "A lifetime with you."

"That's an application I can't turn down," Miranda told him, and threw herself into his outstretched arms.

* * * *

Look out for Back to Eden *by Melinda Curtis, part of the* A LITTLE SECRET *mini-series, available only from Mills & Boon Superromance next month!*

BACK TO EDEN
by Melinda Curtis

Raising her sister Missy's children, Rachel Quinlan has never got over her crush on Cole Hudson, love of Missy's life. And when the past collides with the present, Rachel has to know if there's more to it…

HER SECRET FAMILY
by Sherry Lewis

Jolene Preston faced prejudice as the only female cop in her department, but she feared the truth about her heritage making things even worse. Could she trust Mason Blackfox with her secret

LIES THAT BIND
by Barbara McMahon

Home to see her ailing foster mother, April Jeffries hears some shocking revelations about her parents. But with the help of Hac Palmer, she finds love is easier the third time around.

A TEMPORARY ARRANGEMENT
by Roxanne Rustand

Abby Cahill is in Wisconsin helping out as a nurse for the summer and lodging with Ethan Matthews. As summer draws to a close will Ethan and Abby finally realise what they mean to each other

There's the life you planned and there's what comes next...

A LONG WALK HOME
by Diane Amos

Annie remembers her young niece, Summer, as a sweet girl, and is happy to have her stay. So the wild child with piercings is a bit of a shock. Sullen and scared, Summer turns Annie's life upside down. But Annie is determined to get through to her. For her, the journey to what matters most will be worth every step.

STARTING FROM SCRATCH
by Marie Ferrarella

Elisha Reed loved her job and her life. But when Elisha's world changed over night, it was time for a rethink. With two teenagers to care for, Elisha couldn't disappear in the bliss of a creamy confection...unless she had several forks. She decided to start from scratch...and from here on in, it would be a piece of cake!

Because every life has more than one chapter...

On sale 18th May 2007

Available at WHSmith, Tesco, ASDA, and all good bookshops
www.millsandboon.co.uk

LOVE LESSONS
by Gina Wilkins

Catherine Travis had all the trappings of the good life – except someone special to share it with. Could it be that gorgeous maintenance man and part-time student Mike Clancy would fix her, too?

A WEDDING IN WILLOW VALLEY
by Joan Elliott Pickart

Ten years ago Laurel Windsong had left, cancelling marriage plans with Sheriff Ben Skeeter. But now she's come home – and discovered that it's never too late for true love.

THE RUNAWAY AND THE CATTLEMAN
by Lilian Darcy

Jacinda fled to Callan Woods' remote cattle station in the Australian outback to protect her child. She found Callan attractive and protective, a man she could depend on.

On sale 18th May 2007

THE MATCHMAKERS' DADDY
by Judy Duarte

Zack Henderson was starting over. But he hadn't planned on falling for Diana Lynch. He knew she and her two adorable matchmakers were better off without a man like him…

UNDER THE WESTERN SKY
by Laurie Paige

When compassionate midwife Julianne Martin was accused of stealing Native American artefacts, investigator Tony Aquilon was sure he had the wrong woman…

DETECTIVE DADDY
by Jane Toombs

Fay Merriweather was in labour when a storm stranded her on the doorstep of detective Dan Sorensen's cabin. He gave Fay and her baby the care they needed, but he never intended to fall for this instant family…

Available at WHSmith, Tesco, ASDA, and all good bookshops
www.millsandboon.co.uk

Three timeless tales of love and marriage from international bestseller Betty Neels

Featuring

Heidelberg Wedding

When surgeon Gerard Grenfell offered her the chance to work with him in Europe, Eugenia Smith went happily, but that was before she realised she was falling in love with a man who already had wedding plans.

Wedding Bells for Beatrice

Beatrice told single father Gijs van der Eekerk to marry again, but she hadn't bargained on him offering her the position! Especially when love didn't appear to be part of the deal...

Making Sure of Sarah

Having fallen in love with Sarah at first sight, Litrik ter Breukel vowed to go slowly because of her youth and innocence. But perhaps he simply needed to propose!

Available 4th May 2007

www.millsandboon.co.uk

— *Queens of Romance* —

An outstanding collection by international bestselling authors

16th March 2007

20th April 2007

18th May 2007

15th June 2007

Collect all 4 superb books!

www.millsandboon.co.uk

FRE

2 BOOKS AND A SURPRISE GIFT

We would like to take this opportunity to thank you for reading thi Mills & Boon® book by offering you the chance to take TWO mor specially selected titles from the Superromance™ series absolutel FREE! We're also making this offer to introduce you to the benefits c the Mills & Boon® Reader Service™—

- ★ **FREE home delivery**
- ★ **FREE gifts and competitions**
- ★ **FREE monthly Newsletter**
- ★ **Books available before they're in the shops**
- ★ **Exclusive Reader Service offers**

Accepting these FREE books and gift places you under no obligatio to buy; you may cancel at any time, even after receiving your fre shipment. Simply complete your details below and return the entir page to the address below. You don't even need a stamp!

YES! Please send me 2 free Superromance books and a surprise gif I understand that unless you hear from me, I will receive superb new titles every month for just £3.69 each, postage and packin free. I am under no obligation to purchase any books and may cance my subscription at any time. The free books and gift will be mine t keep in any case.

U7ZEE

Ms/Mrs/Miss/Mr.........................Initials ....

BLOCK CAPITALS PLEAS

Surname ....

Address ....

....

.................Postcode ....

Send this whole page to:
The Reader Service, FREEPOST CN81, Croydon, CR9 3WZ

Offer valid in UK only and is not available to current Mills & Boon® Reader Service™ subscribers to this series. Overseas and Eire please write for details. We reserve the right to refuse an application and applicants must be aged 18 years or over. Only one application per household. Terms and prices subject to change without notice. Offer expires 31st July 2007. As a result of this application, you may receive offers from Harlequin Mills & Boon and other carefully selected companies. If you would prefer not to share in this opportunity please write to The Data Manager at PO Box 676, Richmond, TW9 1WU.

Mills & Boon® is a registered trademark owned by Harlequin Mills & Boon Limited.
Superromance™ is being used as a trademark. The Mills & Boon® Reader Service™ is being used as a trademark.